# A DEBT OF DISHONOR

### Lords of Sussex
### Book 2

## by Lillian Marek

Dragonblade Publishing, Inc. is an imprint of Kathryn Le Veque Novels, Inc.

P.O. Box 7968

La Verne CA 91750

ceo@dragonbladepublishing.com

Produced in the United States of America

First Edition January 2021

Print Edition

## ARE YOU SIGNED UP FOR DRAGONBLADE'S BLOG?

You'll get the latest news and information on exclusive giveaways, exclusive excerpts, coming releases, sales, free books, cover reveals and more.

Check out our complete list of authors, too!

No spam, no junk. That's a promise!

### Sign Up Here

www.dragonbladepublishing.com

*Dearest Reader;*

*Thank you for your support of a small press. At Dragonblade Publishing, we strive to bring you the highest quality Historical Romance from the some of the best authors in the business. Without your support, there is no 'us', so we sincerely hope you adore these stories and find some new favorite authors along the way.*

*Happy Reading!*

*CEO, Dragonblade Publishing*

# PROLOGUE

*London, April 1818*

THE SCARLET CARRIAGE belonging to the Earl of Farnsworth pulled up at the residence of Viscount Newell, and the groom leaped to open the door and put down the steps. The butler, who had been warned to watch for the earl's arrival, opened the door as the earl approached. His eyes widened at the earl's smile, and he could not restrain a shiver. He had never seen the earl pleased before. It was not a pleasant sight.

Still smiling, Farnsworth paused for a moment before the somewhat dingy mirror in the hall to examine himself. He was not an ugly man. Taken individually, his features were not unpleasing, except for the strange redness of his nose. He was well set up, his clothes needing no padding or other tailor's tricks. He always wore gloves, and few could know this was to cover a persistent sore. His hair was his own, and though it had become patchy, it was still brown with no gray showing. His eyes, also brown, were reasonably clear. It would be difficult to fault his appearance.

Newell came into the hall to greet him, looking like a man who has not yet recovered from the previous night's debauch. He rubbed the back of his hand across his mouth and nodded a greeting to Farnsworth without actually speaking.

"And where is your sister? Is she not ready for our little outing?"

Newell shrugged and looked away. "She's locked herself into her room and won't come out."

Farnsworth froze. The smile faded. "And why would she do that?" he asked icily.

Newell shrugged again, without looking at Farnsworth.

The earl spoke with exaggerated patience. "Newell, do not tell me you were so foolish as to tell your sister about our arrangement."

Newell flushed. "I didn't tell her. I…" He pursed his mouth and looked away. "It's not my fault. She was in the library last night and overheard us."

"She overheard us." Farnsworth's voice was flat. "Would I be correct in concluding that she took some exception to our agreement?"

Newell said nothing. He simply stood there, head turned aside, looking both mulish and sulky.

Farnsworth spun away from the viscount, looked off at some sight he alone could see, a muscle in his jaw twitching. After a moment, he turned back. "I should have known better than to leave anything in the hands of an idiot like you. Now, what should have been a pleasant little excursion will, of necessity, turn into an ugly scene."

Newell said nothing.

But then, thought Farnsworth, what could the idiot say? "Have you at least the key to her room?"

Newell shook his head. "She has it in there with her. I've told her she has to come out, but she won't answer when I talk to her." He sounded resentful.

Farnsworth made a sound that seemed half-disgusted and half-amused. "Well then, order your largest footman to break down the door. I am afraid I do not intend to wait for your efforts at persuasion to have effect."

The largest footman, who was also the only footman, did not set about the task he was ordered to perform with any enthusiasm. He had not been paid in the past two quarters for the ordinary footman duties he performed. He could not really see why he should be expected to do something that was clearly out of the usual run of footman duties. However, one look from Farnsworth was enough to persuade him to make an effort.

It was not a painless effort. Though the footman was large, the door was sturdy, and when he ran at it, he bounced right off. That he tried three more times, with equal lack of success, was a tribute to the power of Farnsworth's glare. He was standing there rubbing his shoulder and wondering which would shatter first, wood or bone, when the housemaid appeared.

She had been drawn by curiosity, wondering what the thuds and grunts portended. The butler, who had been peering around the corner of the corridor, trusting that he was too old to be asked to help, whispered to her what was afoot, or rather, ashoulder.

Now, the housemaid had nothing against Miss Russell, the viscount's sister, but she had nothing for her either. On the other hand, she did have a bit of a soft spot for the footman, so she tweaked the butler's sleeve and whispered in his ear. He looked at her in surprise, and she nodded vigorously.

The butler approached the viscount and cleared his throat. When he had Newell's attention, he said, "Excuse me, my lord, but this young person reminds me that the keys in this house are interchangeable."

Newell looked at him blankly.

Farnsworth barked a laugh. "That means, my dear Newell, that any key in the house will open any lock in the house. So if you can produce a key, any key, we can bring this farce to an end."

Newell flushed. "Fetch a key."

While the butler hurried off to do just that, the other two servants backed quietly away and vanished around the corner. Once he had produced the key, the butler prepared to do the same, but Farnsworth waved him to unlock the door. He did so and stepped aside.

Farnsworth stepped in, followed more slowly by Newell. Both were prepared for a storm of fury. Neither was expecting an empty room. Farnsworth was the first to recover his equilibrium, and strolled around the room, using his cane to peer behind curtains and into the armoire in a fair imitation of indifference. It was he who noticed the letter propped up on the writing table.

It was folded and sealed, with only "Humphrey" written across it. Who but Katherine could have left it? Farnsworth had no hesitation about opening it. Then he laughed. It was not a pleasant sound.

"Your sister does not appear to hold either of us in great esteem," he said, with apparent casualness. "She calls you a 'pusillanimous pander' and says you are welcome to starve in the gutter for all she cares, and she would rather die than be sold to a 'disgusting, diseased degenerate'. That would be me, I presume. She is a trifle overfond of alliteration, but one cannot fault her characterizations. How well she knows us both." He turned to Newell with a look of barely controlled fury. "You bungling fool."

Newell looked appalled. "She would rather die? My God, has she killed herself?"

"Do not be an idiot. You will notice that there are no clothes in this room, with the exception of that rather tawdry thing you dressed her in to display her at the opera. She has obviously packed her bag and run away. Now, you will need to retrieve her."

"How the devil am I supposed to do that? I don't know where she went."

Farnsworth looked at him.

Newell blustered, "Well, I don't. How could I know?"

Farnsworth sighed the sigh of an intelligent man forced to deal with fools. "Does she have any friends in London? Does she know anyone in London?"

Newell shook his head. "She's only been here a few weeks and never met anyone except friends of mine here, and she don't like them any more than she likes you."

Farnsworth gave him an impatient look. "Does she have any friends anywhere? She is twenty years old, after all. She must have known people before you brought her here."

"Well, I suppose she has friends back in Yorkshire. Leastways there were people there with her at our mother's funeral." Farnsworth looked at Newell, and got a shrug in reply. "I don't know where else she'd go. She's lived there all her life, so she won't know anyone anyplace else."

"Then you will be taking a trip to Yorkshire to retrieve my property, won't you?"

"But she's run away. She's not going to want to come back, and if she's with friends..."

"That is your problem. You will have to deal with it. We both know you have no other way to pay what you owe me." Newell opened his mouth to protest, but Farnsworth glared at him. "You will leave at once and let me know of your success immediately on your return. You really do not want to disappoint me."

The click of his footsteps on the marble of the stairs and hall was the only sound in the house as Farnsworth departed.

Newell felt sick. How the hell was he supposed to get to Yorkshire without any money? He needed a drink.

>>><<<

A FEW MILES south of London a farmer's wagon was heading for home, the load of cheeses having been delivered. The aging cart horse plodded along slowly but steadily. On the back of the wagon, munching on apples, sat the farmer's son, a cheerful boy of about ten, and a young woman to whom the farmer had given a ride. A few strands of blond hair peeked out from beneath her bonnet, a somewhat battered thing, devoid of decoration. The farmer had at first thought her too delicate, too fragile for the Yorkshire farm girl she claimed to be, but her sturdy brown dress and cloak, and the boots on her feet, to say nothing of her roughened hands, all looked familiar with hard work.

She tilted her head back to feel the warmth of the springtime sun and took a deep breath of the fresh air. Her eyes closed and the corners of her mouth tipped up in a faint smile.

Miss Katherine Russell had escaped.

# CHAPTER ONE

*Sussex*

KATHERINE RUSSELL, KNOWN to those who loved her as Kate, was awakened from a deep sleep by the sun streaming through the window. She lay there in frozen stillness, her eyes wide with panic. Where was she? This was not her home, nor was it her brother's house. Once the silence in the room had assured her that she was alone, she cautiously lifted her head to look around. The room was unfamiliar and it was—she stopped to stare in surprise. Yes, the room was unfamiliar. But it was not threatening. It was actually *pretty*. How remarkable. There were chintz curtains with a pattern of pink flowers on both the bed and the windows. There was a fireplace with a cheerful fire in it to take the chill off the spring morning. And the sheets on her bed were soft and lavender-scented.

The panic began to ease and her heart started slowing down to a normal beat.

She was in her aunt's house in Lewes, that was it. She had reached sanctuary. Frances Darling had not just given her shelter last night when she knocked on the door, close to exhaustion, but had welcomed her. For the first time since her mother's death, Kate had felt safe. The determination—or desperation—that had carried her here from London eased under that welcome and she had tumbled into bed barely aware of her surroundings.

Now she was aware. Someone must have unpacked her bag and pressed her blue dress, because it was laid over the chair, along with a clean shift, stays and stockings. Her half boots had even been cleaned and polished. Sitting on the hearth by the fire was a pitcher of water, still warm for her washing.

Feeling embarrassed—she did not want her aunt to think her lazy—she dressed hurriedly, pinned the pocket with the necklace under her skirt, and ran down the stairs.

As she reached the hall, she was startled by a knock on the door. The sound froze her for a moment and panic returned. He could not possibly have found her so soon, could he? Then she realized it had been a courteous knock, not a demanding hammering. She stiffened her shoulders and opened the door, but then she stood frozen once more, unable to speak.

In front of her was a man, the most spectacular man she had ever seen. He looked like an angel, a warrior angel, with a fierce, proud face, though he was probably only a farmer. His coat was well cut but loose enough for ease of movement and so too loose for fashion, and his boots boasted more mud than polish.

He was tall, much taller than she. Her head barely came up to his chin. If she looked straight ahead, she would be staring at his cravat. That was not where she wanted to look, however. She wanted to look at his face, his wonderful face. How could it be so beautiful and so masculine at the same time? His hair was dark, almost black, and fell neatly into place with no fashionable curls. His chin was strong without being obtrusive, his nose was classical without being hawkish, his mouth was well shaped without being voluptuous, and his eyes were a clear, brilliant blue, sheltered by unfairly long lashes and sharply arched brows. His face was, perhaps, a trifle too long and narrow for perfection, which somehow made it even more attractive. With its stern expression, it was the face of a hero, a Lancelot come to rescue Guinevere or Hector determined to defend doomed Troy.

"Run along, girl, and fetch your mistress," he said, walking into the hall without so much as a glance at her.

Girl? Kate thought, coming to herself. *Girl?* He thinks I am a *servant?* She drew herself up and said icily, "I will see if my aunt is at home. Who shall I say is calling?"

That drew his attention. He stopped abruptly and turned to stare at her. And continued to stare.

There was a muffled snort, and she realized there was a second man, who had been standing just behind the first one. She should have noticed him since he was even taller and broader than the first man, but he was not as beautiful despite his golden curls. At the moment, he appeared to be greatly amused, while the first man continued to stare. It was the second who spoke. "I do beg your pardon." He seemed to be having difficulty restraining his laughter. "This gentleman is Peter Alexander Joseph Bancroft, Duke of Ashleigh, and I am Thomas Wortham, Earl of Merton. We have come to call on Mrs. Darling, if she will receive us."

Kate was reasonably certain that her jaw did not drop. Instead, she dropped a stiff curtsey. "Duke, Lord Merton, if you would be so good as to wait, I will see if my aunt is at home." Opening a door at random, she breathed a sigh of relief when she saw that it was a drawing room. She ushered them in, gracefully, she hoped, and then managed to leave at a ladylike pace when all she wanted to do was run. Aristocrats, a duke and an earl no less, she thought, panic rising again. They must not be allowed to discover who she was. No matter how wondrous, how heroic the duke looked, he was not a hero, not for her. More likely an enemy. No member of the nobility could be anything but danger.

ONCE SHE HAD departed, Merton no longer bothered to restrain himself but collapsed in laughter. "Ashleigh, your face was priceless. What a blow! There is someone around Lewes who does not know you by sight."

Ashleigh, who was still staring after the girl, recalled himself. "And apparently, someone I offended," he said with an effort at carelessness. "Prickly little creature, isn't she? But if she goes around dressed like a servant girl, she can hardly be surprised when people mistake her for one." *Or a sprite. A forest nymph, with those green eyes and that flaxen hair.*

Merton was still smiling. "And if you go around dressed like a farmer, you can hardly be surprised…"

Ashleigh raised a hand. "Pax. I understand your point. But in fairness to me, I had not known that Mrs. Darling had a niece, no less that said niece was staying here."

"And a decidedly pretty niece at that."

*Pretty? What an insipid word.* "Merton, remember that you are a married man."

Merton's smile broadened. "And I have no wish to forget it, but I have not grown blind. Nor have you. I saw you staring at her."

Ashleigh gave a shrug. "Very well. She is indeed pretty, though far too thin." *No, she is not pretty. She is enchanting. And not thin so much as ethereal. Would she vanish on the breeze if I tried to catch hold of her?*

"Mmmm. One might even call her beautiful." Merton grinned at his friend. "Although some might consider her too thin."

"One might also remember that she is Mrs. Darling's niece," Ashleigh replied austerely. That was something he needed to remember himself. Fanciful thoughts about nymphs were not for a man in his position with his responsibilities.

MRS. DARLING CAME bustling in, hands outstretched, with a delighted smile on her face. She was a small woman, no taller than Kate, still slim, her hair more blond than gray for all her fifty years, and dressed in a flattering morning dress of cream muslin with lacy ruffles surrounding her neck and a frivolous scrap of lace on her head. "Ashleigh!" she said. "You have not been here this age! How goes everything at Kelswick? Is Lady Talmadge well?"

"Indeed, she is," said Ashleigh, taking her hands in his, "and sends her greetings."

"And you, Tom? I should say, Merton," said Mrs. Darling. "How goes it with Lady Merton?"

"No, please," he laughed, "in this house, let me ever be Tom." He bent over to kiss her cheek. "And Miranda is in blooming health, driving my steward mad with plans for a new drainage system for the village."

Slipping in quietly behind her aunt, who had insisted that it would only raise curiosity if she did not return, Kate examined the visitors. The earl looked almost embarrassed by his happiness though the duke looked a bit wistful.

"Do not pretend you object. As I recall, drainage in the village was one of your concerns in the first place." Mrs. Darling still smiled, and then realized that her visitors were looking behind her. "What am I thinking!" She took Kate's hand to lead her forward. "Your Grace, my lord, may I present my niece, Kate, who has come to stay with me."

Kate curtseyed once more, just deep enough to be proper, and said, "Your Grace, my lord."

Ashleigh and Merton bowed a bit lower than was absolutely necessary. "We encountered your niece at the door," said Ashleigh, "and I fear I insulted her by taking her for a servant. I do apologize."

"Not at all," said Kate, holding herself stiffly. "But I fear I must have insulted you as well, taking you for a farmer." She could only hope that they had failed to notice her calling him "Duke" at the door. That familiarity would be far too much presumption on the part of a

ااااااااااااااااااااااااااااااااااااااااااااااااااااااااااااااااااااااااااااااااااااااااااااااااااااااااااااااااااااااااااااااااااااااااااااااااااااااااااااااااااااااااااا

mere connection of Mrs. Darling.

Ashleigh looked as if he could not decide whether he should consider this remark amusing or impertinent. Merton had no difficulty and laughed again. "Indeed, Miss Darling, Ashleigh was deeply offended. You must know that no matter how fondly he remembers our being Peter and Tom in this house when we were boys, outside, he is dreadfully high in the instep. He expects forelocks to be pulled on every side."

"Merton, you are an ass," said Ashleigh mildly. "Miss Darling, will you be staying long?"

She started a bit at the name—should she answer to Miss Darling? But when she looked at her aunt, Mrs. Darling gave an approving nod, so she said, "So long as my aunt permits."

"And that will be forever," said Mrs. Darling, giving her niece's hand a squeeze. She turned to Ashleigh and explained, "My niece is now an orphan. Since we, neither of us, have any other family to rely on, she will naturally make her home with me. To my great delight."

"I am, indeed, glad that you will have company," said Ashleigh. "I have worried about you, living all alone here since Andrew's death. But I have come to ask a favor of you, of both of you now. I know it is short notice, but will you join us for dinner this evening? I will send the carriage to bring you, of course, and to take you home."

Mrs. Darling smiled. "Such an invitation can hardly be considered a favor. What is the rest of it?"

Ashleigh looked rueful. "The favor part of it is that the Wiltons decided to descend on us, and my sister beseeches me to dilute the company as much as possible. Merton has promised to bring his wife and I hope to snare Mr. Chantry and Dr. Goddard as well."

"Poor Alice! Of course we will come and protect her from her unwanted suitor," said Mrs. Darling.

Merton turned to Kate with a smile. "It is all Ashleigh's fault, Miss Darling. Since Lady Wilton is his aunt, he is too polite to tell her that she is not welcome. In addition, he insists on the same high level of courtesy from his sister, so she has found it difficult to be cold enough to convince young Wilton—or rather, not-so-young Wilton—that his suit is unwanted."

"And you, my lord?" asked Kate with an answering smile. It was impossible to not smile at Merton. "Are you also so bound by courtesy that you are unable to protect yourself?"

"Not at all," he replied. "That is why Ashleigh takes me about with him. He does not protect himself, so I must do it for him. Thus, all the blame falls on me, and he is universally acclaimed as a model of civility."

"Yet you are unable to prevent the descent of unwanted guests," said Kate. "I do not see that you offer much in the way of protection."

"He offers none at all." Ashleigh seemed irritated. "I simply invite him to join me for amusement, rather as kings of old kept their fools."

"One duty of those fools was to tell the king unpleasant truths that the courtiers hesitated to speak, was it not?" said Kate, turning to the duke. "Is that Lord Merton's task as well?"

"Oh, nicely turned, Miss Darling." Merton smiled broadly. "Well, Ashleigh, is that my task? Or do you receive enough lectures from Lady Wilton?"

Ashleigh stiffened and seemed to cloak himself in formality. Mrs. Darling came to the rescue. "Lady Wilton often feels obliged to lecture one and all about the demands of their station," she told Kate, and then turned back to Ashleigh. "We shall be honored to dine at Kelswick and will do our best to deflect some of her slings and arrows."

The duke nodded to the two women. "Mrs. Darling, Miss Darling. The carriage will be here at six, if that is acceptable. And now we must be on our way." He frowned at Merton before he turned to leave, and Merton followed, still smiling.

As they left, Kate began to worry. She had not expected to meet anyone, not before she had a chance to explain to her aunt what had happened to her, why she had come, and she had no idea how she should have behaved with these visitors. Almost certainly, she had been too forward. They were aristocrats, so if they found out who she was, they could be expected to side with her brother and Farnsworth. She should have been meek and unnoticeable. She should never have followed her aunt into this room. She should have pretended she was the servant they took her for when they first arrived. She certainly shouldn't have spoken as she did. *Stupid, stupid!*

How was she going to hide if she couldn't control her tongue?

Mrs. Darling was smiling at her. "Come sit down, my dear, so we can talk. You must tell me what has brought you here in such a state." When she rang a bell, a maid promptly appeared, and Mrs. Darling requested tea and buns. Then she smiled at her niece. "Cook made some delicious raisin buns this morning. I have always found it simpler to deal with difficulties when they are accompanied by something sweet. And you have not even had breakfast, so we will indulge ourselves first."

Indulge themselves they did, thought Kate. The maid—her name was Molly, Kate discovered—brought in a silver tray with a silver tea service. The cups and plates were of the finest china, almost translucent, painted with tiny flowers and bordered with gilt. And the room, Kate realized, was most elegantly appointed, boasting a ceiling festooned with plaster garlands, walls covered with painted paper, and a suite of gilded furniture upholstered in silk.

She remembered that when she arrived the night before she thought, at first, that she had come to the wrong house. Hawthorne Cottage was a large stone house of—was it three stories or four? And it was set on extensive grounds, a small park, really. With servants. Not just a maid of all work, but a cook and a parlor maid and who knew what else. Nothing like the tiny cottage she had pictured when Mama read her sister's letters to her back in Yorkshire.

What was worse, her aunt was obviously on easy terms with a duke and an earl. How could that be? "They came here as children?" she wondered, and then realized she had spoken out loud.

"Yes, they were inseparable, those two. They were either at Schotten Hall—Tom's grandfather's home—or here, tagging along after Andrew." Mrs. Darling shook her head. "Whenever his parents were in residence, Kelswick was not a safe place for a child."

Kate suddenly realized that her aunt must be rich. Would she think Kate had come here because of that? She couldn't let Aunt Frances think she had come to sponge upon her. She couldn't.

She was still trying to deal with that problem when her aunt began to speak. "Now, my dear, I know from your mother's letters over the years that neither your father nor your brother took any care of you, that they had gambled away virtually everything, and from your presence here, I conclude that your visit to London was not a success. But why ever did you not write to me? I would have come to fetch you and you could have traveled in comfort and safety."

"There was no time." Kate shook her head. As soon as she thought of her brother, the slimy toad, anger and disgust began waging a battle in her stomach. Her hands were clenched tightly in her lap, and she stared at them, determined to keep her voice calm and unemotional. "It seems that when my brother decided to take me to London with him, it was not to share his home or even to be his housekeeper. He intended to use me as payment for his debts. Three days ago, I overheard him making that precise arrangement with the Earl of Farnsworth. He owed the earl £10,000, but the earl agreed to take me instead. He was to pick me up—pick me up like a parcel—the next day. Oh God!" She lost control of her voice. "Aunt Franny, he wanted to make me a whore. My own brother!" She flung her head back and held her eyes closed until the hot fury had been controlled and she could speak calmly again. "I had to leave at once, so I slipped out of the house before dawn."

As the tale unfolded, the color had been draining from Mrs. Darling's face and her hand reached out to Kate, who spoke with militant determination. "I will not let them make me a whore. I will not!"

"Of course not." The older woman pulled her niece into an embrace and hugged her fiercely. "My poor child—I never thought—I thought perhaps you were being pushed into a marriage you did not want or had been separated from a sweetheart back in Yorkshire. How could your brother—even your father would never—and to think I was going to scold you for putting yourself in danger by traveling alone!"

"When I set out, I was so angry, I didn't even think of danger." Kate sat back and allowed herself a small smile. "I could hardly imagine that anything ahead of me could be worse than what was behind. My only fear was that Farnsworth might come after me."

"Is that likely?"

Kate took a deep breath and let it out slowly while she thought. "I don't really know. It is possible." She considered what she had seen of him and could not prevent a shiver. "Yes, it is quite possible. He is not a man who will accept being thwarted. It's hard to say what he might do. He... he frightens me, and I do not like being frightened."

"He cannot have any legal claim on you."

Kate suddenly felt old, much older than her aunt. "Farnsworth is an earl. He cannot imagine that anyone has the right to refuse him what he wants. Should I appeal to a magistrate? I am not of age so, legally, I am under my brother's control. If he says that Farnsworth may have me, who is there to object?"

"Of course. It is so long since I have been subject to the arrogance of such men that I forget. What is just, what is right—none of that matters." Mrs. Darling shook her head sadly. Then she stiffened her back and spoke briskly. "Now, let us be practical. I don't know what the law might be, but your brother cannot exercise any rights over you if he cannot find you. So we must make sure he doesn't find you. Will he think to look for you here?"

"I doubt it." Kate shook her head. "Humphrey never lived with us while I was growing up. Did you know that? He was always with our father. So I can't be sure what he knows. But I think it unlikely he knows your name or even of your existence, and I am sure he does not know your direction."

"Let us see, then. For the time being—at least until you are of age—when will that be?"

"Not until next January."

"Until next January, then, we will be careful. Your mother was the only member of my family to keep in touch with me after I was disowned for marrying Andrew, so even if your brother thinks to go to Locksley Hall, no one there will know where to find me. And now, Ashleigh and Merton have solved a problem for us by assuming that you are Andrew's niece. If people think of you as Miss Darling, they will not identify you as Miss Russell, Viscount Newell's sister. But we will have to be careful in the future. Let me think."

She tapped her cheek as she considered the possibilities. "Yes, if anyone asks, we'll say you are the daughter of one of Andrew's cousins who married the daughter of a country gentleman. That will explain why you have the accent and manners of a lady." She smiled suddenly. "People laugh at cits who ape the manners of their betters, but I can tell you from experience that it is every bit as difficult for one who has been raised as a lady to pass herself off as a cit!"

"Aunt Frances..." Kate felt her throat tighten with gratitude and tried to smile. "Thank you."

"Oh pish." The older woman blushed as she smiled. "And you must call me Aunt Franny, for Franny is what my Andrew called me."

A bump against her leg reminded Kate what she was carrying. "Do wait, Aunt," she called as she reached into her skirt to retrieve the pocket. "I must show you what I have." She pulled out a blue velvet bag, laid it on the tea table and untied it carefully to display a pearl necklace—a double strand of large, perfectly matched pearls.

Aunt Franny looked at it in amazement, and reached out a hand to let the pearls run through her fingers. "I know this necklace. These are my mother's pearls. How…?"

"Her father—your father—sent them to Mama shortly before he died. Then, when she grew ill, she told me to keep them hidden so my brother would not find them."

"A sorry but doubtless necessary precaution." The older woman smiled sadly at her niece. "I expect our father intended this as an apology for having insisted that Mary marry your father. He was not a deliberately cruel man, you know, just a bit blind in some ways. He never saw beyond your father's title, never saw the kind of man he was until it was too late. Just as he never saw Andrew's worth."

"He could have helped us." Kate did not even try to hide the bitterness. "Mama was his daughter, and we were living in poverty."

Franny gave her niece a sharp look. "Did he know that? I never suspected it was as bad as it seems to have been, and if she did not wish to confide in me, she would have been too proud to ask for help from him. And then, I doubt he could have given her anything that would not have been taken by Newell and tossed on the gambling table. My father would not have been able to prevent that. No one could. The pearls—am I correct in thinking that he sent those after your father's death?" At Kate's nod, she continued, "Well, at any rate, you now have a dowry when you choose to marry."

"No, not a dowry. A livelihood."

Her aunt frowned. "What do you mean?"

"I am hoping that they can be sold for enough to give me a start. Perhaps I could buy a cottage with enough land to raise vegetables and keep some chickens. Or I could start a school and earn some money that way. Or I could work in a shop until I learn enough about the business and then start a shop myself."

"Why ever would you want to do such a thing?" Franny looked thoroughly shocked. "You are the daughter of a viscount. You would be ruined."

"Being the sister of a viscount has come close enough to ruining me. Earning my own living would make me safe. If I am not dependent on anyone, I will not be at anyone's mercy."

"But why would you not want to marry? Marriage is by far the safest haven for a woman, I assure you."

Kate lifted her brows. "Was it safe for my mother?"

Franny shook her head dismissively. "I am not talking about a marriage like that, to a man who cares for nothing but his own pleasures. But a marriage where there is respect, where there is trust, where there is love—that is something entirely different."

"Marriage to a man I can trust? I doubt I will ever find such a man, but if I do, perhaps I will consider marriage."

A smile flickered across Franny's face. "As long as you would not refuse it if such a match presented itself. But you will not be forced into marriage. I can promise you that much. And as for the other, well, there is no need to do anything yet. You are more than welcome here, and you may make your home with me permanently if you wish."

Kate shook her head. "I know I have come here and thrown myself on your charity, but I will not presume on it."

"Stuff and nonsense. There is no question of charity. You are my niece, and my Andrew left me more than well provided for."

"But truly, Aunt Franny, I cannot allow you to support me."

"Do not be foolish, child. You heard the duke—I have been in need of company, of a companion. You will be doing me a favor by staying with me." She gave her niece an impish smile. "Now, let us put those pearls of yours in the safe—and yes, I do have a safe. Your treasures can keep mine company."

Kate shook her head. At the moment, she desperately needed the sanctuary her aunt offered—she was not foolish enough to pretend otherwise—but she could not live on her aunt's charity forever. For the time being, she had to remain hidden. But sooner or later, she would have to find some way to support herself.

# CHAPTER TWO

FRANNY LOOKED AT her niece critically, tweaked the limp ruffle at her neckline, and sighed. "We will need to do something—and quickly—about providing you with a decent wardrobe. This is hopelessly out of style, and far too worn to be worth refurbishing."

Kate looked down at her old pink muslin that had faded to almost white and added a theatrical sigh of her own. "This gown has seen plenty of dinners with the vicar and the squire. You would think it would perk up at the prospect of dining with a duke, but no. It is just hanging here limply. It has no pride at all."

Franny looked at her for a moment and then smiled. "That's the spirit. We are the grantors of a favor this evening, not the recipients of one. We are the ones condescending to dine with the unpleasant Lady Wilton and her even more unpleasant son. Anyone who sees only your garments and not your sterling worth is not deserving of our notice."

The two women nodded at each other approvingly, donned their cloaks—Franny's a rich green velvet lined with cream satin, Kate's a sturdy brown wool—and set out for the duke's carriage, waiting at the gate. Kate was almost giddy with excitement. Her life in the past year had been such a series of disasters that to think she might really be safe now seemed almost like a fairy tale. Yesterday, she had been stumbling along a strange road, hoping for nothing more than a safe place to hide. This evening, she was riding in a duke's carriage, sitting in luxury on a well-cushioned seat covered in leather as soft and smooth as silk. This was not simply safety, this was the stuff of fantasy. She was laughing when they arrived at Kelswick, but when she stepped out of the carriage, her breath was taken away. She had seen glimpses of the house from the drive, and she had expected it to be a large building, but this was well beyond large.

Aunt Franny's home, a three-story stone house—it was three, she now knew, and not four—appropriate for the wealthy merchant Andrew Darling had become, was by far the finest house Kate had ever been in. Her home in Yorkshire may have been the largest house in the area, but it didn't even have a name. It was just the manor, shabby and so close to tumbling down that many of the rooms were uninhabitable. Squire Grant's house, where she and her mother had often visited, had been nearly as large as the manor and was more impressive, having been well cared for, but it was not nearly so fashionable as Aunt Franny's.

Kelswick, however, was something quite outside her experience. It must be at least four times the size of the manor, if not more. And "well cared for" did not begin to describe it. The setting sun was glinting off endless rows of windows that sparkled as if they had all been washed that very day. The pale gray stone of the facade looked as if it had been quarried only yesterday. Nothing looked worn. The very steps were as clean and white as if no one had ever trod on them. Even the gravel of the drive was perfectly raked.

Footmen in black and silver livery, complete with powdered wigs, appeared almost magically to open the carriage door, lower the steps and hand them out.

Kate tried not to stare. She had not expected anything like this, not when the duke who had come to call on her aunt had been dressed so simply. She hesitated to take the hand offered by the footman when the glove covering her hand was worn and mended and his was so pristine.

Suddenly, the gap between the Duke of Ashleigh and the runaway sister of Viscount Newell grew into a chasm.

She looked at her aunt, who was going up the steps as if she entered such houses every day. It suddenly occurred to Kate that this might actually be the kind of house Aunt Franny and Mama had known when they were girls. Mama had spoken of dinners, house parties, glittering affairs. Kate had assumed those memories were colored by nostalgia, but perhaps they had been nothing but the truth. In that case, Mama had indeed been thrust out of paradise when she was married off to Newell, who pocketed her dowry and then left her to molder in that shabby manor house near Grassington, married off by a father who saw no further than a title and thought a viscount was a good match for the daughter of a country baronet.

Kate shook off those thoughts and held up her head. She might never before have entered a building this impressive, but she was not about to let anyone know that. She walked in as proudly as a queen, allowed a servant to take her outer garments, and followed her aunt into the drawing room.

There, Kate blinked. She could not help it. The austere grandeur of the outside of the building had been bad enough. Here, there was warmth and color, but on such a scale that the people seemed almost insignificant. Crimson brocade draperies swathed windows at least ten feet high. Panels of silk in the same shade covered the walls. Chairs and settees upholstered in apple green velvet were arranged in groups scattered around the room, a crimson and green carpet covered the floor, and dozens of wax candles, in sconces and chandeliers, reflected over and over again in huge gilt-framed mirrors, lit the room even though it was not yet dark outside. Two fireplaces, on opposite sides of the room, gave out enough warmth to make shawls unnecessary.

Kate blinked again and tried to find the people in all this grandeur. She noticed Ashleigh at once, of course. He was even more austerely beautiful than when he first appeared at Aunt Franny's door. But, this evening, no one could have taken him for a farmer. With hauteur in every line of him, dressed impeccably, with black coat and breeches, a silvery brocaded waistcoat, and a cravat so white it almost glared, he was the very pattern of a duke, superior to all about him and perfectly aware of that fact. He looked straight at her, unsmiling, and she could not look away for a long moment. Was he finding her faded gown disgracefully inadequate to this splendor? So much the worse for him. She raised her chin and held her head even higher. She would not be intimidated.

Near him was the Earl of Merton, looking far less polished despite the fineness of his garments. He kept darting glances at a lady reclining on a settee who seemed to be laughing at him. That, thought Kate, must be Lady Merton. She was talking with a gentleman who bore some resemblance to the duke, though he was less striking. His hair was not so dark, his clothes were less perfectly tailored, and he lacked the air of being monarch of all he surveyed. Instead, he had a kindly look about him. A gentleman but not a nobleman, she thought.

At the moment, the duke was standing stiff and unsmiling between two women. One was a thin woman who looked at the newcomers as if they had brought an unpleasant smell into the room. Her gray hair was styled in an elaborate concoction of curls, ribbons and feathers, and she wore a gown of bright scarlet satin trimmed with gold lace. Its alarmingly deep décolletage might have looked attractive on a woman thirty years younger. The other woman, who was a good thirty years younger, looked too much like the duke to be anything but his sister. She had his almost black hair and clear gray eyes. She wore a fashionable dress of deep blue silk and a matching turban with a plume of white feathers. Beside her stood a young girl with the same dark hair, perhaps fifteen or sixteen years old, in white muslin. The girl looked at the newcomers with a delighted smile, and came hurrying to them, followed more slowly by Ashleigh and the other women. Merton seized the opportunity to travel to his wife's side.

"Mrs. Darling, I am so pleased to see you," said the girl. "And you must be Miss Darling." She turned to Kate with a smile of unaffected pleasure. "My uncle told me you were coming. I am Lady Clara Grammont, and it will be wonderful to have someone young in the neighborhood. I am sure we shall be great friends." She was about to take Kate by the arm and lead her away when her mother gave a slight cough. Lady Clara halted and gave Kate a rueful look. "I am running ahead too quickly again. I do that, I fear." She sighed as she turned to face her mother and uncle with an apologetic look.

Looking less frigid, though not quite smiling, Ashleigh bowed a greeting to the newcomers, who curtseyed in return. "Alice, Lady Wilton, I believe you already know Mrs. Darling." Mrs. Darling and Lady Wilton exchanged frosty nods. "May I present her niece, Miss Darling? Miss Darling, my sister, Lady Talmadge, my aunt, Lady Wilton, and, as you already know, my niece, Lady Clara." Lady Wilton offered an even frostier nod, but Lady Talmadge's smile of welcome seemed genuine.

The encounter drew the attention of a gentleman who had been holding forth to an elderly man who must, by his dress, have been the vicar. The gentleman turned away to stare at the newcomers through his quizzing glass. Having apparently decided that they were worth further investigation, he strolled over to them and struck a pose. It was obviously intended to display his padded shoulders and excruciatingly high collar points to best advantage. Kate found it difficult to restrain her amusement, especially when she saw Ashleigh's pained expression.

"And who might this be, Cuz?" the man drawled, looking Kate up and down in a way that drove all amusement from Kate's face. It was too much like the way Farnsworth had looked at her, as if she were an item being considered for purchase, not a person.

Nor did Ashleigh look amused. He drew in a sharp breath before he spoke tightly. "Miss Darling, may I present my cousin, George

Wilton? He and his mother are paying us a brief visit." Kate was certain that she heard a stress on the word *brief*.

Wilton leaned over in a semblance of a bow and started to reach for her hand. Kate managed to bob an acknowledgement of the introduction while stepping back, putting herself just out of reach, and giving Wilton a freezing look.

Lady Talmadge took Kate's arm and said, "You will excuse us, Wilton. I wish to introduce Miss Darling to Lady Merton." The women were off before Wilton could protest, leaving only Lady Wilton behind.

"Now that's a pretty little slip of a thing," said Wilton, keeping his quizzing glass on them as they walked away. "I don't recall being shown anything that attractive the last time I was here. Have you been keeping her hidden away?"

"Miss Darling has just come to stay with her aunt," said Ashleigh stiffly. He felt a totally irrational impulse to punch Wilton in the nose. "I would ask you to remember that they are gentlewomen and should be treated—and spoken of—as such."

"Gentlewomen!" sniffed Lady Wilton. "Cits, you mean, and stinking of the shop. It is an insult to expect us to dine with them."

"Feel free to depart at any time, Aunt," said Ashleigh. "I would not wish you to stay when you feel uncomfortable with my guests." He turned to Wilton. "I would, however, remind you that they are my *invited* guests and I will not have them treated with discourtesy."

LADY MERTON WAS, indeed, the woman receiving Lord Merton's hovering attentions. She was an attractive woman, not much older than Kate, with a laughing face. Merton was tucking a cushion under her feet when Lady Talmadge arrived with the newcomers. "Forgive me for not rising," Lady Merton said, smiling at Kate, "but Merton is being earl-like and insists I stay put."

"And we all know what an obedient wife you are," said Merton dryly.

She smiled fondly at him before confiding to the women, "I am hoping he will get all his fussing out of the way soon. Six more months of this will drive me mad."

"It's your own fault," said Lady Talmadge with a laugh. "If you didn't want him to fuss, you should have waited until the ninth month to tell him. Miranda, I would like to present Miss Darling. She has come to live with her aunt, and I thought to remove her from George's rather repulsive attentions."

Lady Merton made a face. "He is a loathsome creature, isn't he?" She turned to Kate and smiled. "I assure you that most people in the neighborhood are far more pleasant, and he is here only occasionally. We never need to suffer his presence for long."

A bit confused by Lady Merton's American accent, and not certain how to respond to such frankness, Kate ventured, "There are more offensive people in this world."

"No doubt." Lady Merton gave an airy wave. "However, I do not see why anyone should be required to suffer the bad simply because things could be worse. They could also be a good deal better."

Lord Merton smiled down fondly at his wife. "We are well aware of your limited tolerance for the bad."

"And this gentleman is Stephen Bancroft, a cousin of ours who is the steward for the estate." Lady Talmadge, still holding Kate's arm, introduced the gentleman who had been speaking with the Mertons.

Bancroft smiled and murmured the appropriate greetings, to which Kate murmured the appropriate responses. The duke's cousin. That explained the resemblance. But Mr. Bancroft seemed a far more comfortable personage, not nearly so forbidding, not nearly so overwhelming. What Kate noticed most about him, however, was the way his eyes kept turning to Lady Talmadge, even when he was being introduced to Kate. Whether Lady Talmadge was aware of his attention, Kate could not say. Perhaps she was since she seemed to carefully avoid meeting his eye.

Just then, a butler appeared, indicating that dinner was ready.

"We need not stand on ceremony when we are all friends here," Ashleigh announced to the room at large and walked over to offer Mrs. Darling his arm to lead her in to dinner. Wilton, under his mother's glare, stepped over to lead Lady Talmadge in, but too late. She was already going in on the arm of Mr. Bancroft, who had quickly stepped in as Wilton approached. So he seized on Kate, to his own pleasure but no one else's.

The dinner was excellent, Kate noted with delight, well prepared and well served, with nothing pretentious or excessive, and no more silver on the table than had been found at the squire's home. She had been afraid, given the overwhelming splendor of the house, that dinner would consist of a sequence of exotic and unrecognizable dishes that would make her feel like a country bumpkin. Instead, she could enjoy every bite, with honest pleasure.

She was, unfortunately, seated next to Wilton, who seemed convinced that she must feel honored by such proximity. His hands had a regrettable tendency to find themselves resting on her person. Neither glares nor icy looks made any impression on him, and each time she picked up his hand and removed it, he seemed to think this was some game they were playing.

The conversation, with so small a party, was general and, for the most part, pleasant. Mr. Chantry and Dr. Goddard—the vicar and the doctor—were both intelligent and cultured gentlemen, dealing comfortably with the duke, neither toadying nor denying him the deference due his rank. Ashleigh, in turn, displayed no condescension in his attitude, no arrogant assumption of superiority, but seemed to genuinely enjoy their company and conversation.

Wilton, on the other hand, endeavored to impress all present with his wit and sophistication. His comments, uttered in a loud voice with smug self-satisfaction, frequently had the effect of bringing any discussion to a halt. When the conversation turned to the controversy surrounding the government's purchase of the sculptures Lord Elgin had brought back from Greece, he said, "Ah, yes, beware of Greeks bearing gifts." While everyone paused, trying to puzzle out what, if any, relevance that remark had to anything that had been said previously, he turned to put his hand on Kate's arm yet once more and said condescendingly, "Homer, you know."

Kate had had enough. She was tired of being pawed. She was tired of being patronized. She turned to him and said, "Virgil, actually."

He looked startled, then laughed and patted her again. "Silly girl. Homer was a Greek chap. Wrote about the Trojan War."

"Indeed," said Kate, "but it was Virgil who told the tale of Laocoön warning the Trojans against taking the wooden horse into their city. The line you are thinking of is 'Timeo Danaos et dona ferentes'—'I fear the Greeks, even when they are bearing gifts.' You will find it in Book II of the *Aeneid*." She removed his hand from her arm, turned back to her dinner, and took a sip of wine.

Mr. Chantry and Dr. Goddard were looking at her in surprise. Merton was bent over with his face in his napkin, trying to choke off his laughter. The rest of the company displayed various degrees of amusement except for Ashleigh, who looked enigmatic, and Lady Wilton, who looked outraged.

Merton recovered his composure and smiled. "Sorry, Wilton, but I'm afraid the lady is correct. The reference is indeed to Virgil." He lifted his glass and dipped his head to Kate in a silent toast.

Lady Clara turned to her uncle, eyes sparkling with mischief. "Uncle Peter, I think I must spend more time on the classics myself. I should hate to appear foolish when I find myself in educated and cultured company."

Ashleigh looked at his niece impassively. "I trust that whatever company you find yourself in will be sufficiently well-bred that no one will ever be discomfited."

At that, Kate felt her face reddening in embarrassment. Yes, it had no doubt been rude and impertinent of her to point out Mr. Wilton's ignorance, and worse to have been feeling a bit smug about it. Nonetheless, what she had really wanted to do was stab him with her fork. Mr. Wilton's wandering hands had been far more than impertinent. That remark about discomfiture should have been directed to him. Why had the duke not chastised him? But then, she thought angrily, why would he? Wilton was a gentleman, cousin to the duke. She was a creature of no importance, a woman, someone who could be abused with impunity.

All her pleasure in the dinner and in the conversation evaporated. She kept her head high but held her tongue and simmered in silence until it was time for the ladies to withdraw.

Once they had reached the drawing room, however, Lady Wilton saw no need to hold her tongue. She turned to Mrs. Darling. "I am sure you must be mortified by the outrageous behavior of your niece." Mrs. Darling raised her brows as if she could not imagine what Lady Wilton meant and looked not in the least mortified, so Lady Wilton turned to Kate. "Miss Darling, whether real or pretended, a familiarity with books suitable only for gentlemen is hardly the sort of accomplishment that is becoming to a young woman. Even less becoming is your presumption in attempting to correct one who is your better. Such behavior will make it extremely difficult for you to find a husband."

Kate looked at her icily. This woman, the mother of that boorish idiot, had the temerity to chastise her? Then she saw her aunt shake her head quickly and remembered that she was supposed to be in hiding, and that meant hiding her birth. So she said, with a stiff smile, "Thank you for your instruction, Lady Wilton. It was, no doubt, most kindly meant. I shall endeavor to bear that in mind."

"Nonsense, Miss Darling," said Lady Merton with a laugh. "Pay no attention to such foolish advice. A woman who pretends to be a fool in order to catch a husband will end up with the fool she deserves." She took Kate's arm and reached out for Franny as well. "Now, would you ladies please be so kind as to join me over on that settee in the corner where we can have a pleasant chat?"

Lady Talmadge looked after Kate as she walked away. She had noticed the girl's initial prideful reaction to Lady Wilton's words and the aunt's silent warning. She had spent enough years of her married life sitting dutifully silent while observing others to know there was some mystery here. However, she had no intention of giving any support to her aunt's nonsense, so before she left, she looked into the distance and commented to no one in particular, "It is amazing, is it not, how foolish a man appears when he pretends to have knowledge he does not possess?" She turned and smiled at her aunt. "Perhaps if George were to listen more and speak less, he would not make quite such a spectacle of himself." Then she excused herself and strolled over to join Lady Merton and Kate.

While Lady Wilton continued to simmer, the other women all gathered around Kate to chatter happily, ignoring earlier events. Once Mrs. Darling made mention of her intention to take Kate to the local dressmaker, the others all chimed in with advice.

"You are truly fortunate in your coloring," said Lady Talmadge, looking at her consideringly. "You can wear virtually any color except perhaps scarlet."

"What about me? Could I wear scarlet?" Lady Clara looked hopeful.

Her mother laughed gently. "Someday, perhaps, but I'm afraid that for the next few years it is white for you, my pet, or very pale colors."

The ladies' warmth and friendliness had almost made Kate forget the embarrassment of the dinner table by the time the gentlemen came in, chatting cheerfully. At least, most of them were chatting cheerfully, Kate noticed. Mr. Wilton rather pointedly avoided looking at her, and went to sit apart from the others with his mother.

When Kate wandered over to admire one of the paintings, a rather fanciful depiction of classical ruins, Ashleigh came over to join her, a slight frown on his face. He must expect an apology, she thought. He was entitled to one, she supposed, since it was at his table that she had caused that little scene. She would not, however, apologize to that contemptible worm Wilton, even if the duke asked her to. So she held her head high and spoke to the duke's cravat. "I must apologize, Your Grace. It was wrong of me to embarrass Mr. Wilton in company that way."

Ashleigh shook his head, flushing slightly. "Not at all. It is I who owe you an apology, Miss Darling. Merton told me what I should have noticed, that my cousin was making himself offensive to you at the dinner table."

Kate looked up at him in surprise. She wished that she did not have to look up quite so far—his height made her feel at a disadvantage. Nonetheless, a duke apologizing? "You need not apologize for Mr. Wilton, Your Grace. You are not responsible for his behavior."

"But you are a guest in my home. I should not have allowed him to make you uncomfortable. Had I realized..."

Ah, he was apologizing because she was a guest in his home. Was it the offense to his position that rankled? That made some sense. Kate smiled slightly. "Nonetheless, it was not well done of me to embarrass him."

Ashleigh also smiled slightly. "I doubt you managed to do more than put even a small dent in his self-esteem, and I am certain his mama is presently repairing any damage. By tomorrow, he will be fully recovered, though I fear he is unlikely to renew his attentions to you. But then, I do not think you will find that too great a loss."

She did not know quite how to respond to that slightly flirtatious remark, so she turned back to the painting, and Ashleigh did the same. There were groups of figures, in costumes of perhaps two hundred years earlier, set in a landscape of ruined columns and arches. In the distance was a city of red-tiled roofs and ochre buildings. "It is a scene in Rome," he said, "perhaps by Claude, more likely only a copy." He smiled deprecatingly. "But I have always liked it. Does it appeal to the classicist in you?"

"I am hardly a classicist, Your Grace."

"There is no need for modesty. You seem to have a familiarity with Virgil that is unusual for a young lady, Miss Darling."

Kate regretted again having spoken out, not because she had been rude to Wilton but because she had drawn far too much attention to herself. It could be dangerous for her to stand out in any way, especially in any way that might be identified with Katherine Russell from Grassington. But then, she could not deny that there was a part of her that did want the duke's notice. She certainly noticed him. Who could not?

She tried a dismissive shrug. "Our vicar was a scholarly gentleman, exceedingly fond of the classics. There was no one else in our village who wished to study with him, so he taught me."

"He provided you with a respectable start. There are not many young women who have mastered enough Latin to be able to read Virgil."

He seemed to think he was paying her a compliment, but his amused smile was a bit too condescending for Kate's taste. She drew herself up and snapped, "To say nothing of Caesar and Livy and Tacitus. And enough Greek to be able to read Homer and the playwrights." She thought better of it a second later—would she never learn to hold her tongue?—but pride did not allow her to wish the words unsaid.

Ashleigh seemed taken aback, but not insulted. A bit of amusement remained in his face, however, and he said, "You had indulgent parents, then, to allow their daughter to have such an unusual education."

She chose her words carefully this time. "My mother considered that education was a benefit to children of both sexes, and my father did not concern himself with my upbringing."

"He must have been startled, then, to find himself with a daughter who recited Homer to him of an evening rather than play a minuet on the pianoforte."

She could not suppress a bitter sniff. "I cannot recall that my father ever passed an evening with us. My mother and I spent our evenings with our needlework or reading when we could." *Needlework sounded more ladylike than mending, and they did read whenever someone had lent them a book.*

"You must allow me to show you the library here." Ashleigh led her to an enormous room with space enough for massive columns of pale gold marble dividing it into sections and case upon case of books. The room was so high that a spiral staircase led to a balcony giving access to the upper shelves. Kate had never seen so many books. She took a deep breath. She could smell the leather bindings and the slightly dusty scent old books could not avoid, the most glorious perfume in the world, she thought.

"They are not all of great interest." Ashleigh grinned at Kate. "The north wall is devoted to collections of sermons and theological debates of the past few centuries. I suspect that the only person to so much as touch them in the last fifty years has been the housemaid assigned to dusting." He picked up a candelabra and led her to a section off to their side. "This is where you will find the classics."

Kate followed and once she was close enough to see what was there, she could not restrain a gasp. It was not only that there were so many books, but that they were such beautiful books. Here was everything that Dr. Finley, the vicar who had been her teacher, had even so much as mentioned. His own library had included only a few dozen volumes, and those in the cheapest board bindings. But here, everything was bound in leather, in jewel colors of red, green and blue, stamped with gilt letters. The very scent was the smell of luxury. "The plays are all here," she half-whispered. "You have Aeschylus, Euripides, the comedies of Aristophanes—and all of Sophocles." She turned back to look at him. "I have read only his *Oedipus*. Dr. Finley did not have any of his other plays."

She saw the startled expression on his face. It did not last long—he covered it well—but it was enough to betray him. She knew. He had not believed her when she said she read Greek. He had assumed she was boasting. After all, ladies do not read Greek. He had thought she would not be able to even decipher the Greek letters on the spines. The insult stiffened her spine.

He reached out to remove one of the books. "This is the *Antigone* of Sophocles. I have always thought that it poses profound questions about duty. If you would care to read it, I would be interested to hear your thoughts." He proffered it to her, perhaps as an apology for his doubt.

The volume was a thing of beauty, bound in dark red calf with heavy, deckled pages. Her irritation dissipated as she found herself hungering to touch the book itself, to caress that smooth leather, not just devour the contents. When she looked up to meet his eye, she saw no mockery there, no condescension, only interest and curiosity. Perhaps too much curiosity. Perhaps too much interest. "Thank you, Your Grace. It would give me great pleasure to read it. And I assure you, I will take the greatest care of your book."

Their fingers touched as she took the book, and her eyes widened. She could have sworn she felt something in that touch, some reaction she did not recognize or wish to acknowledge. She did not want to feel any attraction to him, to feel any spark between them. It was impossible. That was a complication she did not need in her life. She should feel nothing but wariness. Anything else was dangerous, foolishly, stupidly dangerous. It would be safest to have nothing—or at least very little—to do with him. She offered him a polite smile of thanks and hurried away.

HE WATCHED HER walk away, head held high. She had felt it, too, that spark between them, that connection. Had he expected that? Perhaps he had. Certainly, he knew he had been aware of her the moment she arrived, and he thought she had been equally aware of him. There was the way their eyes had locked as soon as she entered the room.

It was inappropriate, he knew. He had tried to avoid looking at her during dinner, but all that effort had accomplished was to allow that pig, Wilton, to paw at her. He smiled as he remembered the shocked look on Wilton's face when she corrected him, and the tiny little bit of smugness on hers. It shouldn't have been necessary. He should have prevented her discomfiture, but he had to admire the way she had defended herself.

She was an odd little creature, with her unusual learning, odd but fascinating. He could not remember ever being so intrigued by a woman. She spoke and behaved like a lady, and had the pride of a lady of high birth, though the shabby dress betokened a lack of fortune. Her father had, it seemed, taken little care for her future. The difference between her breeding and her present circumstances might explain her quickness to take offense. She was fortunate to be taken in by Frances Darling, a generous woman and a sensible one.

Whatever her fortune, she was remarkably lovely. There was that mass of pale hair, with glints of gold in the candlelight. There was so much of it, it would tumble past her waist when she took it down, he thought. And those green eyes—it was the way they tilted slightly at the outer corners, and the slant of her brows that gave her that elfin look. She was not tall but she moved with grace. Still, she was so thin that she appeared fragile, in need of care, in need of protection. In need of a protector?

He stopped smiling and mentally shook himself. That was no way to be thinking of Andrew Darling's niece. The Darlings had been the sole source of warmth in his childhood. He had escaped to their house whenever he could to play with the dog, to be fed jam tarts, to be a child. Later, when he had inherited the dukedom, Andrew Darling had helped him make sense of it, to bring it back to order.

Most of all, Andrew Darling had taught him to be an honorable man.

Now he was the Duke of Ashleigh. He was not some careless libertine like Wilton who would prey on innocents. And Miss Darling was clearly an innocent. He could offer her the protection of his friendship, of his interest, but nothing more.

〉〉〉〈〈〈

THE NEXT DAY, Wilton asked for an interview with the duke. It was granted, and some twenty minutes later, Mr. Wilton could be seen leaving the duke's office with hasty steps, his face flushed with humiliation.

Shortly thereafter, Lady Wilton marched angrily into the duke's office. It required only ten minutes for her to march even more angrily out.

Within the hour, their coach was carrying them down the drive, followed by the second carriage, carrying their bags, her lady's maid and his valet, all tossed in hastily. Lady Talmadge watched this from the window of her sitting room with no little surprise. It was not that she regretted their departure in the least, but good manners normally required parting guests, even uninvited ones, to at least bid farewell to their hostess.

She returned to the menu the cook had sent up. If they no longer had the Wiltons to entertain, and no other guests were expected for dinner, a much simpler meal would suffice. She crossed off the second soup, three of the side dishes, and one of the roasts. When the footman came in response to her ring, she handed him the revised menu and asked him to tell the cook that there would be only four for dinner.

Then she went down to see her brother.

He was at his desk as he usually was at this time of day, reading reports on his various interests and looking over the recommendations from Stephen Bancroft in preparation for their daily conference. He was also looking cheerful, almost smug. When she stepped in, he stood up and smiled.

She made herself comfortable in the leather armchair facing him. "I see that our guests have departed."

His smile broadened as he settled back into the comfort of his own chair.

"You look so pleased with yourself that I conclude you had something to do with the discourteous haste of their departure," she continued.

His smile persisted. "Wilton asked for an interview to request your hand. I told him that I would never give my permission and that I considered him a totally unfit suitor. Quite apart from his personal failings of character there is the fact that you are, after all, the daughter of a duke. Then his mother stormed in. If he was not high enough for you, she proposed a match with Clara, since her father was only an earl. I told her that even if Clara were not young enough to be his daughter, I would never allow her to marry a dissolute fool like Wilton. Apparently, they took it all amiss."

Lady Talmadge frowned slightly. "You seem quite proud of yourself."

He gave a deprecating wave. "Merton told me that I have been overly courteous in the past, that I raised false expectations. It seems he was correct in that they were surprised at my refusal of Wilton's suit. I shall try to avoid raising false expectations again."

Lady Talmadge continued to frown. "I do not suppose you stopped to consider that you are not the one to be either raising or lowering expectations? That perhaps I am fully capable of refusing his suit? That decisions about Clara's future should be my decisions?"

He stared at his sister and his smile faded. There was a sharpness in her tone he had not heard before. "Really, Alice, you cannot mean to tell me you wished to encourage Wilton."

"Of course not. I do, however, think that you are being more than a bit high-handed here." She blew out an angry breath. "Besides, I had prepared a number of blistering setdowns to give him, and now I will not have an opportunity to use them."

Ashleigh relaxed again. "Fear not. I am certain that when we re-move to London next spring there will be quite enough insolent creatures hanging about you to give you ample scope for your blistering setdowns."

"And I trust you will not interfere. You really must stop treating me like a child. I am quite capable of distinguishing a rake from an honest gentleman, and of knowing a fortune hunter when I see one."

"I am certain that you are," he said soothingly, "but you cannot think it an insult when I seek to protect you. Is that not what a brother is for? I was unable to do so while you were married to Talmadge. Do not deny me the privilege now."

"Yes, but... but try not to overdo it."

He smiled.

She closed her eyes. She knew perfectly well that he wanted only the best for her, but she sometimes felt as if she were suffocating. He was her younger brother, after all. How would he like it if he was treated like a child, an incompetent child, all the time?

One of these days, she needed to give him a taste of that medicine.

# CHAPTER THREE

*Yorkshire*

NEWELL STUMBLED THROUGH the front door of his ancestral mansion and grasped hold of the door jamb to keep himself upright. He swayed as he peered through the gloom. Night had not fallen, but he had consumed a large quantity of ale at the Ring o' Bells, the nearest tavern. That had taken nearly the last of his coin, but after the hellish trip to get here—nearly three weeks on public stages, selling off his spare clothes to pay the fare, with nights spent in fields more often than not—he felt entitled to any comfort he could get.

Not that there looked to be much comfort awaiting him here in the gloom. God, he hadn't lived here since the day his father had taken him off to school, and he hadn't wanted to. Even the few nights he had spent here when he came to see what there was after his mother's death and when he had come to fetch Katherine had been a nightmare. Sleeping in the bloody butler's pantry, for God's sake, because the rest of the house wasn't fit to live in. The manor, he thought bitterly. It didn't even have a name. Just the manor. How his mother and Katherine survived it all those years he didn't know.

He pushed himself off the wall and staggered through empty rooms, inhabited only by insects and vermin. Eventually, he found his way to the kitchen, which was no more welcoming than the rest had been. The fire in the hearth was only a memory. He stumbled down the passageway and found the butler's pantry where there was still a cot, though the sheets and blankets had vanished. He didn't care. He lay down and was oblivious in moments in a state half-sleep and half-stupor.

Come morning, the world showed no improvement. If anything, it was worse, for now his head was splitting, his stomach was tossing, and he was cold. Bitterly cold. He should make a fire. Unfortunately, he did not actually know how to do that. He knew he needed wood, but it probably needed to be chopped or something. Didn't wood need to be chopped? To hell with it.

He rubbed his cheek. He needed a shave. His razor was in his bag, but where was his bag? Ah, yes, he'd put it down at the tavern. It was probably still there. He doubted these clowns would dare disturb a bag belonging to the viscount. And the tavernkeeper could provide him with hot water, perhaps even a bath. He'd doubtless be honored to be of service.

A few hours later, Newell had revised his opinion of the clowns. They had not touched his bag, to be sure. However, they showed not the slightest glimmer of deference to his station. The tavernkeeper had the audacity to offer hot water for a price, and that price to be given before the water was supplied. He had been of a mind to give the lout a good thrashing, and would have done so had he been feeling more himself.

Then when he had asked where his sister was, the lout had denied all knowledge of her, had even been surprised to hear she had returned. Impossible. In a village this size, Katherine's return could never have passed unnoticed. She was not in the house. No one had been living there in months—that had been obvious from the layers of dust everywhere. Someone had to be giving her shelter.

He stomped out of the tavern and looked around. He didn't even know who lived in this godforsaken place. There was a church, however. He could see a steeple in the distance. That meant there was probably a vicar, and a vicar was the sort of person Katherine might turn to. He seemed to remember her going to church on Sundays in London. God, she was so prissily self-righteous. He turned back to the tavern, opened the door and bellowed, "Where does the vicar live?"

Jason Powell, the tavernkeeper, stepped outside and closed the door behind him. He was no taller than Newell, and there would be no more than a few ounces difference in their weight. However, much of Newell's weight was fat. Powell's was solid muscle. In no hurry to assist the viscount, he stared for a minute before saying, "Dr. Finley lives in the vicarage."

Newell huffed in exasperation. "And where might the vicarage be?"

Powell didn't bother to hide his sneer as he looked at Newell. "Next to the church."

Newell waited for a "my lord". It didn't come. He was about to demand it, but the look in Powell's eyes dissuaded him and he turned away in silence.

The vicarage, however, proved to be of no assistance. The vicar was there, right enough. Dr. Finley was a small man, bent over in a scholar's hump, with snowy hair, an angelic smile, and absolutely no idea where Katherine could be. The news that she was missing caused him great distress, great distress, indeed. He was horrified, in point of fact. He had been expecting to hear from her, and had been worrying when no letters arrived. Yes, he agreed, if she had returned to Grassington, she would most certainly have come to him, most certainly. Or, of course, to the squire.

"The squire?" Newell demanded.

"Oh, yes," said Dr. Finley. "The squire and his family are very fond of Katherine. They will be most upset to hear that she is missing. You really should have taken better care of her, you know. She is your responsibility now."

The old man paid no heed to Newell's grimace. He was hobbling around as he spoke, collecting a scarf and a cape, and then he headed for the door. He paused and looked at Newell. "Well, come along then," he said.

"Where are we going?"

"To see the squire, of course. He needs to be told Katherine has been lost."

The vicar moved with surprising speed, and Newell had to hurry to keep up with him. It was close to two miles before they turned into the gates, and another mile before they reached the house. Newell was limping, and annoyed that Dr. Finley did not seem even a bit winded.

"Tell the squire that we must see him at once," Dr. Finley told the butler as he walked in and hurried down the hall. "We will wait in the library." Newell followed. He did not seem to have any choice.

Nor did he have a chance to sit down before a sturdy gentleman of middle years hurried in wearing a worried frown. "Finley, what is the matter?"

Dr. Finley waved at Newell. "This is Viscount Newell, Katherine's brother. You will remember him from his visit after Lady Newell's death."

The squire turned to the younger man and gave a nod. "Ah, Newell. Horatio Grant, at your service." Then he sniffed and looked more closely, making Newell uncomfortably aware that he was not smelling particularly fresh. "Where is Katherine? Is she with you?"

"He seems to have misplaced her," said Dr. Finley, frowning at the young man.

"No, no," said Newell. "The silly creature has run away, and I'm trying to find her."

"Run away? You mean to tell us she eloped?" asked Grant. "Bless my soul."

"Elope? Katherine? That doesn't sound a bit like her, I must say. Whom did she elope with? Whoever it was, she can't have known him very long. I'm quite sure she had formed no attachment with any of the young men around here." A sensible-looking lady entered the room and the conversation.

"This is Katherine's brother, my dear, and he's come looking for her. Newell, my wife."

Mrs. Grant nodded coolly to Newell. "Why are you looking for her here if she has eloped?"

"She hasn't eloped," said Newell, finally getting a chance to speak. "She ran away, and I assumed she had returned to her old home. I've come to take her back."

"Well, dear me, this is the first I've heard of it," said Grant. "Run away, you say? How extraordinary. She certainly isn't here, is she, my dear?" He turned to his wife, who was looking at Newell.

"Why would she have run away, my lord?" asked Mrs. Grant. She was looking at Newell in a decidedly unfriendly manner.

Newell flushed. She sounded as if it were his fault Katherine was gone. "No idea, I've no idea at all. You know how girls are, silly creatures. Get all upset about some trifle."

"Really?" Dr. Finley shook his head. "Perhaps it's the air in London. She always seemed a very sensible, levelheaded girl when she was living here. Not at all silly."

"Indeed, it is most unlike her to get upset about trifles. If she ran away, it must have been over something serious." Mrs. Grant was still looking at Newell in a way that made him quite uncomfortable. She reminded him of one of the masters at school, the one who had always known when he was lying. "You've no idea what could have upset her?"

"No idea whatsoever," he insisted, "but I must get her back." That second part he managed with great intensity since it was perfectly true. He was terrified at the thought of facing Farnsworth if he was unsuccessful. "Have you any idea where she might have gone? I must find her. It is vitally important." He could hear himself pleading now, pleading to these bumpkins. He hated it, but could not seem to help it.

"Important? Of course it is important," said Grant. He frowned at Newell. "A young girl like that all on her own. I must say, you don't appear to have taken very good care of her. Not at all."

"Well," said Mrs. Grant thoughtfully, "she did always long to visit the Lake District. She was quite fond of Mr. Wordsworth's poetry. Could she have saved up enough of her pin money to enable her to travel?"

Newell looked at the woman with intense dislike. Pin money! She was taunting him, he knew. She probably didn't know where Katherine was—they had all seemed honestly surprised to learn of her disappearance—but he was sure she had an idea and was not going to tell him. Perhaps that would be enough for Farnsworth. He hoped so, for apparently it would have to do.

THE SQUIRE LOOKED at his wife thoughtfully. Something was clearly going on here, but he was not about to try to bring it into the open. He trusted his wife's judgment, and he had no reason to trust Newell. On the contrary. He had disliked Newell when he turned up for the first time in years after his mother's death and he had been very sorry to see Katherine leave with him. He did not seem at all the sort of man to be in charge of a young woman, for all he was her brother.

Right now, however, he wanted to get Newell out of here. Finley seemed to be of the same opinion, for he was dithering away at Newell to urge his return to London.

Grant drew the viscount to the side for some private conversation, with his wife's nod of approval. It did not take long to discover that the only reason the viscount might linger in the neighborhood was that he lacked the funds to get him back to London. That problem was easy enough to solve and, very shortly, the viscount was in the Grants' own carriage, being taken to Leeds, where the coachman had orders to buy him a ticket and see him safely on the London stage.

They waved him off, waiting at the door until the carriage was out of sight. Then Dr. Finley ceased to dither and turned a sharp glance at his hostess. Grant asked his wife, *"Do* you know where Kate is?"

"No. I assure you, and you, too, Dr. Finley," she turned to the vicar, "I have told no lies. I have no actual knowledge. I will not deny that I have a suspicion, but that is because Lady Newell was my friend. And because she was my friend, I have my doubts as to the new viscount's suitability as a guardian for his sister. Kate is not a fool. If she ran away, she must have had good reason."

"I can't say I took to him myself," said Grant, "but she can't be left out there on her own with no one to protect her."

Mrs. Grant nodded. "If I find she is not safely where I suspect, I will tell you. But meanwhile, I will leave you to plead ignorance in all innocence." Then she thought again. "There is another place she may have gone, and you may be the best one to make inquiries there. Her mother's family—I know Mary's father is dead, but she had at least one brother. Kate may have turned to him."

Grant scowled. "Never even came to the funeral. No sense of responsibility, any of them, her family or his. How they produced two good ladies like Lady Newell and Kate, I can't imagine. I'll ride over myself, just in case."

# CHAPTER FOUR

*Sussex*

L̲ADY CLARA WAS dining with her mother and her uncle, who appeared greatly amused as she recounted her recent adventures, having been allowed to join in the discussions at the dressmaker's where Miss Darling was ordering some new gowns. Lady Clara's opinion had even been solicited as they chose fabrics and trimmings.

"Do you mean to tell me that a young lady who can read Greek and Latin and quote Virgil—quite accurately—is unable to choose a new dress without assistance?" asked Ashleigh as he carved the mutton into neat slices.

His niece looked at him in exasperation, and Lady Talmadge said, "Don't be difficult, Peter. The two things have nothing to do with each other." Then she looked thoughtful and added, "And do be sure to take some peas. You are eating far too much meat of late. I fear it is distressing your digestion."

He looked at his sister incredulously.

She smiled—*see how he likes being treated like a child*—and continued, "It is of great importance for an unmarried young woman, especially one with neither fortune nor connections, to present a proper appearance. I am glad she is doing something about it."

Ashleigh frowned slightly as he resumed his seat. "What was

wrong with her appearance? I thought she looked quite pretty when she came to dinner, though I suppose her dress was a trifle drab."

Lady Clara sighed dramatically. "Uncle Peter, really! Her dress was faded and years out of date. That sort of thing is dreadfully depressing for a girl. I promise you that when you see her at the Assembly Ball next week, you will be struck dumb with amazement. 'Quite pretty' indeed!"

"The Assembly is next week? Oh, good. Ambruster is coming to visit. He wants to talk to me about investing in some canal project. He's bringing his wife and daughter, and that will give them something to do."

She would be at the Assembly Ball. Ashleigh had not seen her since that dinner. She had, however, managed to pop into his thoughts with alarming frequency, and every time he thought he had succeeded in banishing her, Alice and Clara brought her name up. They seemed to be making something of a pet of her, and he gathered that Miranda had also taken her up. Perhaps she would dwindle into the commonplace when he saw her again, and would stop sending his thoughts, his highly improper thoughts, down paths they should not take.

And perhaps not. He frowned at his plate.

Lady Talmadge smiled at him. "A canal project? Really, Peter, how can you be so naive? The only project the Ambrusters are interested in is a marriage between you and Selina."

"Selina Webster? Eeew!" said Lady Clara. "Please, Uncle Peter, not her. She's horrid."

Ashleigh raised a brow. "Miss Webster is a very beautiful young woman of considerable poise and elegance, with a very nice sense of decorum. Some might suggest that my niece could take her for a pattern."

Lady Talmadge looked at her daughter. "If you ever start behaving like Selina Webster, I will disown you." Then she turned to her brother. "You can't possibly want Clara to be like Selina, can you?"

The question was half-amused, half-worried.

"No," said Ashleigh with a rueful smile. "For all her virtues, Selina is so icily correct that the temperature drops immediately when she enters a room. Her mother's conversation is devoted to pointing out the many ways in which Selina is suited to being a duchess. Selina's conversation, on the other hand, seems to be devoted to pointing out the faulty behavior of everyone else."

Lady Talmadge tilted her head and looked at her brother. Dinner progressed through the next course and the plates were being removed when she turned to her daughter. "You may go upstairs, Clara. I need to speak with your uncle."

The girl gave a long-suffering sigh and rolled her eyes but went.

Lady Talmadge returned her attention to her brother. "You give a misleading impression, you know. The last time you encountered the Ambrusters, you were so courteous that they clearly thought you were on the verge of making an offer. And I was hideously afraid they might be right."

Ashleigh sat back and gave his sister a look of alarm. "Really, Alice, you know me better than that. I was simply trying to keep from showing how tiresome I found them."

"I hoped that was so, but I was beginning to fear you might be considering Selina Webster simply because she would never indulge in behavior that could cause a scandal."

"There's nothing wrong with wanting to avoid gossip and scandal. Our parents provided quite enough of that to last this family for generations," said Ashleigh sharply. "When I marry, I will want a well-bred wife, to be sure, one whose birth and education will enable her to fulfill the position of duchess with decorum, but that is not enough. I want a wife who understands and accepts the duties, not just the privileges, of her position. Miss Webster is well aware that those below her have a duty to her, but does not seem to consider that she might have a duty to them as well."

"And you think that is enough? Birth, decorum, and an acceptance of duty?"

Enough? He thought of a girl who looked like a sprite, a prideful girl with a surprising education. A slim, graceful girl with green eyes. He shook his head sadly. "No, I know it is not. After all, you brought all of that and more to your marriage to Talmadge, and I cannot think that was an example to emulate."

A shadow crossed her face and she gave her head a small shake.

Ashleigh tore himself from thoughts of green eyes and looked at her with real concern. "Do you think to marry again, Alice? You have no need to do so, of course, but you are still young, and you do not need me to tell you that you are beautiful. You could have your pick of suitors."

"I truly do not know what I want. At first, after Talmadge died, I was simply relieved to be free of him. But sometimes, when I see Miranda so happy with Merton, I am reminded that not all marriages have to be like mine."

"If you wed again, it will be your choice, Alice. I promise you that it will be your choice and there will be no pressure from me."

"And will it be Clara's choice, too, when she is of an age to wed? You will not be like Franny Darling's father, who disowned her when she wed a cit?"

"Is that what happened? I never knew." Ashleigh shook his head. "Andrew Darling was the kindest, most honorable man I ever knew."

"But he had no title. He was not even a gentleman." Alice looked steadily at her brother.

He smiled. "Very well. If that is what you are asking. If Clara falls in love with a man as good and honorable as Andrew Darling, I will not forbid the match. Should she declare herself in love with a libertine, however, that is an entirely different story."

Alice laughed. "You need not worry. In that case, I will forbid the banns myself. But we have strayed from our topic, which was a marriage for you. Do you seek a love match then?"

Thoughts of Miss Darling leaped into his mind. They had been doing that all too frequently. He shrugged them aside. "What man does not hope, at least secretly, for a wife he loves? But that is not always possible. I have responsibilities to the estate, to the title, to the country, that I cannot ignore. Were I to make a foolish marriage, I could lose the respect of my peers. That would mean that I would lose any influence I might have in the Lords and elsewhere. Still, at the very least, I want a wife who will share my life, be a companion, someone who is not a fool. I don't know that I must be in love with her, but I will need to like her."

His sister smiled fondly at him as she rose to depart. "I hope for far more for you but, at the very least, I hope she makes you laugh. You have not been laughing nearly as much in recent years as you should."

THREE DAYS LATER, Lord Ambruster and his family arrived at a nicely judged hour of the afternoon. It allowed time for a cup of tea while their servants unpacked and then a sufficiency of time for Lady Ambruster and Miss Webster to dress for dinner.

Their appearance at dinner was also nicely judged. Miss Webster, as an unmarried young woman, albeit one approaching her twenty-third birthday, wore white muslin with small puffed sleeves and carried a Kashmir shawl of pink and gold in case the evening proved chilly. Her golden curls were elaborately entwined with ribbons and pearls, and her rosebud of a mouth was fixed in a small smile. Lady Ambruster, a handsome woman, chose to present a subdued appearance in shades of gray, intending perhaps to serve as a foil for the springtime freshness of her daughter.

Their jewelry was also understated. Miss Webster wore only a cameo on a ribbon about her neck, but it was a very fine, very ancient cameo. Her mother wore a simple brooch of amethysts and pearls, but they were flawless amethysts.

Their appearance proclaimed, "We know precisely what is appropriate for a small dinner at the splendid country home of a duke." Lady Talmadge could not help but acknowledge that they had judged it to a nicety. The duke noticed only that Miss Webster looked much like a china doll and was equally expressionless.

Lady Talmadge had planned dinner with equally nice judgment. There were sufficient dishes, of sufficient quality, to welcome the guests without being too welcoming. After all, she had spent the fifteen years of her married life doing little but making such judgments. It was pleasant to know that those years had not been entirely wasted.

There had been an awkward moment when the Ambrusters realized that Stephen Bancroft, who was to dine with them, was the duke's steward. They were only slightly mollified to discover that he was also the duke's cousin. Lady Ambruster and her daughter managed to get through dinner without ever actually directing a remark to him. Since their conversation consisted almost entirely of remarks about the weather, comments on upcoming marriages and minor scandals in the *ton,* and praise for what they had seen of Kelswick so far, Bancroft was more amused than offended.

⋙⋘

BY THE FOLLOWING afternoon, Ashleigh, suffering from a surfeit of nicely judged civility, felt the need to claim a previous appointment and escaped into Lewes. He avoided the center of town, where the milliner and draper had shops across from the Crown Inn, the most likely attractions in the town should the Ambrusters decide on an excursion. Leaving his horse at the livery stable, he walked up the hill to the crooked old building that held Mr. Prufrock's bookshop.

A bell signaled his entrance, but he did not expect any notice to be taken of that. Prufrock spent his days ensconced in a corner, his cane next to him, surrounded by piles of books with a lamp providing just enough light to enable him to read. If any customers actually needed him or wished to make a purchase, they generally knew where to find him.

Ashleigh paused, waiting for his eyes to accustom themselves to the gloom. Once they did, he was surprised to see that he was not the only visitor to the shop. Miss Darling was standing by one of the tables with a book in one hand and a cloth in the other, staring at him with her mouth open. It appeared she had been in the process of dusting and arranging some of the books. How very odd.

Odder still, Prufrock was standing beside her leaning on his cane.

"Good day, Your Grace." The old man nodded a greeting. Miss Darling said nothing but bobbed a quick curtsey.

"Prufrock, Miss Darling." Ashleigh nodded in return. He was not comfortable. He did not care for surprises. He did not need Miss Darling stepping out of his dreams and appearing in person. This bookshop had always been a refuge for him. He had been able to come here and browse through the stocks of books, occasionally coming across a hidden treasure. Well, perhaps not a hidden treasure. Prufrock always knew what he had and knew its value as well. But he had been able to explore these shelves in peace and quiet, with no one bothering him, no one demanding his attention, his assistance, his decision. How could he do that with Miss Darling here? How could he possibly ignore her presence?

"You know Miss Darling, do you?" Prufrock was beaming at the young woman. "She's been trying to convince me that I need an assistant, that I could do more business if I straighten the place up a bit, maybe have some chairs and offer tea or some such to bring more people in. What do you think, Your Grace?"

Ashleigh frowned. He liked the shop just the way it was. "I don't see why you would want to change at all." Miss Darling seemed to be recovering from her surprise, but had returned to her dusting and was not looking at him. Why wouldn't she meet his eye? She had not seemed at all diffident at their last meeting.

"I don't know, maybe I should make some changes. That cousin of yours was in here the other day."

"My cousin? Bancroft?"

"No, no, not him. I know Mr. Bancroft well enough. The fancy one with the quizzing glass."

"Ah. Wilton."

"That's the one." The old man nodded, smiling.

"I confess myself surprised. I would not have thought Wilton much of a reader."

"No, nor do I think he is. He wanted to know where I keep the special books. The ones that wouldn't be out on display." Prufrock shook his head. "I offered him Catullus, but he seemed to need pictures."

Miss Darling did not manage to suppress a snort of laughter. "That is not at all the sort of change I was suggesting, and you know it, Mr. Prufrock."

Ashleigh frowned slightly. She could at least disguise the fact that she knew who Catullus was, a most inappropriate poet for a young lady. But when she looked up with an impish smile, he had to smile back. "I don't suppose he was interested in Ovid's *Art of Love* either," he said.

Prufrock was happily chuckling away and did not notice that though their smiles had faded, his visitors were staring at each other.

Miss Darling broke the spell first and returned to her dusting. "One change I was suggesting to Mr. Prufrock is that he set up a lending library. What do you think of that idea, Your Grace?"

"A lending library?" Ashleigh frowned. "Whatever for? Why not just sell the books?"

She looked at him in exasperation. "Because, Your Grace, not everyone can afford to buy all the books they would like. Let us say that a subscription to the lending library costs a guinea a year, and that allows the subscriber to borrow ten books. That is just over two shillings per book, and even inexpensive Minerva Press books cost at least six shillings."

He smiled at her. "I can see how that benefits the borrower, but how does it benefit Mr. Prufrock?"

"Because he can lend the same book out over and over again. Suppose he has ten Minerva Press books for which he paid three pounds. They provide reading matter for ten subscribers for a year, and those subscribers have paid ten guineas for the privilege of borrowing those books. He has a clear profit of more than seven pounds."

Mr. Prufrock chortled. "You must admit, Your Grace, that's a neat little profit. Very neat, indeed. I don't say that it would work out quite that way. Some books would be more expensive, and some won't be as popular as I expect, and people don't always treat books with the respect they deserve. Can't guarantee that some books won't come back a bit worse for the wear. Still, it's not a bad idea, is it?"

"No, no, I don't suppose it is a bad idea." Ashleigh spoke slowly in an effort to give himself time to get his mind around the idea of Miss Darling proposing ideas like this at all. And it wasn't a bad idea. He supposed it might be a very good idea if one wanted more customers. But he didn't want more customers in Prufrock's bookstore. He liked it just the way it was.

His musings were interrupted when he realized that Miss Darling was putting on her gloves and bonnet.

"I fear I must be on my way. I will come by another day, Mr. Prufrock."

"Aye, do that," he said. "It's always a pleasure to hear you trying to convince me."

"You are going home?" asked Ashleigh. "Allow me to accompany you."

She hesitated, as if she was about to refuse him, but instead said, "Thank you, Your Grace."

They stepped out onto the pavement. Ashleigh offered his arm, which Miss Darling took. He was pleased that she did not look so very thin as she had the first time he saw her. Though she still looked delicate, even fragile, she was definitely more sprite than waif now. It helped that her clothes were not so shabby. Her gloves may not have been of the finest French kid, but they looked new and clean. Her dress of some sort of blue stuff had little green leaves all over it and her spencer was green, too. Quite pretty. Her bonnet, though, had one of those deep rims that hid her face unless she was turned to him. Annoying.

He cleared his throat. She turned to look at him. Those eyes of hers were truly amazing. She started to turn away, so he said the first thing that popped into his head. "Was the lending library the only change you were proposing for Prufrock? I'm not at all sure I like the idea of an increase in his business. I have always enjoyed the peace and quiet of his shop."

"Mr. Prufrock, however, might enjoy a little more income." Her tone was a trifle sarcastic. "I also pointed out that if he did that, he could then hire an assistant. The increase in business would pay for the assistant and give him more leisure."

"More leisure?" Ashleigh smiled. "Whatever would he do with more leisure? I cannot imagine old Prufrock away from his books."

"Perhaps you cannot, Your Grace, but Mr. Prufrock has expressed a desire to retire, and I suggested an assistant instead."

"Retire? I confess I am surprised. I had never thought about it, but I suppose he must be getting on in age." He smiled ruefully. "I suppose there is a part of oneself that expects those about one to go on forever unchanged. Yet where could he find an assistant hereabouts?"

"I was suggesting myself."

"You? Really, Miss Darling!" He chuckled.

"You think me incapable?" Her tone of voice was suddenly frosty.

"Not at all. I was in no way mocking you." He did not wish to sound as if he thought her foolish, though he did, so he tried to choose his words carefully. "It is only that it does not strike me as a suitable occupation for a young lady."

"Not suitable." She seemed to find that amusing. "Your Grace, there are very few occupations available to a 'young lady' in my position. My aunt has kindly given me a home, but I cannot impose on her charity forever. I have no trade and I do not wish to be a servant, even so genteel a servant as a governess or companion. It appears to me that employment in a shop is perhaps the most honorable alternative available. It would provide me with independence."

"Miss Darling, I am certain that your aunt does not find you a burden. Indeed, she seems delighted to have your company."

"And I am very grateful to her. However, it cannot be more than a temporary arrangement, I fear."

She was turned away from him, and he could not see her expression. He would have to speak with Mrs. Darling to see what this was all about. Find employment as a shop assistant—it was ridiculous even if Prufrock were fool enough to agree to such a plan. Miss Darling had clearly been raised as a gentlewoman and she had been educated at a level far above that of most women of his acquaintance. He could not stomach the notion of her waiting upon her inferiors in a shop. He would not permit it. There must be something he could do for her.

"Ah, look, the primroses are already fading. At home, they would scarce be in bloom so early." She had halted to look at the clusters of yellow flowers growing at the edge of the hedgerow.

He looked around him, relieved by the change of subject, and realized that they had turned into the lane leading to Mrs. Darling's house. "Do you know, I cannot recall ever having walked along this lane before."

"But you have often visited my aunt's house, have you not?"

"Yes, but if I walked, it was across the fields to approach from the rear, and if I came this way, I was on horseback. It is easy to overlook things when one is atop a horse. I never even noticed that primroses grow here." He smiled at her, relieved at the change of topic. "And what would be blooming at home?"

"At this time of year, we would have ragged robin and lousewort perhaps."

He gave a shout of laughter. "Charming names!"

"We are not mealy-mouthed in the north." She smiled.

"In the north. Northumberland?"

"Not quite that far. Yorkshire." Her smile faded and she began walking again. "But that is all in the past."

Her past was not a subject she wished to pursue, it seemed. Ah, well, there was time enough. He would sort her out sooner or later. They walked along in a companionable silence.

As they neared the house, Miss Darling said, "It is most convenient that we have met this way. It gives me the opportunity to return your book."

"My book? Oh, the *Antigone*. You have finished? What did you think of it?"

"It is, of course, a powerful dramatic work."

When she seemed disinclined to continue, he said, "What of Creon and Antigone? Which one of them did you think had the right of it—he with his insistence on the rule of law or she with her devotion to family duty?"

"In all honesty, I thought them both fools." He looked at her in surprise, and she continued, "Oh, the conflicting demands make for wonderful tragedy, but all quite needless. If Creon had any sense at all, he would never have felt obliged to make one brother the hero and the other the villain and order death for anyone who buried the bad brother. He should have said something like, 'Here we can all see the results of excessive ambition. Let us take warning from their example and go on with our lives.'"

Ashleigh could not help but laugh. She had surprised him again. She had a mind and she used it. "Indeed, such common sense would be the death of tragedy. But what of Antigone? You cannot so easily dismiss her obligation to give her brother burial, can you?"

"Why should she feel any obligation to her brothers at all when they had clearly felt no obligation to her?"

He was taken aback by that. "They were her brothers. Surely some family feeling is natural. The ties of blood are strong."

She shook her head impatiently. "Think about it. There they were, plunging into a civil war. One of them was sure to be killed and, as it turned out, both of them died. Did either of them think to do so much as remove her to a place of safety before they began the fighting? To make any provision for her? No, they took no care of her and left her to survive as best she could. Should she then be expected to give her life for them? If she thought so, she was a fool."

He blinked. "Ah. That is a viewpoint I had not heard before. You dismiss family obligations so easily then?"

"Not at all. But family obligations must be mutual obligations. I simply say that when one has been deserted, ignored, left to survive as best one can, one would be foolish to feel any sense of obligation to the deserters."

By then, they had arrived at the house, and Mrs. Darling appeared to offer tea and cakes. Under the soothing application of civility, thoughts of tragedy were smothered, and the book, neatly wrapped in brown paper to protect it, was returned to its owner.

However, while Ashleigh walked back into Lewes to retrieve his horse and then on the ride home, he could not stop wondering how Miss Darling had been betrayed. He had no doubt that her reaction to Antigone was based on her own experience. There had been real pain in her face. Anger as well. Her words were too bitter for mere philosophical speculation.

But it was his own pain and anger at the thought of her suffering that frightened him.

>>><<<

ONCE THE DOOR had closed behind Ashleigh, Aunt Franny turned a worried look on Kate. "Had you planned to meet?"

"Not at all," said Kate, taking her aunt's arm as they returned to the drawing room. "It was entirely accidental. He came into Mr. Prufrock's bookshop while I was there. I promptly made to leave, but he proposed to accompany me, and I did not think I could refuse without appearing rude."

The older woman sat for a while, gnawing her lip, before she spoke again. "I do not know how to advise you. It would, of course, be a wonderful match for you..."

"Don't even think it."

"I can't help but think it when I see the way he looks at you, the way he is aware of you. And I see you quite as aware of him. There are difficulties, of course."

Kate laughed. "To say difficulties does not begin to describe the situation, Aunt Franny. He is a duke. It would be impossible for him to marry a merchant's niece."

"Not so impossible," said Aunt Franny robustly. "You are a merchant's niece only by my marriage. Your father was a viscount. That means your birth is quite high enough for you to be considered an acceptable match for a duke."

"Oh, Aunt Franny, think about it." Kate stood up and began to pace up and down the room. "My father may have had a title, as my brother does now, but they are men of such contemptible disrepute that I do not believe Ashleigh would be willing to even admit their acquaintance no less ally himself to such as they. He takes his duties and responsibilities seriously and would sooner, I am sure, ally himself with the family of an honorable merchant like your husband. And that, we know, would never happen."

Aunt Franny heaved a sigh and nodded. "You may be correct. But there is the way he looks at you. It is worrisome." She shook her head. "I have known Peter since he was a child and cannot imagine him acting dishonorably toward you. I do not think it is in him. Nonetheless, I think perhaps it would be wise for you to avoid any private encounters with him."

It was Kate's turn to sigh, but instead she laughed softly. "Why is it that wisdom and inclination so rarely go hand in hand? But I will be practical. I must. And once I convince Mr. Prufrock to take me on as his assistant, I am unlikely to ever have any more to do with Ashleigh. Unless he comes in to buy a book."

Nonetheless, as she sat with her needlework—a pillowcase that required mending—she could not keep impractical thoughts and desires away. He had given her his arm as they walked. It was a perfectly ordinary courtesy. A gentleman always offered his arm to a lady when they walked together. But it was not a courtesy that a gentleman would offer to a shopkeeper.

If her brother had been at all a decent man, if he had introduced her to society in London and she had met the Duke of Ashleigh at a concert or at a ball... she could imagine herself meeting him on equal terms, being taken in to dinner on his arm, perhaps even waltzing with him at a ball. She could imagine what it would feel like to be held in his arms. Her eyes closed and she felt a surge of... of something... she was not sure what it was, but a surge of something swept through her and she felt her cheeks grow hot.

Just walking beside him had been wonderful. She had been able to feel the strength of him through all the layers of cloth in his sleeves. And he listened to her. He actually asked her opinion and heard what she said. He talked of things like honor and obligations as if they mattered. She closed her eyes and gave herself up to the fantasy for a moment.

Her eyes stung with tears of anger at her brother. It was not that he had tried to sell her, to turn her into a whore. She had been able to escape that. But he, and her father before him, had stolen her life. They had taken the life she could have had and tossed it away on the gaming tables. There was no way she could ever recover that. She could never enter society. She could never have the kind of marriage to which her birth might have entitled her.

She gave herself a mental shake. Had she lost her mind? Was she longing for a man she barely knew just because he was honorable and responsible, so unlike her brother? Just because he was so handsome, so very beautiful?

The most beautiful man she had ever seen.

*Stop that!* she told herself. She was not some mindless little fool to fall in love with a handsome face.

The duke was not for her and never could be.

To have found refuge with Aunt Franny, to have the possibility of owning a shop that could provide her with a living for the rest of her life—this was more good fortune than she had any right to expect. Owning the bookstore would make her safe. She would have escaped her brother's control. She would have escaped any man's control. She would be the one in charge of her own life.

She would not have to be afraid.

That would be enough. That had to be enough.

Even if it made the future she truly wished for impossible.

Her neglected needle pricked her finger.

She would be safe, but surely she could spare a moment to regret what might have been.

# CHAPTER FIVE

Lady Clara Grammont was going to attend the Assembly Ball, to be held in the ballroom of the Crown Inn.

To most people, notice of this fact would have brought, at most, a smile of acknowledgement. To Lady Clara, however, few announcements could have brought greater joy, for she was not officially out, and this would be her first ball. She had a new dress—white muslin, of course, but with lovely embroidery on the flounce at the hem and around the neckline. And she had silk stockings and kid slippers as soft as the stockings.

Her excitement made it difficult for her to sit still which, in turn, made it difficult for her maid to put the finishing touches on her toilette.

"If you do not sit still, my dear, you will not be ready in time to leave with the rest of the party," said Lady Talmadge, trying to conceal her amusement at her daughter's enthusiasm.

That froze Lady Clara in place. "Oh, Mama, do not say such things."

A relieved maid quickly tweaked the last curl into place and tucked the last silk flower into the curls. "There you are, my lady."

Her mother nodded approval and trailed behind as Lady Clara flew down the stairs to the hall where the rest of the party was gathered.

"I am here, Uncle Peter, and you mustn't scold me for being late."

Ashleigh smiled fondly down at her. "How could I possibly scold anyone who looks as enchanting as you do?"

"Do I really?" Lady Clara grinned. "Then you must promise to dance with me, so that all the other young men will."

"Really, Lady Clara, you must try to remember your position," drawled Miss Webster, smoothing a nonexistent wrinkle out of the pink kid gloves that matched her silk gown so perfectly. "Your uncle may be generous enough to grace the local assembly with his presence, but there is unlikely to be anyone there who would be considered an acceptable partner for his niece."

Lord and Lady Ambruster nodded approvingly at their daughter. Bancroft looked at her with distaste.

Lady Clara turned a stricken face to her uncle. "Oh no, Uncle Peter, you can't mean that I am to go to my very first ball and not be allowed to dance!"

Ashleigh smiled reassuringly at her. "Never fear, pet. You will wear out your slippers dancing." He turned to the Ambrusters. "We are not so high in the instep here that we cannot share in the pleasures of our neighbors."

"If you say so, my lord," said Ambruster, "but I fear it sets a poor example. There's too much noise about reform abroad these days. Men like you need to see that people keep in their place and don't get ideas above their station. To do that, you need to remember your own position."

Lady Talmadge saw the mutinous look on the face of her daughter, to say nothing of the flash of irritation in her brother's eyes at Ambruster's presumption. She put a firm hand on her daughter's shoulder and announced, "I believe the carriages are here."

Ashleigh caught himself up, nodded to his sister, and said, "Yes, we must be on our way. It would not do to delay everyone's pleasure."

Rather to the annoyance of all the Ambrusters, the duke did not join them in their carriage. Nor did Bancroft, but he did not matter, being only a distant cousin.

AT HAWTHORNE COTTAGE, Kate was also preparing for the ball, with quite as much eagerness as Lady Clara had shown. She tried to subdue herself but it was not easy, especially with her aunt encouraging the enthusiasm.

"It's just that I've never been to a ball before," she said, trying to explain away her delight, "and I've never had such a beautiful new gown." She looked down at the pale green muslin with the three rows of ruching on the skirt, each one a darker green. She poked out a foot to smile with delight at the kid slipper with a green rosette.

Franny looked at her niece with pride. Kate looked positively regal with her hair in a crown of braids.

That might be a problem, she thought. Kate not only looked like a princess, she held herself like a princess. In Yorkshire, whatever society Kate had moved in was doubtless severely limited, and unlikely to have held anyone of superior station to a viscountess and her daughter. Mary would have held on to her pride, even if she had little else—or *because* she had little else—and had clearly instilled that pride in her daughter.

It was difficult to know what to do. It had taken years for Frances to stop thinking of herself as a gentlewoman, a baronet's daughter, and to think of herself instead as a merchant's wife. In truth, she had difficulty doing so to this day. Could Kate remember to humble herself, at least for these months while the masquerade was necessary? She spoke hesitantly. "My dear, you will remember that for the present you are Miss Darling and not Miss Russell?"

Kate stilled in her admiration of her slippers, then she looked up and smiled. "Don't worry, Aunt Franny. I will treat the duke with all due deference and keep my distance," she said. "It should not be difficult. He is an honorable man, if a trifle stiff." *It will be exceedingly difficult, but I will manage it. I must.*

Mrs. Darling sighed. "There will be others at the ball, you know. And you may need to grant them precedence, and not feel insulted."

"I know, Aunt Franny. I will be polite and deferential to any Lady Wiltons who appear." Kate grew serious for a moment. "It is not as if I have ever derived any great benefit from my father's title. At least Miss Darling need not fear that her family will be so impressed with a title that they will marry her off to a dissipated viscount as my mother was. Instead, Miss Darling will be able to dance happily with tradesmen and farmers' sons and enjoy herself thoroughly."

"I can't help but worry. You must remember that there are villainous merchants as well as villainous viscounts, and a man who is well-born may nonetheless be an honorable gentleman."

Kate smiled fondly at her aunt. "You fear I may be both too mistrustful and not mistrustful enough?"

"Yes," said Frances, "and, sad to say, mistrust is doubtless safer than foolish trust."

A knock at the door announced the arrival of Dr. Goddard. The kindly doctor had offered his carriage for the ladies of Hawthorne Cottage, lest their finery get spattered with mud on the walk to the village. For this, Kate, thinking of her lovely slippers, was most grateful. Seeing the color in her aunt's face as the doctor handed her into the carriage suggested to Kate still another reason to be pleased with the arrangement.

THE BALLROOM AT the Crown Inn did not resemble the ballroom of the Duchess of Richmond, whose ball in Brussels the night before Waterloo had gone down in history, nor could it equal the ballrooms in which any of the celebrated hostesses of London welcomed their glittering guests. There was not a marble pillar in sight, and the floor had given up all pretense of gleaming with polish decades ago. Instead of huge bouquets of hothouse flowers, the room was decorated with modest nosegays of primroses and narcissus and the flowering branches of cherry trees. Champagne did not flow from lavish fountains, and footmen did not carry trays of crystal glasses, though there was a bowl of punch for the gentlemen and another of lemonade for the ladies.

The greatest difference, however, lay in the demeanor of the guests. There were no faces of frozen ennui, no graceful fingers trying not too hard to cover yawns of boredom. Instead, all present seemed delighted to be there. Franny and Kate had barely been able to remove their cloaks before they were engulfed by a sea of welcoming faces. Kate had already met many of the women and was promptly introduced to those she did not know. They, in turn, introduced her to their husbands, brothers and sons, so that half a dozen partners had claimed dances before she could catch her breath, and before the party from Kelswick entered.

Harold Marshall, an attorney and a round tub of a man who tended to see himself as the man responsible for everything in Lewes, bustled over to greet the duke. "Your Grace, you do us great honor, great honor, indeed. Your presence, and that of your lovely sister and niece"—he bowed low to Lady Talmadge and Lady Clara—"sheds a luster over our gathering not to be equaled."

Ashleigh smiled and shook his head. "And we have delayed everyone's merriment by our lateness, so you had best tell the musicians to begin. Clara, will you do me the honor to stand up with me for the first set?" He held out his hand to his niece, who turned pink with pleasure, and took his hand, too excited to speak.

As they took the floor, followed by easily a dozen other couples, Miss Webster turned to Lady Talmadge with a rather frozen smile. "The duke is quite an indulgent uncle to your daughter," she observed.

"I wonder you do not fear that she will grow spoiled and willful."

"Indeed," put in Lady Ambruster. "She does seem remarkably forward for such a young girl."

Lady Talmadge's lips tightened, but she contented herself with a look of such icy disdain that Lady Ambruster flushed.

"But Clara is completely charming in her enthusiasm. Far better than being an insipid twit without a thought for anything but fashion and propriety, don't you think?" said Bancroft. He smiled coldly at the Ambrusters, then turned his back to them and bowed to his cousin. "Lady Talmadge, would you honor me with this dance?"

For him, Lady Talmadge had a smile of pure pleasure. Dear Stephen, who was always there when she needed him. They went to join the set that was forming, stepping perfectly in time with each other.

Miss Webster started to frown, but then remembered that frown lines led to wrinkles, and arranged her face into a small smile instead.

⤜⤛⤜⤛

AS THE SETS came and went, Lady Clara and Kate danced with all the young men under thirty, and Lady Talmadge and Frances danced with their fathers. Ashleigh and Bancroft danced with all the wallflowers. To be invited to dance by the duke was undoubtedly a great honor, but the young women so honored seemed to find it a terrifying experience. Miss Brockman, for example, did not dare look him in the face and, with her head averted, found it difficult to meet her partner in the dance. Miss Carter, on the other hand, could look nowhere except in his face, and giggled in response to each of his comments.

Bancroft had more success at putting his partners at ease. He had each of his partners smiling happily before her set was ended. By the time he returned Miss Prentiss to her mother's side, the girl had quite forgotten that her carroty curls were unfashionable, and she looked so delighted with life that she was soon claimed for all the remaining dances.

Ashleigh wished he knew how his cousin managed it. He could smile and relax easily enough with his family, or even with the men of the town, but with shy young ladies? He searched again for a topic of conversation.

"Do you enjoy music, Miss Hunter?" he tried.

"Yes, my lord," Miss Hunter whispered.

"And do you play yourself?"

"Yes, my lord."

"What instrument? The pianoforte?"

"Yes, my lord."

"Ah, an excellent choice. It offers the opportunity for such a wide choice of music."

"Yes, my lord."

The gods were merciful, and the set came to an end. He returned Miss Hunter to her parents and looked around. The Ambrusters formed a little island to themselves, having frozen off anyone with the temerity to approach. He berated himself for his neglect. They were, after all, his guests. He led Miss Webster to the floor. But conversation with Miss Webster proved no easier than conversation with his earlier partners. Each of his comments in praise of the company, the music, even the weather was met with a raised eyebrow or a sniff. Then as the set ended, they found themselves face to face with Kate and Bancroft, both of them smiling happily. For a moment, Ashleigh was struck dumb with amazement, as Clara had promised. Fashionably dressed and with her eyes bright with pleasure, Miss Darling did, indeed, look extraordinarily beautiful. The sight of her struck him like a blow.

"Your Grace," she said, with a graceful curtsey.

Ashleigh acknowledged the greeting with a bow, which gave him a chance to recover his breath. "Miss Webster, may I make known to you Miss Darling, the niece of an old friend." Turning to Kate, he continued, "Miss Webster is visiting Kelswick with her family."

The two women exchanged wary nods.

"I trust you are enjoying your visit, Miss Webster."

"Kelswick is, indeed, a most beautiful estate, and Ashleigh's kindness cannot be faulted." Miss Webster fluttered her fan and glanced about at the company. "His affability is almost excessive when he brings his guests to an affair such as this."

Kate started to stiffen, and then forced herself to smile. "Oh, Miss Webster, I am sure everyone here knows precisely how to value your condescension in gracing our ball with your presence this evening."

Ashleigh choked down a laugh. She had done it again. The girl clearly had no idea when to hold her tongue. He had himself found Miss Webster's comment offensive, so he could hardly be surprised that the prickly Miss Darling reacted as she did. On the other hand, he really could not allow an insult to his guest to pass. What on earth could he say that would not sound insufferably priggish?

Before he could say anything, however, Kate excused herself to return to her aunt, leaving Ashleigh to lead Miss Webster back to her parents.

"She is quite nicely spoken, and has pretty manners," said Miss Webster. "Is she a gentlewoman? At an affair of this sort, one cannot be certain."

Ashleigh looked at her in surprise. Miss Webster had not realized she had been insulted? She had given him a reprieve. He smiled slightly. "As I said, Miss Darling is the niece of an old friend."

"Really, Ashleigh, that is no answer at all. You speak of farmers and tradesmen as your friends, yet you must know that there can be no friendship where there is no equality of station. To say there is encourages presumption. I only asked about Miss Darling because she seemed on such easy terms with your steward. He is, after all, a connection of yours, though distant. If she is not someone he can marry, he may be raising her hopes unfairly and find himself in an untenable situation."

"I am sure Miss Darling would be very grateful for your concern," he said stiffly. He had not noticed anything beyond ordinary civility between Bancroft and Miss Darling. Of course, she had been smiling and looking happy, and he had not seen her smile often, but Bancroft was always good at teasing people into relaxation. Should he have noticed something more? Surely Bancroft was much too old for her. He must be what? Thirty-six? More? Old enough to be her father.

Miss Webster closed her eyes and endeavored to look calm, not exasperated. "It is not Miss Darling who rouses my concern, but your cousin. His situation is precarious at best. You seem to have some fondness for him, but if he marries foolishly, he could sacrifice all claim to your concern. Your affability may already have given him ideas above his station. I was quite shocked to see him dancing with your sister and speaking to her quite familiarly."

Ashleigh stopped abruptly and looked at her coldly. "Miss Webster," he began.

"No," she said, holding up a hand. "I know you do not like what I am saying, but you cannot deny the truth of it. You are a duke, and your position imposes obligations as well as privileges—obligations to your peers. I will now return to my family, and we will return to Kelswick. You and your family are welcome to indulge yourselves with your tenants, your bucolic neighbors, whatever they are. Just remember that you may be doing more harm than good. They are not your equals. Your cousin may fend for himself, but you may be doing your niece a great disservice by encouraging her to befriend people so far below her. When she makes her come-out, people will judge her by her companions, and they will be less tolerant than you."

She turned and walked away, head high. Ashleigh regarded her with a mixture of irritation and a certain reluctant admiration. She had, for once, spoken honestly—or had spoken her honest beliefs, not quite the same thing. He still could not like her, but she had earned more of his respect than he would have thought possible. Of course, these people were not his equals and they were as aware of that as she. However, they were his responsibility. Did she not realize that the welfare of this entire area depended to a great extent upon him? What he did or failed to do could mean prosperity or decline for this town and all of those around it. And if he was to guide these people, he had to understand how they thought, what they needed, what they wanted.

Still, was it possible that there was something of the truth in what she said, at least insofar as it affected Clara?

He looked around the ballroom. Bancroft was now dancing with Miss Shelton, whose father was a country gentleman, prosperous, though far from wealthy. His cousin seemed no less friendly with her than he had with Miss Darling. He found that comforting. Then he frowned. Bancroft was not married. Why was that? Did he want to marry? There had been several discrete arrangements over the years, but that was no reason why he should not marry. He lived in rooms at Kelswick now, but there were several houses on the estate that he could have if he wished. Was he looking for a wife?

It bothered Ashleigh that he did not know. He relied on Bancroft tremendously, on his judgment, on his knowledge. They talked together daily about the estate, about investments, about everything concerning the dukedom. Bancroft knew all his plans. But now, he realized that he knew nothing of Bancroft's plans, of Bancroft's hopes. Was Bancroft preserving his privacy, or had he just never asked, never noticed?

He turned back to the dancers. Miss Darling was a bit farther down the room, partnered with Mr. Marshall. She was no longer smiling so broadly, but she looked no less happy than she had with his cousin, Ashleigh was pleased to see. She still looked remarkably lovely. Bancroft faded from his thoughts. He could not help noticing that the slight flush on her face as she danced made her eyes look particularly brilliant, and her figure, as she moved through the steps... her body... her rounded... he caught himself. Graceful. The girl was simply graceful as she danced. That was all he noticed.

He turned away and looked for his niece, and found her throwing herself with enthusiasm into the country dance with a group of youngsters of her own age. They reminded him of nothing so much as a litter of puppies, and he could not help but smile. But as he watched them, Miss Webster's strictures came to mind. Clara was the daughter of an earl and the niece of a duke. The rest of them were, at best, the children of minor gentry. Was he making a mistake in allowing her to be friendly with people so far beneath her socially? He did not want her to grow up as isolated as he had been, but had this gone too far?

Clara had been only fourteen when she and her mother came to live here after the death of Lord Talmadge, Alice's elderly and autocratic husband. Both of them had been so dreadfully subdued. Alice was intimately acquainted with matters of etiquette and precedence, but had not dared to voice an opinion on anything else. Clara had seemed afraid to speak about anything at all. It was a delight to see them blossoming over the course of the past year.

Clara was laughing happily as she danced with farmers' sons. He would not wish to silence that laughter. Besides, mingling with people who were dependent on her family could only give her a greater sympathy with them so that she would come to understand her responsibilities.

Then there was Clara's friendship with Miss Darling. Was this something he should discourage? There was nothing in the least vulgar or pushy in Miss Darling's behavior. Her manners, her speech, her carriage—everything about her proclaimed her a gently bred lady. The uncertainty about her background was a problem. Still, Alice liked her, and apparently so did Lady Merton, not that that was much of a recommendation. An American like Miranda could hardly be expected to recognize what was and was not acceptable.

No, Miss Webster was simply seeking to build up her own consequence by denigrating those around her, he decided. He could see no sign of any special fondness between Bancroft and Miss Darling any more than between Bancroft and Alice. He frowned. Bancroft and Miss Darling...it would be a perfectly acceptable match for both of them, even with the discrepancy in their ages. The notion should not bother him. He had no right to be bothered.

Miss Darling seemed to have no lack of partners this evening, but Ashleigh came up to her just in time to engage her for a quadrille. He held her hand and her eyes as they circled around. She was smiling with what he was certain was genuine pleasure. As he circled about with her, he realized that he was truly enjoying himself. He could not remember the last time this had happened.

LADY AMBRUSTER WALKED into her daughter's room later that evening and sat down. Selina was already in her nightgown and her maid was brushing her hair. She looked at her mother and dismissed the maid.

"He is not going to make you an offer," Lady Ambruster said flatly.

"No," Selina agreed, "but I am glad we came. Now, I can see that we would not suit at all. It is a magnificent house, and it would make an excellent setting for me, but Ashleigh would drive me mad. His behavior is impeccable, but he seems indifferent to society. He is as willing to attend this trifling country assembly with these vulgar merchants and attorneys as a London ball in the company of his peers."

"You could perhaps persuade him to change," her mother said speculatively.

"No." Selina was quite firm. "I have no wish to marry a man with whom I will be in constant battle, and I do not think he would be easily led. I will be better off with Lord Carrisbroke. He will come to the point as soon as I give him a hint of encouragement. He is only a viscount, and his estate is not so magnificent, but his fortune is enormous and he prefers London, as do I. It will be a better match."

Lady Ambruster nodded her agreement. "However, we should stay through the week. It would not do to cut our visit short."

"Of course," said Selina, slightly shocked. "If we left early, it would appear we only came in search of an offer and left in defeat. We shall stay, and I will dress most magnificently and flirt with all the eligible gentlemen, if Ashleigh can manage to provide a few. And once we are home, we will arrange a house party of our own."

"At which Lord Carrisbroke will be a guest."

"Along with a number of other eligible gentlemen."

Mother and daughter smiled at each other, in perfect accord.

AT HOME IN Hawthorne Cottage, Kate lay in bed, unable to sleep, smiling as she relived every second of that dance. It had been glorious. She could still feel the touch of his hand at her waist. She could still see his smile as he looked at her, looked as if he really saw her. If she had ever believed in the possibility of a Prince Charming coming to her rescue, he would have looked like the Duke of Ashleigh. He would have been tall and fiercely beautiful, with heavy dark hair and blue eyes that seemed to see into the very heart of her. He would have been a man who took care of people, who would protect her, not think of her as simply another chip to toss onto the gambling table.

Could the duke possibly be what he appeared to be? Could he possibly be as honest and honorable as he seemed? Or was she deluding herself? Was she so dazzled by his beauty, so drawn by it, that she saw in him only virtue?

Her smile turned into a mocking laugh. Did it really matter? He was a duke, and could have no honorable interest in her. He would expect to marry someone like Miss Webster, whose perfect facade could not even be broken by a smile, no less a laugh. Or a thought.

Perhaps she was underestimating Miss Webster. Perhaps she did actually think. It didn't really matter. The duke could marry Miss Webster, the daughter of a not-particularly-impressive but respectable viscount, but not the sister of someone as contemptible, as scandalous as Viscount Newell.

More importantly, a duke could have no serious interest in the Darlings' niece, and that was the woman he thought her to be. What she thought she had seen in his eyes had to be simple courtesy, not interest, not attraction.

If she thought she saw anything more, she was mistaken.

If she wanted to see anything more, she was a fool.

But still, she could not rid herself of this longing ache.

# CHAPTER SIX

L ADY CLARA HAD insisted that Kate come to visit the day after the ball so that they could talk about it, and Lady Talmadge had laughingly seconded the invitation. It was an odd experience, Kate found. She was years older than Lady Clara—in some ways she felt herself decades older. Yet in other ways, they were on the same precise level, and Kate found the novelty of a young friend enchanting. They had quickly dropped all formality.

It had been the first ball for Kate just as it had been for Clara, and their excitement and pleasure were identical. So they spent a highly enjoyable hour curled up cozily in Clara's room dissecting the ball. They agreed that Mr. Marshall was too kind to mock, and Miss Shelton was too dimwitted to tease. Mr. Gibbons was by far the best dancer—other than the duke and Mr. Bancroft of course—but far too proud of his cravat. Mr. Dobbins was a danger to his partner's toes, but so shy that one could not in good conscience refuse him when he worked up the courage to ask for a dance. Miss Webster—they rolled their eyes and agreed to think no more of her.

Kate felt rather guilty listening to Clara disparage Miss Webster. It wasn't that she didn't want to do so herself. She just wasn't sure it was quite right of her to encourage Clara to speak ill of her. Although she had to admit to herself that she was extremely pleased to hear that Ashleigh's family disliked the oh-so-proper, oh-so-perfect Miss

Webster. She was even more pleased to hear that Ashleigh himself found Miss Webster trying.

Kate could console herself that she was only thinking of Ashleigh's happiness. He would be miserable married to a china doll. Any man would.

Having decided to take advantage of the sunny day, they set out for a walk and were almost at the bottom of the stairs when they heard Selina and Lady Ambruster above. In a moment of panic, Clara grabbed Kate's hand and dragged her into the nearest room. She shut the door and leaned against it, holding a finger to her lips and listening in silence until she heard the two women leave the house.

Clara stood up with a sigh of relief. "I'm sorry, Kate. I just couldn't bear another lecture on the deficiencies of my behavior."

"Perhaps a lecture on the importance of making one's guests feel comfortable and welcome might be in order." The deep voice came from the side of the room. Clara and Kate spun around to see Ashleigh rising from his desk with a frown and the Earl of Merton standing beside him, half-laughing as usual.

"That's not fair, Uncle Peter," Clara protested. "I have had them for the past week. Lady Ambruster keeps suggesting so very sweetly that I might try to moderate my enthusiasms, and Selina keeps pitying me for being so countrified and telling me how I must change if I wish to be accepted by the *ton*. Meanwhile, you get to hide here in the library all day long and only have to see them at dinner."

"That is, of course, one of the advantages of being a man," said Merton, grinning. "We arrange our schedules to avoid the more onerous social duties, which the ladies fulfill so much more graciously."

It took Ashleigh a moment to comment. He realized that he had been staring at Kate—Miss Darling—and he could swear she was staring back. "You make it sound as if we are hiding away in here," said Ashleigh, irritated with himself. What was wrong with him that he could not keep from staring at the girl? "Ambruster has proposed this canal project, and Merton is going over it with me. We need to determine whether it is worth an investment. I cannot spend my days dancing attendance on Lady Ambruster and her daughter."

Kate raised an eyebrow at this, but managed to keep silent. Clara, however, did not. "I can't believe you are seriously considering any investment with him. You know the only reason they came is to push Selina on you."

"All the more reason for your uncle to hide," laughed Merton.

"You do not think you might be raising Miss Webster's hopes by giving her father's project serious consideration?" Kate said. Ashleigh looked at her incredulously and she flushed. "Pardon me, my lord. I had no business commenting on your affairs."

"But it's perfectly true," said Clara. "And I, for one, would never invest in a project of his. I don't like him."

"And that, my pet, is why it is the gentlemen who make the decisions, and not the ladies, who are far too emotional." Ashleigh gave her an indulgent look. "Whether I like my partners or not has nothing to do with my investment decisions."

"Truly, my lord?" asked Kate. "Suppose you distrust the man arranging the project, or doubt his honesty. Would that not make you hesitate?"

"Of course, if I had some valid reason to doubt those involved, I would hesitate to join them. But not for a frivolous reason, such as a dislike of a man's waistcoat—or of his daughter, which appears to be Clara's complaint."

"You think a woman too foolish and frivolous to be able to determine a man's character?" Kate's posture had grown rigid and her tone was frosty.

Ashleigh smiled placatingly. "I think women are far too apt to value a man for his dancing or his flattery. It is part of their charm that they react emotionally." As you are reacting now, Miss Darling, he thought, but did not say.

"Men, of course, always act calmly and rationally." Kate sounded increasingly irritated.

"More so than women, I believe. That is why their fathers and brothers and uncles"—he bowed to Clara—"are charged with their care and protection."

Kate glared at the duke. "How lovely that must be. All those gentlemen gambling away their fortunes in the clubs and hells, or just frittering the money away on their own pleasures can assure themselves that they are taking the best possible care of their wives, sisters and daughters because they are men and therefore are calm and rational."

"Obviously, there are men who do not live up to their obligations," Ashleigh said, growing irritated himself, "but that does not mean the obligations are not there. Any man who calls himself a gentleman must always put first the welfare of the ladies of his family who have been entrusted to his protection."

"And is that what Lord Ambruster is doing? Is he dangling his daughter before you in an effort to entice you to invest in his canal scheme or is he dangling his canal scheme in an effort to entice you to marry his daughter? In either case, is it her welfare that concerns him or his own social and financial benefit?"

"Really, Miss Darling, that is a most improper remark." Ashleigh was truly outraged. The girl had no sense of propriety. And to be speaking this way in front of a child like Clara.

"Yet it is precisely the kind of determination a woman must make if she wishes to survive," she snapped. "A great many noblemen think a title simply means that they are entitled to self-indulgence. Any woman who finds herself at their mercy had best see to her own protection."

Merton stepped into the breach with an attempt to defuse the situation. "Assuredly, there are selfish men who do not always live up to their responsibilities. That is something on which we can agree, can we not?" He turned his charming smile on Kate.

She did not look charmed, but she took a deep breath and subsided. "Please forgive me, Your Grace, my lord. I fear I was carried away. That is no doubt a sign of my feminine weakness."

Clara was staring at Kate, wide-eyed and nervous. "I think the Ambrusters have gone now," she said. "I heard the carriage. So we can leave." She took Kate's hand and almost pulled her from the room.

Merton and Ashleigh stared at the empty doorway in silence. "Well," said Merton at length, "what just happened here?"

"I have no idea, but such anger suggests that the topic is a sensitive one."

"Anger indeed," said the earl slowly, "but you can't deny that what she said is perfectly true. I've known too many titled wastrels, as have you."

"That is beside the point." Ashleigh was angry but he was not entirely certain why. "She has no sense. She should never have spoken that way in front of Clara, who has no need to know such things."

"No?" Merton tilted his head consideringly. "You think there is no danger in ignorance?"

"Not for Clara," said Ashleigh firmly. "I am here to protect her."

Merton looked inclined to argue, but shrugged instead. "Was Miss Darling speaking from personal experience, do you think?"

"I can hardly doubt it. It would appear that the men of her family were less than dutiful in pursuit of their obligations. She said something the other day that suggests her father paid little attention to his family." He was still staring at the door through which she had departed.

"A bit of a mystery, isn't she?"

A mystery, indeed, thought Ashleigh. She was too bitter to be complaining of nothing but carelessness. But an attractive—a beautiful—young woman like Miss Darling with guardians who failed to protect her.... he did not like to think of the kind of betrayal that could have befallen her. He turned and realized that Merton was watching him with a knowing smile. He scowled.

"But she had a point about Ambruster," Merton said. "He wants you to take either his daughter or his canal. I doubt he cares which one."

Ashleigh gave a sour little laugh. "Lady Ambruster most decidedly cares."

"But that does not affect me. Now that I have Miranda, I am protected from attacks of that sort. Nonetheless, I think I shall decline this investment opportunity. It is a family I would just as soon avoid."

⤏⤏⤏⤏⟨⟨⟨⟨

LATER THAT AFTERNOON, alone in his library, Ashleigh tried to concentrate on the details of the canal project, but failed. Thoughts of Kate—Miss Darling—kept intruding. He turned his chair around and stared out the window. He really ought not to let his mind dwell upon her. She was Andrew Darling's niece, and to the Darlings he owed every bit of warmth and kindness in his childhood. Miss Darling was not someone he could marry, so he should not think about her at all.

But she was a mystery. Everything about her—her speech, her manner—proclaimed her to be a lady. Remembering Clara's comments, he smiled to himself. Everything except the garments in which she had first appeared, perhaps. Still, when he had met her in company, he had seen the difficulty she had in showing deference to those who could be presumed to be her superiors.

Was she truly a gentlewoman? But why did she not say so? Why did she say nothing of her family? He could think of no reason why she should be ashamed of her birth. She did not have the hesitancy, the careful speech of one trying to rise above her station.

What if it was not she who was ashamed of her family, but her family who was ashamed of her? That could be the explanation.

Suppose she had been seduced, betrayed by some scoundrel. God knows she was attractive enough, with those eyes and that graceful figure. He doubted there was a man alive who would not be tempted by her. Then like as not, she would have been disowned by her family. That happened often enough—all the blame fell on the girl, when the real disgrace belonged to the family that had not protected her.

Mrs. Darling had also been disowned by her family. She would have sympathized with her niece. She would have offered her a home, a refuge. And they would say nothing of her family, of her background, if that was necessary to protect her from any scandal.

If that was true, he thought, if that was true, then he still could not marry her but he could offer her his protection. He could keep her safe, offer her security.

Good God, what was he thinking? He leaned back and closed his eyes. There was absolutely no reason to suspect that Miss Darling was anything other than innocent and virtuous, but here he was concocting a tale that would give him an excuse for seducing her. He was no better than the "gentlemen" she had been excoriating.

He turned back to the canal project, but gathered up the papers and put them aside. Merton had declined the opportunity to invest. He would decline as well, he decided. He did not wish to associate with Ambruster.

⟫⟫⟫⟪⟪⟪

WALKING BACK TO Hawthorne Cottage, Kate berated herself yet once more. She had to keep control of her temper and her tongue. There had been no reason for her to lash out at the duke. He was in no way to blame for her father's behavior, or for her brother's. Why did she keep sniping at him? What he said was what any honorable gentleman thought. The fact that he thought in such honorable terms was one of the things she loved about him.

No.

Stop right there.

She had no business thinking of love and Ashleigh at the same time. She had no right. Thinking that way was beyond stupid. He was not for her, and she was not for him. That had been decided by her brother.

And that was over. What her brother had done had set her life on a course that could not be altered. But that did not mean she had to be miserable. She could be happy.

She could not let her anger at her brother poison her life. She had to forget him. Forget everything about her past. She needed to begin anew, as if her life were just beginning. Here in Lewes, she could have a good, decent, safe life. Not a life as a duchess, but a life as the owner of a bookshop. It might not fulfill all her dreams, but it was far better than the degradation her brother had planned for her. She had escaped the fate he had planned for her. She would not be a whore.

She held her head up and put a determined smile on her face. She could be happy with the bookshop. That would have to be enough.

*London*

FARNSWORTH SAT BEHIND his desk and regarded Newell with disgust. The viscount had obviously spent hours in a cheap tavern trying to soak up enough courage to come here and recount his failure.

"Did my best," Newell muttered drunkenly. "Beastly place. They didn't know anything. No respect."

It was a waste of time sending Newell, thought Farnsworth. I did it to punish him, and that was foolish. I need to send someone with at least a modicum of intelligence.

"Your sister, she is the only family you have?" Farnsworth asked.

Newell nodded and sniveled.

Farnsworth subdued his impatience and persisted. "I know your father had no other family, but your mother? Had she no relatives?"

Newell started to shake his head but stopped. "She must have had a family." He shrugged. "No help from them. Never even saw them."

"Who never saw them?" asked Farnsworth with exaggerated patience. "You? Your father? Your mother?"

"Don't know." Newell frowned petulantly. "Never met them. My mother might have seen them or written."

"And if she wrote, your sister might know them as well," Farnsworth spoke in his silky tone. "And might you at least know their names? Their locations?"

Eventually, he pried the information from the recesses of Newell's wine-soaked brain. Lady Newell had been a Miss Langley, daughter of Sir Bertrand Langley, baronet, of Locksley Hall in Somerset. There also came the grudging admission that Mrs. Grant, wife of the Yorkshire squire, quite possibly knew more than she had been inclined to tell Newell. Farnsworth could hardly blame her. Only a fool would tell Newell anything, and there was no reason to assume Mrs. Grant was a fool, even if she did live in Yorkshire. He rang for his butler.

When the man appeared, Farnsworth waved at the now comatose Newell. "Remove him."

"To a guest chamber, my lord?"

Farnsworth grimaced. "Do not be preposterous. Just get him out of here. Take him outside and leave him anywhere, so long as he is out of my sight."

THE NEXT MORNING, Farnsworth sent for Howard Hall, a man whose talents he had used before. Farnsworth smiled when Hall entered his office. He recognized the man when he saw him again. But before that, he had found it difficult to remember just exactly what Hall looked like. That, of course, was Hall's stock in trade. His face was ordinary. His clothes were ordinary. His demeanor—in whatever society he found himself—was ordinary. People who met him, even people who conversed with him, dined with him, drank with him, found it impossible to give any sort of clear description of him.

Hall was ordinary. He almost defined ordinariness, except for one thing. Hall was extraordinarily gifted at drawing out confidences. People found themselves divulging all sorts of things to him, betraying secrets they thought they would never betray. But it didn't really count. Hall couldn't possibly be trying to discover those secrets. He was so ordinary.

At the moment, Hall looked like a perfectly ordinary gentleman. After all, he was calling on a nobleman. Anyone other than a gentleman calling at this house would be noticeable, like the rather disreputable creature he had seen outside, pulling himself up out of the gutter. Hall had recognized Newell. He had encountered the viscount a number of times. Newell had not, of course, recognized Hall.

Farnsworth waved his visitor to a chair. He could have kept him standing—Hall was only an employee—but he had done that once and felt vaguely uncomfortable. These conversations were more comfortably conducted informally.

"A young lady has gone missing," Farnsworth began.

Hall nodded. "You refer to Miss Russell?"

Farnsworth frowned. "People know about this?"

Hall shrugged. "I hear things. I make it a point to do so. Your... arrangement was known to the servants. I doubt anyone of importance to you knows."

Farnsworth continued to frown and tapped his fingers on the desk. "No matter," he said finally. "I want her back. Do you know where she went?"

"No. She seems to have managed it quite effectively. Vanished in the night, and no one knows where. Impressive for a young gentle-woman."

Farnsworth scowled. "I don't care how impressive you find it. Can you find her?"

Hall shrugged again. "Probably. Unless she vanished into the river. Or the brothels. I assume you wouldn't want her then."

"Let us presume she survived her vanishing act intact. She had no resources, she knows no one in London. She must have managed to get out of the city. And someone must be helping her."

"Fair enough," said Hall. "But who would help her?"

"There seem to be only two possibilities. She had friends in York-shire, where she lived. Newell went there. They claimed to know nothing, but they may have been lying."

Hall nodded. "The viscount does not always impress people as trustworthy."

Farnsworth gave a twisted smile. "Then there are her mother's people. She was from Somerset. Her father was a baronet by the name of Langley. Newell seems to think they were estranged, but he might not know. See if you can find the family. If no one there knows anything, you will have to try the Yorkshire connection again. When you find her, let me know."

Hall nodded and left.

The butler showed him out. Later, when he went downstairs, the housekeeper asked about the visitor. The butler couldn't quite remember what he had looked like, except that he had been a fairly ordinary gentleman, with an ordinary kind of name.

# CHAPTER SEVEN

*Sussex*

AT FIRST GLANCE, Stephen Bancroft appeared a somewhat pale reflection of his cousin, the duke. His hair was not so dark, his eyes were brown instead of blue, and his figure was sturdy rather than elegantly slim. He was the elder by some ten years, and tended to be self-effacing in his manner, as befitted a steward.

Yet when the cousins stood together in the library studying the papers spread out on the broad mahogany desk, the intelligence and intensity in their expressions seemed identical. They shared a commitment to the estate and its inhabitants. There had been lean years for the tenants before Ashleigh inherited and installed Bancroft as steward. Ashleigh's father had been pleased to collect rents but had made no improvements on the estate for years, and the old steward had not dared to challenge him. The farms had yielded less each year, but the rents remained the same. When Ashleigh took over, under Andrew Darling's guidance and with Bancroft's support, he had ploughed every penny he could back into the estate and, for a few years, things had flourished. Then the end of the war brought not only a collapse in farm prices but an influx of discharged soldiers, all looking for work with none to be found.

Ashleigh was determined to do right by his people and by the returning soldiers, and Bancroft shared that commitment.

They had been investigating possible industries they could bring to the area, much as the Earl of Merton had begun a shipbuilding enterprise on his estate. When Lady Talmadge came into the study, they had their heads together over plans for a brewery.

Bancroft sensed her nearness immediately. He straightened up and offered a small bow by way of greeting, and she returned a nod. He was struck anew by her beauty every time he saw her. She had been a pretty child when she had married Talmadge—far too much of a child for marriage, he had thought—but now she was simply the most beautiful woman he had ever seen. Like her brother, the duke, she had dark hair. But she had startlingly gray eyes. Her features were soft, delicate, refined, and she moved with such grace. He shook his head in bemusement.

She met his eye and smiled slightly before she turned away quickly. There was a slight flush on her cheek.

Ashleigh, realizing he had lost Bancroft's attention, looked up and saw his sister. He, too, smiled. "Alice. How may I help you?"

"I was wondering if you could tell me about my estate."

"Your estate?" Ashleigh looked at her blankly.

"My estate. Longwood. The estate I inherited from Talmadge. It is mine, is it not?"

"Ah, yes, of course." Ashleigh smiled at his sister. "You need not worry. There is a good steward in charge." He turned to Bancroft. "What is his name? Carter? Carson?"

"Carstairs. Robert Carstairs."

"Yes, that is it." Ashleigh turned back to his sister. "This Carstairs seems to know his business. It appears he has established a good mixture of crops and stock raising, and the estate is producing a healthy income. So you see, there is nothing to worry about."

"I was not worried. It is only that I know nothing about it. I do not know what my income is, or what the estate is like, or even precisely where it is, and I think I really need to know."

She seemed nervous, Bancroft thought. Why is that?

"There is no need for you to worry," Ashleigh assured her. "You and Clara are perfectly safe here. You will always be taken care of."

"I am not worried," she repeated, "but I do not actually know what my situation is. It has been more than a year since Talmadge died. It is time for me to get on with my life."

"Ah." Ashleigh smiled as if he understood now. "You are thinking that you might marry again. Well, that will be as you wish. You have your jointure as well as Longwood, so you are well set in your own right. You need not fear. You have no need to marry, and no one will pressure you to this time."

Bancroft frowned slightly. He had not thought that was what she meant, but it could be. There was no reason why she should not be thinking of marriage. She was a young, beautiful and wealthy widow. Suitors would be swarming around her the moment she set foot in London. His frown deepened.

Lady Talmadge was shaking her head. "No, this is not about marriage, this is about the estate I have been told I own. I would like to know about Longwood. I have never even seen it. What does it look like? What is the house like? Who are the neighbors? Will I like them?"

Bancroft's frown eased into a smile.

"I could take you there to see it, I suppose," Ashleigh said slowly. "I have not seen it myself, but I understand that there is a fairly modest manor house, not far from Moreton-in-Marsh. A bit isolated, I should think. Why do you wish to see it?"

She was smiling at him as if he were somewhat dim-witted. "For one thing, simply because it is mine, and I have never before had a house of my own. For another, because one of these days, you will wish to marry, and I think we will all be more comfortable—I am sure your wife will be more comfortable—if I am established in a home of my own."

"What nonsense, Alice. This is your home. For heaven's sake, Kelswick is big enough to house a dozen families. Do you think I would even consider marrying the kind of woman who would turn my sister out of the house?"

"It is not a question of turning me out. It would be one thing if I had no choice, if I had to make my home with you. We would all make the best of it, I am sure. What I want to know is, do I have a choice? Is Longwood a place where I would like to live? If not, could I sell it and buy some other estate? What sort of income do I command?"

Ashleigh scowled at her. "This is foolishness. There is no need for you to worry yourself about such matters. You know I will always take care of you and Clara."

She closed her eyes, took a deep breath and let it out slowly. "You are being insufferably obtuse." Then she turned to the steward. "Stephen, do you understand what I am saying?"

He smiled gently. "I believe so, my lady."

"Then please be so kind as to try to make my brother understand." She turned and left the room, head held high.

Both men looked after her, Bancroft with admiration, Ashleigh with something approaching shock.

"What on earth has come over her?" Ashleigh asked. "Has Lady Merton been infecting her with her odd notions?"

"I believe her ladyship is beginning to realize that she can have control of her own life."

"But she knows I will take care of her, and Clara as well. There is nothing she needs to worry about."

"It seems that she no longer wishes to be taken care of."

"Does she not trust me to know what is best for her?" Ashleigh was looking affronted but also stricken.

Bancroft was close to feeling sorry for the duke, so he picked his words with care. "It is not a question of trust, Your Grace, but of independence. Lady Talmadge would, I am sure, always welcome your advice, but it appears that she considers it her right to make the final decision."

"When have I ever questioned her decisions? She is perfectly free to do whatever she chooses."

"Like decide to live at Longwood rather than here?" Bancroft felt obliged to point it out.

"But that would be foolish!" Ashleigh stopped and seemed to listen to himself. "That is what you mean, I collect."

"Yes, Your Grace."

Ashleigh scowled and stared at nothing. "Very well. If Alice wants to know about Longwood, you will have to be the one to tell her. I have never paid it much heed."

"Yes, Your Grace."

He grimaced. "I did not like to think about it. It came to her from Talmadge, and I cannot forgive him for the way he wore down her spirit. She has regained some of herself since she returned home, do you not think so?"

"Yes, Your Grace."

"And stop 'Your Grace'-ing me. You do that only when you think I am being pompous." He picked up the paper he had been studying earlier, frowned at it, and threw it down. "We will have to come back to this later. I need to go for a ride."

Bancroft smiled as he watched the duke stride from the room. Ashleigh was a good man, a responsible man, perhaps too responsible. He sought to take care of all about him, which was no doubt admirable. However, his conviction that he was best suited to make the decisions for all about him could be trying for others.

Now, he wanted Bancroft to be the one to talk to Lady Talmadge about her estate, to explain how to manage it? To be closeted with her for hours on end?

For a protective brother, Ashleigh could be incredibly blind.

﹥﹥﹥✕﹤﹤﹤

As Ashleigh strode into the hall, he encountered his sister, bearing down on the door with Clara in tow. Before he could ask, she sailed past him, not meeting his eye as she announced, "I have promised to take Mrs. Darling and her niece to see Miranda." He could only watch as she flew down the steps and into the carriage, her daughter scurrying to keep up.

Ashleigh shook his head. She was annoyed with him, and he was damned if he knew why she was in such a taking. He was only trying to protect her, and she would have been a sight better off if their father had done the same.

It was only when he was in the stable yard, waiting for his horse, that he realized his sister had said she was to take Miss Darling with her. He could have offered to accompany them. He could have said that he needed to speak to Merton. That would have provided an excuse. He might have been able to discover what was bothering Alice. And he could have furthered his acquaintance with Miss Darling.

Not that he wished to pursue Miss Darling's acquaintance, of course. That would be pointless. No matter what tales his imagination spun about her, what he knew was that she was the niece of a merchant, and that merchant was Andrew Darling, a man to whom he owed both respect and affection. Miss Darling was too high for a mistress and too low for a wife. She should be treated with courtesy and respect, and that was all. No matter that she was lovely, with those eyes, those incredible green eyes.

He wanted to drown in those eyes.

And fascinating. She not only read books, she thought about them. Had he ever before been fascinated by a woman's mind?

Mysterious. So prickly, so defensive—he could not keep from wondering why. What secret was she hiding? She had the manners and bearing of a lady—was she ashamed of her connection to the Darlings, ashamed that she needed to turn to a merchant's widow for help? But she seemed genuinely fond of Franny Darling and grateful to her. It was a puzzle.

No.

He had to stop thinking about Miss Darling.

This was madness.

# CHAPTER EIGHT

THE CARRIAGE RIDE was a trifle awkward. Lady Talmadge stared out the window at the passing scenery, responding with barely a shrug while the others produced trifles to fill the silence. Each of the ladies was relieved when they arrived at Schotten Hall after a journey that had seemed interminable but, in fact, lasted less than half an hour.

Kate's first glimpse of the house was reassuring. It was hardly an insignificant house, but its Elizabethan brick facade seemed warm and welcoming after the chilly perfection of Kelswick, just as Lord and Lady Merton had always seemed warm and welcoming. Still, Lady Talmadge was clearly upset about something, and that kept Kate on edge as they entered the house.

Mrs. Darling and Clara may have been as hesitant as Kate to comment on Lady Talmadge's mood, but the lady of the house had no such qualms. The moment the visitors were ushered into the cozy sitting room where she was reclining on a chaise, Lady Merton said, "Good heavens, Alice, what has you in such a state?"

"And hello to you, too, Miranda," said Lady Talmadge, bending over to kiss her friend's cheek before collapsing inelegantly in the chair by her side. "It's my brother, of course."

"Ah, he is being his overbearing and pompous self? I regret that I have not been about to humble him, but even though this creature is not expected to put in an appearance for another four months, Tom is in a tizzy if I so much as step outside the house without him. Ashleigh himself could not be more insistent." She patted her belly, which was just beginning to be rounded, and grinned, not looking at all put out by her husband's strictures. "You English make a great deal of fuss over this sort of thing."

"Yes, we have heard your tales of women in the colonies giving birth in the fields and then getting up to continue with the plowing, but I am sure you would much prefer to be in a bed when the time comes." Lady Talmadge smiled at her friend.

"Do they really do so in America?" asked Clara, her eyes round.

"I think it unlikely," said Mrs. Darling. "I suspect that tale is akin to the frontiersman killing a bear with his bare hands."

"Or Alexander strangling a serpent in his crib," added Kate.

The friendly chatter seemed to be having an effect on Lady Talmadge, who was already looking less distressed. "Oh, I know I am probably making too much of it, but it is so frustrating," she said. "He treats me as if I am a child, incapable of doing or even understanding anything."

"Well, that is the way he treats everyone," Lady Merton pointed out. "One does have to remind him constantly that he is not the only adult in the universe."

"But I am so tired of it! First my father—well, I *was* a child then—and then Talmadge and now Peter. I have no say in my own life."

"Has anything in particular happened?"

"Oh…" Lady Talmadge sighed and waved her hand. "Nothing dramatic. When that toad Wilton asked for my hand, Peter sent him off with a flea in his ear."

"But surely you did not want to accept him." Mrs. Darling looked horrified.

"Of course not. But I did want to put the flea in his ear myself. It is as if he thought I might actually accept if left on my own. And then just now I asked him about Longwood, the estate I received from

Talmadge, and he told me I need not worry. It was all taken care of."

Kate frowned. "Do you suspect that something is wrong?'

"Of course not. If there is one thing that is certain, it is that my brother will take even more care of my inheritance than he does of his own estate. If I leave all in his hands, he will doubtless make me a rich woman."

"I can just hear him," Lady Merton said with a laugh. "There is no need for you to worry. I will take care of everything." She captured his intonation exactly.

Kate continued to frown. "I don't understand. What is it that worries you? Do you think he will force you into another marriage you do not like? I would not have thought it of him."

"Oh, no, my dear, Peter would never do that to me, and I have no fear that he will do it to Clara either. He is truly desirous of our happiness."

Kate began to laugh. "My lady, you have a brother who protects you and guards you from insult, who is solicitous of your happiness, who sees to it that you are safe from care, and you wish to complain? This kingdom is full of women who would gladly take your place."

Lady Talmadge smiled ruefully. "When you put it that way it begins to sound foolish."

"No, not foolish at all. There is a point at which protection becomes oppression. The shackles of kindness and good intentions are still shackles. This should prove interesting," said Lady Merton with a delighted smile. "But this is a discussion that definitely calls for refreshments beyond tea." She called to the footman, "Harold, please bring us some cakes and Madeira." Then she caught sight of Clara and added, "And a pot of tea as well."

The wine was poured and passed around along with little cakes sprinkled with caraway seeds. The ladies all settled down in expectation of enjoyment.

"We shall have a proper debate," proclaimed Lady Merton. "The topic is this: which is worse, a man who smothers you with his protection or a man who fails to protect you at all? Since this is the sort of topic that can be discussed honestly only among friends, I suggest that we dispense with formality and call each other by our first names. Is that agreeable?"

She directed the inquiry at Kate with a smile to accompany it. Kate could feel herself flush, but it was with pleasure rather than embarrassment. "Most agreeable," she said.

"Good. My name, if you do not already know, is the Shakespearean Miranda. My mother called me so because she found herself in a brave new world in America."

Kate laughed. "My name is Shakespearean as well. My mother called me Kate after Shakespeare's shrew. She said that 'shrew' is just the name men give to women who stand up for themselves, and the world would be better off if all women were shrews."

"Bravo!" Miranda clapped her hands in delight.

"Oh, that is my Mary," said Franny. "It is good to know she did not lose her spirit." She reached over to clasp her niece's hand.

"Then let us drink a toast to friendship," said Alice.

Miranda raised her glass. "And may we all endeavor to be shrews!"

They laughed and drank the toast—even Clara with her tea.

Alice sighed. "I think I need lessons in shrewishness. At present, I feel smothered by my brother's protectiveness."

"But is protectiveness such a bad thing?" Kate asked. "A brother who was indifferent to your welfare, to your safety, who thought only of his own benefit, might put you in actual danger."

Miranda cocked her head to the side. "But the smothering protectiveness that keeps a woman from making any decisions, from even knowing the situation of her family, can be a danger in itself. Should she suddenly be tossed out into the world, she has no idea how to manage."

Clara, who had been listening carefully, asked, "Why would

someone who had been taking care of a woman suddenly throw her out?"

Miranda smiled at her. "He might not, but death, illness, all sorts of disasters can intervene. Far too many widows find themselves with no one to turn to and no notion of how to proceed on their own."

Kate raised her brows. "You would say then that indifference from the start is preferable to loving care?"

Miranda shook her head. "No, I would never say that. But I would say that truly loving care does not keep a woman in ignorance and does not keep her from doing things she is perfectly capable of doing. Would you have been happy if instead of being allowed to read Virgil, you were told that the classics were much too demanding for a woman's brain and you should go embroider a cushion instead?"

Kate nodded an acknowledgement of the point and took another sip of her wine. Her glass was nearly empty, as were the glasses of the other women. She was unaccustomed to drinking in the middle of the day and was feeling a trifle lightheaded. The other women seemed to be in a similar state. She smiled fondly at them.

"I know that far too many women are tossed out on the world with no one to help and protect them, but that does not prevent me from resenting the arrogance of men who insist that they always know best." Alice frowned at her empty glass. She reached over for the decanter to refill it and the other glasses as well. Then she continued. "What they know best is what suits them. When my father told me to marry Talmadge, I do not believe he was thinking of me at all. Talmadge was his friend, and it was Talmadge he wished to please."

"I know what you mean," Kate said, nodding owlishly. "It is as if we are not quite human, as if we are *things*. We can be either toys to be protected and kept wrapped up, away from the real world, or tools, used for their profit or pleasure. But in either case, they behave as if we are not quite real."

Franny had a dreamy look about her as she shook her head sadly.

"Don't be too harsh. It is not always selfishness or greed that makes fathers choose badly. At times, they make dreadful mistakes with the best of intentions, through pure foolishness. My own father would not listen to Andrew's suit, and disowned me when we eloped. Father never stopped to consider Andrew's sterling character." She turned to her niece. "And then he insisted your mother marry Newell without stopping to discover that he was a total wastrel. He assumed marriage to a viscount would be enough to guarantee her security at the least."

There was a sudden silence.

Then Miranda smiled and said, "I confess I had noticed that there is a remarkable resemblance between you and your niece."

Franny closed her eyes. "I am such a fool. Forgive me, Kate." She looked at the others then. "I beg you, forget what I said. This is no trivial matter. Please do not mention it to anyone."

"Of course not," said Miranda, "if that is what you wish."

"Did you say something?" Alice smiled. "I must have been wool-gathering. I cannot recall a word of it."

Kate's shock must still have been obvious, for Alice looked at her and said, "Do not worry, truly. Nothing said in this room will ever be repeated. But be assured, if you need our assistance, you may have it."

Miranda nodded agreement, and Kate began to breathe more easily.

Clara, who had been sitting silent and had therefore been over-looked, was finding all of this most confusing. She continued to sit still and silent.

"What I have been woolgathering about is my brother," said Alice. "I know his intentions are of the best, but he is overly arrogant and sure of himself."

"Hear, hear," said Miranda.

Alice acknowledged her with an inclination of her head and continued. "I shall simply have to assert myself. I cannot wait for him to allow me to take charge of my life. I will simply have to do so."

The others all applauded, but Kate could not help but feel a trifle melancholy. Alice had the right, the power to take charge of her life. It would be more than six months before she would have the same right. And when she did declare her independence, she would lose these friends because she would put herself out of this circle. Out of Ashleigh's circle.

⇛⇚

WHEN THEY RETURNED, Ashleigh was relieved to see that his sister no longer seemed annoyed at him. Indeed, she seemed quite cheerful, as if smiling at the world in general. In fact, if it had been anyone else, he might have thought she was a trifle foxed. Then he remembered that she had been visiting Lady Merton, so anything was possible. With a small smile, he took her arm and suggested a turn around the garden.

Clara, who accompanied them, also seemed to have enjoyed the visit immensely, though she was looking a trifle serious, as if puzzling over something in her mind. She frowned. "You know, the way people are named is really very strange."

Ashleigh asked, "Strange in what way? Do you mean to ask why you are called Clara? I believe that was in honor of one of your father's aunts, was it not, Alice?"

Lady Talmadge nodded dreamily.

"No," said Clara, "I mean last names. For example, it would be much simpler if names and titles were all the same. How could a stranger know that Selina Webster is Lord Ambruster's daughter? Or that Lady Talmadge is my mother when I am Lady Clara Grammont?"

Her uncle smiled slightly. "One might suspect that part of the reason is to make it immediately apparent who is a stranger."

Clara continued to frown. "And then, how can Kate be Miss Darling if her mother was Mrs. Darling's sister?"

"Clara!" The dreamy expression fled from Alice's face and she

100

spoke sharply. "When one is asked to forget something, one forgets it completely. One never mentions it again."

Clara looked at her mother in confusion. "I didn't think that meant at home."

"It means everywhere, at all times, and under all circumstances." Lady Talmadge turned to her brother. "You did not hear that. This is not a joking matter." She sounded so angry that Clara was on the verge of tears.

Ashleigh smiled to reassure both of them. "Hear what?"

---

IT WAS NOT until much later, after dinner, that Ashleigh had a chance to think about what he had been told to forget. There is nothing like being told to forget something to imprint it on the memory. He sat long at the table, sipping his port slowly while he considered.

Miss Darling was not really Miss Darling. Instead, she was the daughter of Franny Darling's sister. If she was going by the name of Darling, she was not using her real name.

There might be a number of reasons for this. There might be any number of perfectly innocent and honorable reasons. It was possible, he supposed, though he could not think of one. He could only think that the most likely reason was that she had no name of her own, that she was a bastard.

He could not remember Franny Darling ever speaking of her sister. For that matter, he could not recall Franny ever speaking of her family at all. He had heard somewhere that Franny's father was some sort of country gentry and had disowned her for marrying Andrew Darling. Such a father would doubtless have been even more harsh with a daughter whose child was born out of wedlock.

Was that Miss Darling's secret? After her mother died, with no father to provide for her, to protect her, she might well have sought out her mother's sister. Then Franny Darling, with her generous heart, would certainly have taken the girl in. Franny would have had sympathy in plenty for a girl cut adrift by her family. She would also have helped the girl to keep silent about her origins.

That would explain so many things.

Miss Darling had clearly been raised as a lady, but if she was illegitimate, a suitable marriage would be difficult, if not impossible. Few gentlemen would be willing to take a bastard for a wife, especially one with no dowry, and she would find marriage to a tradesman an uncomfortable fit.

That, in turn, would explain why she would consider taking employment in a shop. Miss Darling—Kate—would seek independence. Her pride would demand it. Franny might be more than willing to give her a home, might be delighted to do so, but Kate would see that as charity. She must have been in truly desperate straits to have come seeking even temporary shelter from her aunt.

That would also explain why Kate was so prickly, so quick to take offense. He could easily forgive that. Indeed, he could only admire her pride, her refusal to be cowed. She was quite a little warrior, his Kate. His beautiful Kate.

No, not his Kate, of course.

Still, she could not be left on her own, no matter what she thought. She was too fragile, too vulnerable. She should be cared for, protected.

There must be some way.

*Yorkshire*

THERE HAD BEEN an exchange of letters.

Mrs. Grant had written to her friend's sister, mentioning that a viscount had appeared searching for his sister, who had run away. Mrs.

Grant had, of course, no notion where the sister might have gone, but she hoped that a young woman with such an unpleasant brother had found a safe haven.

Mrs. Darling had written to her sister's friend, assuring her that the unpleasant fellow's sister had found a safe haven. She trusted that her sister's friends would be discreet should anyone else come in search of the young woman.

Mrs. Grant told her husband and Dr. Finley that she was quite assured that Kate was safe. She did not, however, say anything about where Kate was. She did not think men capable of keeping a secret.

Thus, when Hall appeared, purporting to be a Somerset neighbor of the Langleys who had known Lady Newell when she was a girl, he was received civilly, even graciously, and received no information at all beyond the fact that Lady Newell had died the year before and the daughter had gone to live with her brother in London.

He had not expected anything else. These people were friends to Miss Russell, and they had met Newell. That was enough to assure that they would not help anyone searching for her. However, just to be certain, he spent a few days in the village, presenting himself as a tradesman thinking to retire to the country.

The questions he asked about the land and conditions were sufficiently intelligent to convince the townspeople that he was serious in his search, so it was natural that he should also ask about the inhabitants of the neighborhood. A bad landlord, for example, harmed far more than his own tenants.

He raised the question with the regulars over a mug of ale at the Ring o' Bells, and noted the morose silence that followed. The tavernkeeper, Powell, finished polishing the pitcher he was holding and put it down carefully.

"Well, now," Powell said slowly, "Squire Grant, I doubt you could find a much better landlord. Takes care of his tenants, makes repairs as needed, keeps a good eye on the crops and brings in new breeding stock when it's needed."

Hall nodded judiciously. "That's good to hear. I was a bit worried when I rode out to the west today. There seemed to be cottages just falling to pieces, and the fields looked as if no one was taking notice."

"Ah," said one of the regulars. The others nodded. They looked at Powell, seeming to expect him to speak for them.

"That'd be Viscount Newell's estate." Powell turned aside to spit.

"Not such a good landlord then," said Hall, nodding sagely. "Too miserly mayhap?"

Powell snorted. The others sneered.

"The old one turned up here maybe once every five years or so," said one of the men.

"Happen he'd run out of money," put in another.

"The old one?" asked Hall.

Powell nodded. "Him and the son lived in London. Left the wife and daughter here to run the place."

"Too big a job for a woman," said Hall.

Powell shrugged. "They did the best they could, but he took every penny and left them nothing."

"Ah, well," said Hall easily, "women never have enough money. It's always frills and furbelows with them."

One of the men grunted. "My wife has more in the way of frills and furbelows than Lady Newell and her daughter ever did. If squire hadn't paid old Tomlinson to stay on at the home farm, they'd not have had enough to eat, and if he hadn't run their sheep with his own, there'd have been no money coming in at all."

Hall managed to look shocked. "Mayhap the viscount had no money himself."

"He took every penny they made from the wool and sold the furniture from the manor out from under them. After he died, the son did the same," said Powell.

"The son doesn't manage the estate himself, then?"

Powell snorted. "He came up after his mother died and took his sister away. Then he came back a few weeks ago looking for her."

"Happen the lass had sense enough to run away," said the oldest of the men.

Hall frowned. "Run away? Sounds foolish. Where could a lass run to?"

That was met with shrugs.

"If she'd come back here, she could have gone to the squire. The Grants would have taken her in quick enough. They offered when her mother died. But no one's seen hide nor hair of her." Powell shrugged again.

"To her mother's people," Hall suggested.

That was met with disbelief.

"If they'd been willing to help," said Powell, "those ladies wouldn't have been living hand to mouth all these years."

# CHAPTER NINE

*Moreton-in-Marsh*

LADY TALMADGE LAY down on the broad bed provided in the best chamber the White Hart Inn had to offer. It was quite comfortable, with a feather mattress atop the woolen mattress. Lady Talmadge would not have objected to such a bed in her own home. At the moment, however, it had one supreme virtue to her mind.

It did not move.

It did not bump and bounce her about.

It did not cause bruises on various parts of her anatomy.

It remained stationary.

She gave a sigh of pure pleasure and closed her eyes.

Clara sat in a chair by the window, looked out at the people bustling about the town, hurrying home at the end of the day, and gave a sigh of boredom. "You wouldn't be so tired, you know, if you hadn't insisted on making the trip in two days. It's so late now that we won't be able to see anything of this town either."

Lady Talmadge did not open her eyes, but her sigh changed in tone. "Do not sulk, Clara. It is most unbecoming. Worse than that, I find it very irritating, and since I am both sore and tired, you really do not wish to irritate me."

Her daughter looked at her, affronted. "You were the one who wanted to travel so quickly. Had we taken three days or even four as Cousin Stephen suggested, we would have had time to explore other places and even this town before going to Longwood. And you would not be sore and tired."

It had seemed a good idea at the time. Her brother had insisted that she and Clara could not make the trip alone, and she had agreed. However, Stephen had looked so uncomfortable at having to be their escort that she had not wanted to impose on him longer than necessary.

That did not prevent her current irritation.

They were staying at an inn. She could not tell her daughter to go to her room because her daughter was sharing her room. She could not tell her daughter to go occupy herself elsewhere because they were in a public inn. She sighed once more, opened her eyes and sat up. She glared at her daughter. Clara smiled back angelically.

A knock at the door signaled the arrival of her maid with their bags. Susan was importantly directing the porter to be careful with my lady's cases, and casting a scornful eye about the room. She sniffed and supposed that the cases should be put there, pointing to the corner by the wardrobe. Lady Talmadge caught her daughter's eye and both did their unsuccessful best to repress smiles.

After shaking her head in despair at the clumsiness of the porter, Susan closed the door behind him and curtseyed to her mistress. "Mr. Bancroft has ordered dinner to be served in the private parlor in an hour, my lady, if that is acceptable to you. And he told them to bring you a tea tray now." Another knock on the door brought the tea, which was followed in short order by hot water and a bathing tub.

By the time she and her daughter joined Bancroft, Lady Talmadge no longer felt bruised and battered, and Clara's high spirits at the prospect of a new adventure had returned. A table had been set up by the window to which Clara promptly hurried, eager to see all there was to see.

Bancroft smiled at her indulgently before he turned to her mother. "She reminds me of you when you were a child. You were always ready for something new, always eager to see whatever there was to see."

"Was I? I can scarcely remember myself at that age. How tiresomely boring I have become."

"Do not go fishing for compliments, my lady."

"Stop that. I do remember that you called me Alice when I was a child. I wish you would do so now."

He looked at her with an expression she could not read. "You are no longer a child, my lady."

She felt suddenly self-conscious, but determined to continue. "And I am no longer Lady Talmadge. Not really. It is simply a label left over from a part of my life that brought me little pleasure. Were it not for Clara, I would gladly forget it completely. I know you call my brother Peter. Please call me Alice."

He was still looking at her with that odd expression. Then he smiled. It was an odd smile, too, a combination of pain and pleasure somehow. "I would be honored to call you Alice."

"Honored nonsense, Stephen." She could feel a flush rising in her face. "We are old friends, are we not?"

"Friends," he repeated, still with that odd smile.

They sat down to enjoy a meal that was not, perhaps, the best any of them had ever eaten, but that was certainly one of the pleasantest. Any discomfort from their earlier conversation dissipated under Clara's eager chatter and speculation about everything she saw from her seat by the window. They were soon all laughing together at the sight of a large dog being chased away from a shop entrance by a cat he had disturbed at her ablutions.

As they neared the end of their dinner, Clara asked, "Will we be leaving for Longwood first thing in the morning?"

Alice was about to say yes when she caught a look of uncertainty on Stephen's face.

"I was wondering if you might care to first spend a day exploring the town, perhaps taking a ride about the area," he said slowly.

"That sounds to be an excellent idea," Alice said, taking a cue more from his face than from his words. Clara looked for a moment as if she might object, but then seemed to decide she had no real objection. She simply nodded and finished off her pudding.

Once Clara had retired for the night in Susan's care, Alice turned to Stephen expectantly.

He did not need to hear the question. "It is nothing I know," he said, "just a feeling I have. I mentioned Longwood in the common room without saying anything of your connection to it, and noticed some odd looks being exchanged. I would like to learn a bit more before you present yourself."

She looked at him sharply. "Is that why you did not want me to write to say that I was coming?"

He made a slight face. "I truly do not know of any problems, and the reports and accounts that Carstairs has sent have been unexceptionable. Your brother has always checked them over and everything has been in order."

"But?"

"But I have always had an odd feeling about it all. I am not familiar with this part of the country, and Carstairs is. He was here for many years under your husband—your late husband," he amended at her grimace. "I would like to see a bit before you are handed more impeccable books."

She thought a moment, and then grinned. "We shall be like that sultan who wandered around Baghdad in disguise to hear what his subjects really thought. What fun!"

IN THE MORNING, the travelers strolled about the town, buying ribbons at the drapers and buns at the baker, eavesdropping where people were chatting, and listening politely when people responded to their own mild inquiries about families in the neighborhood.

Longwood?

Well, what can you expect when the owner never comes? West of town it is, on the road to Worcester, with the drive just before the toll gate.

Toll gate?

Ah, doesn't that fill the coffers of the earl. And none of it coming back here.

It was all said with a nod and a sigh.

They walked back to the inn with Stephen scowling and silent, and Alice feeling an unexpected disappointment.

"In all those meticulously prepared and presented accounts, there was never mention of a toll gate," he finally said. "Now I am wondering what else might have escaped mention."

"Indeed. I very much wish to know." Alice thought a moment, and then smiled. "You know, I quite fancy a drive. Along the Worcester road. We should be able to see something of the farms at least, perhaps some of the tenant houses."

THE LANDLORD WAS pleased to rent them a gig and provide a picnic for their jaunt. He recommended two drives, one to the north and one to the east, that would provide pleasant views, and the one to the east led along a bit of an old Roman road, it was said. His face fell slightly when Bancroft said they intended to go west, but he wished them a pleasant afternoon nonetheless.

They had not gone far when they began to see the reason for the landlord's fallen face. Moreton-in-Marsh may not have been the wealthiest town Bancroft had ever seen, but it was reasonably neat and prosperous. Built of the golden Cotswold stone, it had gleamed in the sunlight. West of the town, things began to deteriorate.

The fields they could see looked well enough, green with young crops, and the sheep looked fat enough. The cottages, however, looked sadly dilapidated. A few had chickens as well as children in the yard, but none had a cow or even a pig. Alice hoped at first that they had not reached her estate, but Stephen stopped to ask. These cottages did indeed belong to Longwood.

Clara looked shocked. Never, not on her father's estate and certainly not on her uncle's, had she seen such neglect.

"Carstairs should have said something," Alice said. "These cottages should have been repaired long ago. Even Talmadge would have approved such a necessary expenditure."

"He did," said Stephen grimly. "The accounts for years past were forwarded to your brother after Talmadge's death. Funds enough were allocated every year to keep all the tenants' homes in excellent repair."

When they came to the entrance to Longwood, he turned to ask her if she wanted to drive in, but she shook her head. "No. When we enter, it will be to take possession. I do not wish to give any warning."

Stephen smiled his approval and they continued to the toll gate. This, and the toll keeper's cottage, were in excellent repair. When Anne commented on this, a bit acidly, he pointed out that the road was in excellent repair as well. At least some of the money for the repair of the cottages had been invested here.

They pulled up at the toll gate and an elderly man limped out. Stephen raised his brows at the tariff—a shilling seemed a bit steep for a gig, with only one horse, but the man showed him the printed bill.

"I don't recall this toll gate. How long has it been here?

"Ah, the earl built the road, oh, three years ago. It goes over his land, so it's a private road, but it cuts off a good twelve, fifteen miles of the old road. And it's a good, safe road, too, so those going any distance are glad to pay for the convenience, you might say."

"The earl?"

"The Earl of Talmadge, he is."

"The earl lives here, does he?"

"No, no. It's Mr. Carstairs, the earl's manager, who lives at Long-wood."

"In one of the cottages?"

"Ah, no, not Mr. Carstairs." The toll collector grinned. "Mr. Carstairs lives in the manor house itself, he does."

They rode away in silence. Eventually, Alice said, with a small smile, "So Talmadge was cheated for years, and never knew it. Wouldn't he have been furious. I wonder if he is looking down and gnashing his teeth."

They found a pleasant hillside for their picnic, beside a stream that made Stephen regret that he did not have a fishing pole with him. Clara, however, found it excellent for dangling her feet and, on her own, she was not too old to enjoy racing sticks down it.

The following morning, the two grooms who had accompanied them had the carriage and horses waiting for them when Alice and Clara came downstairs. The landlord was there to wish such well-paying customers a safe journey, but they made his face fall once more when he heard that they were going to Longwood.

"Mr. Bancroft," he said hesitantly, "are you certain you wish to go there? It is not really a place you would wish to bring ladies. It is Mr. Carstairs' place, you see, and he is a single gentleman."

"Actually, it is my place," Alice said pleasantly. "I am Lady Talmadge."

The landlord's eyes grew round and he looked at Stephen for confirmation.

"Yes," he said with a smile. "But before we leave, could you tell me, who is the local magistrate?"

"That would be Mr. Sommerfield, over at Millcrest, about two miles from here."

"Sommerfield," repeated Stephen. "And would you by any chance know if he is in residence at the moment? Just in case he should be needed."

The landlord nodded, still round-eyed and now speechless.

⇻⇺

THE CARRIAGE STOPPED on the crest of a hill in the drive. When Alice looked at him questioningly, Stephen said, "I thought you might like to see the house before we arrive, so I asked them to stop as soon as it came into view."

"What a good idea."

He helped her down, and Clara as well. The three of them stood there, looking down at a house of the same golden stone that had built the village. It was a good-sized house, though not on the massive scale of Kelswick, or even the Earl of Talmadge's Wharton Court. The turrets and multi-paned windows seemed to belong to the house's own history, not to the newer fashion for the gothic. The gardens around it seemed sadly neglected, but of a pleasant size, with a massive oak anchoring the side garden.

"Do you wish to go on?" asked Stephen.

"Of course," Clara said, as if astonished that any other course could be possible. "It looks perfect!"

Alice smiled at her. "Yes, I certainly want to go on."

"There might be an unpleasant confrontation with Carstairs," Stephen warned. "I could take care of it for you, if you like. Then you could come after Carstairs has been removed."

"No," she said. "This is my responsibility. I will handle it."

Stephen smiled, approvingly, she thought, and handed her back into the carriage.

No footmen came running to the carriage when they drew up before the house. No one appeared when the party disembarked. It took several minutes before anyone opened the door in response to their repeated knocks. When the door was finally opened, it was leaned on by a somewhat disheveled individual in shirtsleeves who peered bleary-eyed at the newcomers.

Lady Talmadge sailed in with a slight nod to the doorkeeper. She was followed by Clara, accompanied by Susan. They, in turn, were followed by Bancroft and Perkins, the larger of the two grooms. Collins, the other groom, remained with the horses.

"Have someone bring in the luggage and take it to our rooms," commanded Lady Talmadge, taking off her gloves as she looked critically around the hall. It was pleasantly shaped, she thought, though the housekeeping left much to be desired. "Then summon Mr. Carstairs."

"Bring in... summon..." the doorkeeper began to sputter. "Madam, who do you think you are?"

Bancroft stiffened but Lady Talmadge held out a hand to restrain him while she turned slowly to look at the doorkeeper. She saw a paunchy fellow looking somewhat the worse for wear. It appeared that neither he nor his clothing had been in the vicinity of soap and water for some time. She looked at him until he began to shrivel. "I," she said, "am Lady Talmadge, the owner of this estate. Are you by any chance employed here?" Her tone suggested that if he was, it might not be for much longer.

"Employed?" He looked affronted. "I should say not! A guest. Robbie's guest. And he never said a word about you coming here. You never come here. Are you sure you were expected?"

"Obviously not." She looked around again and shook her head. "Where is Mr. Carstairs?"

"In bed, of course, like the others. Made rather a late night of it. Only reason that infernal banging of yours woke me was that I fell asleep down here. I say, are you really Lady Talmadge?"

She looked at him, and he shriveled again.

"Robbie's not going to like this. Not one bit." He shook his head.

She sighed. "I suppose there are some servants in this place?"

No sooner had she spoken than an older man appeared, buttoning his vest with one hand and smoothing his hair with the other. He had apparently heard at least some of the conversation for he promptly said, "My lady, I am Blenkinsop, the butler here. I regret that we were unprepared for your arrival." Having gotten that far, he paused, unable to think what to do next.

"Blenkinsop?" Clara started to giggle, but Bancroft put a hand on her shoulder and she stopped.

"Well, Blenkinsop," Lady Talmadge said, "would you have our luggage taken up to our rooms." When the butler blanched, she said, "There are habitable rooms, are there not?"

"Yes, of course, my lady, but Mr. Carstairs' friends…"

"Will be leaving." She finished the sentence for him. "Immediately. Susan, you can oversee the distribution of the luggage and the preparation of the rooms. Clara, you may go with her."

Susan drew herself up and a militant gleam came into her eyes. Clara seemed to suspect that she was going to miss some excitement, but the prospect of choosing her own room appealed.

"And then, Blenkinsop, if you would rouse Mr. Carstairs and direct him to meet me in the steward's office…" She stopped at the look of confusion on Blenkinsop's face. "Mr. Carstairs does conduct the estate business, does he not?"

"Oh, yes, my lady, but he uses the library."

"Of course." She smiled slightly. "Then you will direct me to the library and instruct Mr. Carstairs to report to me there immediately."

As the party swept out after the butler, the doorkeeper could be heard muttering, "Robbie ain't going to like this. Not half he ain't."

THE LIBRARY WAS a square room, paneled in oak, with long windows leading to a terrace. Books occupied a few shelves, but did not intrude themselves on the space. In the center of the room was an enormous desk with a high-backed throne-like chair behind it.

Lady Talmadge's nose wrinkled at the smell of stale cigar smoke lingering in the room. She drew the curtains and flung open the windows while Blenkinsop scurried off to find Carstairs. She walked slowly around the room, looking at the shelves. Then she looked at the desk. "I don't even see any account books. I believe it is now your turn to take charge, Stephen."

He had been standing in the center of the room, taking it all in as well. "Not take charge," he said with a smile. "Merely to provide some assistance." He opened the drawer in the center of the desk and moved things around until he found some keys. In response to her look of surprise he shrugged. "It's the usual place to keep keys."

Then he turned his attention to the cabinets beneath the bookshelves. "I don't see our friend exerting himself overmuch, so I would expect the current books to be in the closest cabinet." He tried a few keys until the lock opened, and then gave a satisfied grunt. "Good. Both sets." He picked up half a dozen books, looked them over quickly, and set two of them on the desk.

Alice leaned over to look at them. Then she frowned.

"Notice anything?"

She looked up to see him grinning. "They have the same dates."

He nodded. "Quarter Day is not long past. He had to create the set to go with the report he sent to your brother. Shall we see how he did it?"

It did not take long, and it was really quite simple, though a bit curious. Some income that appeared in the real accounts, like the income from the tolls, never reached the fictitious ones. And expenses that were listed in the fictitious accounts, like repairs to the cottages, never appeared in the real ones.

At the same time, the fictitious accounts showed far more income from rents and agriculture than the real accounts showed. So much more that the final difference was not above three hundred pounds. A goodly sum, but not more than the income of a prosperous shopkeeper might be.

"How very strange," said Alice. "He could surely have stolen far more."

"Indeed, he could." Bancroft was frowning at the accounts. "I do not understand it."

Alice had just seated herself at the desk with the books side by side in front of her when they heard the commotion. A number of people seemed to be running down the stairs. There were angry voices and slamming doors. Then the door to the library opened and Perkins came in, holding a man by the arm.

"Beg your pardon, my lady, but this gentleman is Mr. Carstairs. He didn't seem to believe me when I told him you wanted to see him and he was trying to leave."

Lady Talmadge thought that Perkins managed a remarkably innocent expression.

"Let go of me, you oaf," said Carstairs. He pulled his arm free and straightened his jacket. "I was simply seeing my guests off. I am sorry, my lady. Had I known you intended to visit Longwood, I would have seen that everything would be ready for you."

"I am sure that you would," she said, looking at him thoughtfully. He was a small man with a pouter-pigeon chest. Most surprising, he had a moustache. She had never seen a man with a moustache except for those odd soldiers who came to London with the tsar for the peace celebrations. Cossacks, she thought.

Carstairs was looking increasingly nervous. She was surprised that she had that effect but then she realized that Stephen was smiling at him. That smile would have made her nervous, too.

"This is my cousin, Mr. Bancroft. He has been explaining your rather imaginative bookkeeping system," she said.

"Now, I can explain," Carstairs began.

"Can you really?" she asked. "I confess to a considerable amount of curiosity."

He glared at her and then burst out, "Do you have any idea how long I have been here? More than 20 years, that's how long. And do you have any idea how often the late earl came here? Never, that's how often. Never an inquiry, never a word of praise or blame, nothing. All he wanted was to have the income deposited to his account."

He stepped closer to the desk, shaking a finger at her. "Did he want to hear about it when I warned him that the end of the war would mean a drop in agricultural prices? No, he did not. Did he want to hear about it when I told him the tenants wouldn't be able to pay the rent increase he demanded? No, he did not. I suggested the toll road years ago, but he wouldn't hear of it."

When the steward put his fists on the desk and leaned toward her, Bancroft stepped up, about to pull him away, but Lady Talmadge raised a hand to stop them both. "Mr. Carstairs, I think we will need to have a lengthy talk. Please be seated. Perkins, tell Blenkinsop that we would like some tea, and also some breakfast for Mr. Carstairs."

A lengthy talk it was, indeed. With no oversight or interference from the Earl of Talmadge, Mr. Carstairs had grown accustomed to thinking of the estate as his. So long as he sent along the expected income, no one questioned his decisions. He began to relax as the countess and her cousin listened without comment. As for the house, well, the earl never visited. It seemed foolish to leave it empty. It was, he pointed out virtuously, easier to make certain all necessary repairs were made if he was on the spot, so to speak.

And the repairs to the tenants cottages? The repairs that had not been made?

Well, he had lowered their rents, hadn't he? And then, he realized the earl was growing older. It might not be long before his heir took over, a stranger who might pay more attention. He decided he needed a bit of a nest egg, so to speak, in case he had to retire suddenly.

Alice's fingers tightened on the cup she was holding. "How pleased you must have been to discover that the estate had passed to a woman."

Carstairs suddenly realized he had relaxed perhaps too much, and began to voice stumbling apologies. Alice waved them away.

"Enough," she said. "I must think on this. I will give you my decision in the morning. You will not mind sharing the grooms' quarters tonight, I am sure."

He offered no objection at all, and bowed his way out with Perkins holding his arm once more.

After dinner, Clara went off to bed in a mixture of exhaustion and excitement. She had finally chosen her room and was torn among the half-dozen color schemes she had devised. A tea tray had been brought into the small parlor where Alice and Stephen were sitting. She eyed it dubiously and then looked at the decanter half-hidden in a corner.

"Do you know, I think I would like a brandy," she said.

Stephen poured two glasses and brought her one. "Does that mean you have decided what to do about Carstairs?"

"Yes. It was foolish of Talmadge to leave him here on his own for so many years. Foolish and unfair. It is no wonder he began to think of the estate as his own. I would not punish him for the deceptions he employed to keep Talmadge satisfied. At least he ignored the order to raise the tenants' rents. However, there remains the deplorable state of those cottages. I cannot allow him to profit at the tenants' expense."

"So?"

"So I will not have him imprisoned. However, he must leave and hand over his nest egg. I can use it to make repairs immediately, and there are doubtless other improvements that will benefit the estate."

Stephen smiled at her, and she smiled back. "Does that mean you approve of my decision?"

"No, I applaud it," he said. "A mixture of justice and mercy."

She collapsed back in her chair with a whoosh. "I was not at all certain I could do this, you know."

"You were not, but I was."

"But you offered to do this for me, to deal with Carstairs and"—she waved her hand—"and everything."

He shrugged. "I knew you could do it, but I was not certain you knew that. I didn't want to force your hand if you weren't ready."

"It was easier, having you here. Not only because you trusted me. I suspect it was also easier making people obey me when I had a large, strong man standing beside me."

Stephen threw back his head and laughed. "Do not underestimate yourself, Alice. You had that foolish fellow who opened the door and Blenkinsop trembling in their boots when you sailed in so majestical-ly."

"Did I really?"

"Indeed."

"That's good to know, because I was trembling in my boots as well."

⫸⫷

THE NEXT TWO weeks were spent in constant activity. Repairs were undertaken, tenants were met, neighbors came by and offered welcome, and moments were snatched to enjoy the beauty of Longwood's situation. Stephen sent for his assistant to come and supervise until decisions were made about the administration of the estate.

By the end of the first week Alice had decided that Longwood would be her home. Actually, she had decided the moment she first saw it, but she did not want to admit that she had decided so impulsively.

Of course, much of the pleasure she found here was brought about by Stephen's presence. They worked well together, they were comfortable together—more than comfortable. Clara found in him a father she had never known. He protected them both, but he never smothered her. She knew she could rely on him whenever she needed help, but he never tried to take everything out of her hands. He never assumed he knew what she wanted, what she needed, better than she did.

What she wanted...

That was becoming complicated.

She would look at him, standing at his ease, so strong and solid, so comfortable in his strength. She would start to imagine what it would be like to be held by that strength. She would look at his hands, his strong, gentle hands. She would start to imagine what it would be like to be touched by those hands.

She lay awake at night and wondered what it would be like with a strong young man to share her bed. Her husband's visits to her bed had been infrequent and brief and, to be honest, boring. She wondered what it would be like with someone else. She wondered what it would be like with Stephen.

SHE WAS SO much more than simply beautiful. She was wonderful. She had stepped up and taken charge with common sense and sympathetic understanding. The tenants could hardly believe their luck. He was so proud of her that he thought his heart would burst.

She was ready now to take on the world. She could spend her days here or go to London for the Season. Whatever she wanted.

He would remain back at Kelswick, her brother's steward. Always a friend, though she would no longer need him. Still, he would have the memory of these weeks here, these weeks when he had been able to pretend that he was not simply a steward, that they were a family, he and Alice and Clara.

Not really a family, of course. He was lying here alone in bed, alone and longing.

Ah, Alice!

# CHAPTER TEN

*Sussex*

T HE HAWTHORN WAS blooming. Hedgerows were white with flowers, and the sweet scent filled the air along the road. Kate stood there, her face lifted to the sun, drinking it all in—the scent, the warmth, even the sounds. There was a bird singing. She had heard it here before, but it was not a familiar sound, not a song she had heard in Yorkshire. One of these days, she would have to ask someone what it was, that little bird singing in the hedge.

She smiled as she realized what she meant. She wanted to know the name of that bird because this was where she was going to stay. This place was going to be home. Mr. Prufrock was going to take her on as an assistant and eventually sell her the shop—she was sure of it. She would be able to stay here, she would have a home of her own, she would have Aunt Franny, and she would be happy.

Feeling content, she set out on the chalky footpath on the bank above the lazily flowing Ouse River. The shade trees were on this side, with a water meadow on the other side allowing a clear view of a chalk cliff on the Downs. Someday soon, she would walk this footpath all the way to its end, wherever that might be. She had always gone for long treks in Yorkshire, sometimes on errands and sometimes for the sheer love of exploring.

Walking was something she had missed in London, where the only time she left the house was to go to the market. Humphrey had insisted that it wasn't safe for a young woman to wander around London alone. For all she knew, he was right. Heaven knew London had not proved safe when she stayed indoors.

Lewes and its environs, however, seemed perfectly safe. Sussex was a haven of safety. Here, she no longer had to be on her guard all the time. When she walked here, she not only felt safe, she felt happy. Yes, this was a place where she could be happy. More important, she was free.

That freedom was a bit of a problem. Now that she had escaped her brother, now that she had taken her future into her own hands, she was free to determine what that future would be. But, she had come to realize, any choice she made meant that other futures were no longer possible.

Once upon a time, she had dreamed of marriage. Not a nightmare marriage like her mother's, where the wife was nothing more than an unpaid servant, and—even worse—a servant who could not leave. When she had been old enough to understand her mother's situation, she had urged her mother to leave. But vows were vows, said Mama. The fact that her husband ignored his did not mean she could ignore hers. By the time his death set her free, Mama was too ill to leave.

Now that she was old enough to see the world realistically, she knew that without a respectable portion she could have no hope of the kind of marriage she had dreamed of, marriage to an honorable gentleman who would give her a respectable place in society. Even if she had a decent dowry, she had no family to bring her into society, to see that she was introduced to the right sort of young man. Worse than that, the sort of young man she had once dreamed of marrying would probably recoil in horror when he heard about her brother. And if he did not recoil, his family would.

To be honest with herself, the real problem was Ashleigh. If she had never met him, perhaps she could consider marriage as a solution to her problems. Since she was in no position to turn up her nose at a solicitor or tradesman, marriage would have been possible, with the pearls providing an adequate dowry. But now? When every night she dreamed of Ashleigh, when she longed to be in his arms, when he filled all of her dreams, how could she ever consider marriage to someone else? It would be horrendously dishonest, a violation of her vows before they were even spoken. She could not be that dishonorable.

No. For her, marriage might one day be a possibility if she never saw Ashleigh again and the memories somehow faded, but that was unlikely. Her future had to lie in some other direction.

That was why she visited Mr. Prufrock so often, making herself useful by cleaning up and arranging the books in attractive displays. She had almost convinced him to take her on as an assistant, to teach her the business, so that he could gradually let her take over. She was not sure how much he would want for the shop when he was ready to retire, but she had those pearls. It might be possible to sell them for enough.

She was well away from the town now, though still walking along the path by the river. It was a warm day, and the slight breeze felt pleasant. She was wearing one of her new dresses, a pale green muslin with a lemon yellow stripe in it, and a yellow spencer. It was becoming and made her feel pretty. She knew men had in the past found her attractive and desirable but that was different. The way Farnsworth had looked at her had made her feel soiled.

Today, she felt young and pretty and even hopeful. She had convinced herself that she could look forward to the future. She did not have to fear it. And if she simply avoided Ashleigh, she would somehow manage to forget him. She stepped forward cheerfully, but then came to an abrupt stop. Up ahead, where the river veered close to the road, the duke was standing, watching her. He was very much the country gentleman today in his buckskin breeches and boots, holding a low-crowned hat. His horse was beside him, looking around as if to ask if this spot was really worth a lengthy visit.

Ashleigh smiled as he bowed to her. "Good day, Miss Darling. I did not mean to startle you, but I thought I caught a glimpse of you through the trees."

"Yes, well, I was just out for a walk." Good heavens, she sounded like an idiot. Why was she so flustered? "It is a lovely day, is it not?" Worse and worse. Now she was talking about the weather like some insipid miss.

His smile faded to a frown as he looked about. "You are alone? Do you not at least have a maid accompanying you?"

"Hardly." She could not help laughing at that. "I have been walking alone all my life, Your Grace, and my aunt's maids have better things to do than to tag along after me. Surely you do not think there is danger lurking along the river here."

He continued to frown. "One never knows. A public road runs along here, and strangers, travelers pass along here every day. It is not suitable for a young lady to be walking unaccompanied. I will walk you home, if you will permit."

He held out his arm for her to take, as if there was no doubt that she would permit it.

She shook her head. Did he not know that for her, *he* was the danger? "Really, Your Grace, does it never occur to you that someone might refuse? That I might not desire you to walk me home?"

He flushed and stepped back. "I apologize," he said stiffly. "I did not intend to inflict my company where it is not wanted."

She sighed. As if his company could ever be unwanted. Unwise, perhaps, but never unwanted. "No," she said, reaching over to take his arm. "I am teasing you. Anyone would welcome your company. It is only that I am unaccustomed to such solicitude."

He looked down at her hand on his sleeve and covered it with his other hand, tucking it more firmly into place. "Anyone?" He looked at her with a half-smile. "Only the welcome anyone would give?"

She blushed slightly. "Do not fish for compliments, Your Grace. It is not becoming to your dignity."

"No man's dignity was ever anything but enhanced by a welcome from a beautiful young lady."

Kate looked away to hide a frown. These were empty phrases, empty compliments, the sort of courtesy mere acquaintances exchanged. Is that all they were? Perhaps that was for the best. Very well then. Polite acquaintances it would be.

He signaled to his horse, which stepped up to his side so that Ashleigh could take hold of the reins to lead him along.

"He is quite a beauty," she said coolly, admiring the bay gelding. "Will he not object to being asked to dawdle along beside us?"

"Hector has already taken me to Schotten Hall and back today. He will not object to a relaxing stroll."

"Hector?"

He smiled more broadly. "I have a fondness for classical allusions myself. I have always been somewhat in awe of Homer, making the most admirable character in his epic Hector, the prince of Troy, the enemy of the Greeks."

"Homer was wise in that. It is foolish to underestimate one's enemies." Remembering her own enemies—Farnsworth and her brother—she felt chilled, as if the sunlight had dimmed.

As if he had noticed the change in her spirits, his voice sounded deliberately cheerful. "Besides, had the Trojans been pitiful, the Greeks would have won no honor in defeating them. David wins glory by defeating Goliath. Had the giant defeated the shepherd boy, we would not know the story."

Kate made an effort to maintain a playful tone. "Nor would it have been remarkable had the hare beaten the tortoise."

"Or if the dragon had defeated St. George."

They continued on the way, keeping the conversation carefully lighthearted. Kate had always been given free rein to rummage through the squire's library as well as Dr. Finley's, and she had read widely if erratically. It was liberating to discover that Ashleigh did not seem annoyed when she could toss out examples from legends or the classics to match his. He seemed to actually enjoy it, and she found herself relaxing, enjoying his companionship. She would enjoy his friendship while it was still possible.

When they came to Hawthorne Cottage, Ashleigh reverted to his original concern. "I cannot but mislike it that you are wandering about the countryside unprotected. It is one thing when you walk into the town—it is not far and there are always people about. But you should not be walking alone beside the river."

Kate wondered what he would think had he known that she had traveled alone from London, walking most of the way and accepting rides on farm carts the rest of the time. She could not suppress a little laugh. He seemed to have no idea what life was like for other people. "Really, Your Grace..."

"No, hear me out," he interrupted. "I would not ask you to forgo your walks, but I do suggest that you take them on Kelswick land. Your aunt's property borders mine, so there would be no problem for you in walking there."

"Truly, there is no need for you..."

"Please," he interrupted again, "you would relieve me of the need to worry about you if you would promise to walk at Kelswick."

She shook her head impatiently. "Your Grace, I fear you worry about far too many people." He said nothing, but continued to look at her solemnly until she finally had to smile. It seemed almost cruel to disappoint him, so she said, "Very well, Your Grace, I will take my walks at Kelswick."

When he rode off on Hector, she watched, bemused. She had never before known a man who sought to protect her. Oh, at home,

Squire Grant and Dr. Finley had certainly not threatened her, but they had not seen any need to protect her either. Or perhaps they had not felt they had the right. After all, she was the daughter of the fiercely independent Lady Newell. She did not need protection.

She shook her head. This was what Lady Talmadge—Alice—had complained of? Someone concerned about her, wishing to see her safe? It was like complaining about a fire to chase away the cold or a roof to shelter you from the rain. Could such protection turn into smothering? Perhaps, but for all Alice and Lady Merton—Miranda—had said of smothering, she could not but think that they had no idea what it was like to have no one to protect you, no one.

To have someone, someone who cared about you, someone you could rely on, someone you could trust—she could barely imagine such bliss.

»»»«««

THREE DAYS OF rain followed. Heavy rain. Jem, the coachman and gardener, could be seen, hurrying out to care for the animals. Other than that, no one ventured out of doors if they could stay within. No one left Hawthorne Cottage, certainly not to go for a walk. Ashleigh was reasonably certain of that. Several times each day, whenever the rain had seemed as if it might let up, he had ridden over to a hill from which he could see Franny Darling's house. Hector bore up patiently and stood for half an hour and more under the sheltering branches of the cedar while his rider sat and stared at the cottage. No one was out and about.

On the fourth day, no rain fell. By late morning, the mist had dried off. In the early afternoon, Miss Darling left the cottage and walked through the rear garden gate to enter the grounds of Kelswick. From his vantage point, Ashleigh saw her. His pulse quickened as he watched to see which way she would go. He rode down to a spot she would soon pass, tethered Hector in a grassy spot, and leaned against a tree to wait for her to appear.

She was wearing a dress he had seen before, the blue one with the little green leaves on it. And she had that annoying bonnet again, the one that hid her face unless she was looking straight at him. He knew the moment she noticed him. She stumbled and looked surprised. Perhaps not entirely surprised. Then she looked pleased. He was almost sure of it.

"Your Grace, as you can see, I am taking advantage of your invitation to walk at Kelswick. I hope you do not mind."

"On the contrary, I am delighted. Perhaps you will allow me to show you some of the more attractive views."

He could have sworn he heard his own heart beating as he waited for her answer. There was a look of uncertainty on her face. He waited. It cannot have been more than a few seconds before she smiled and said, "I would be delighted."

It had seemed like eons.

He breathed more easily once she was walking beside him, her hand on his arm. He looked down at the hand. It was such a small hand, and it hovered over his arm rather than resting there. He covered it with his own and pressed it. She started nervously, but then relaxed and did not pull away. Their eyes met, and she smiled. Tentatively, he thought, but then his own smile doubtless seemed tentative as well. It was as if they were both feeling their way, stepping onto an unfamiliar path, not knowing where it would lead them.

Neither spoke but after those first awkward moments, it was a comfortable silence. There was much he wanted to know about her, much he wanted to tell her about himself. Perhaps she felt the same way. But he felt no need to rush. He was simply enjoying the moment—not, he realized, something he often did.

Just then, they came to a break in the woods and, with a cry of delight, Kate stopped to look out over the prospect. Her pleasure surprised him. There was no dramatic scene before them, no crashing waterfalls, no soaring cliffs. It was nothing but fields of grain, still green. Not at all the sort of sublime, romantic landscape that was supposed to appeal to young ladies.

"How beautiful," she said.

"It is only grain. Nothing in the least spectacular or unusual."

"But look how lush, how healthy the crop is, how fertile the fields. That wheat will make bread for many hungry mouths this year." She turned to look at him. "You need not laugh. I have seen enough dramatic scenes with rocky scarps and barren landscapes, where people scrape at the earth to persuade it to give them a few cabbages or onions. Fields like this..."

She shook her head, wordlessly.

He looked out over the fields, remembering the past. "When I inherited the estate, these fields were barren, neglected. It took years to return them to health. I confess I take pride in them now, in the knowledge that my lands and my tenants flourish."

"And you should. Too few landowners do."

They continued on their way. "I had to make up for my parents' neglect, you see. I inherited all this, all this wealth, all this power. The only justification for it is that I take care of those who live here, who work here. I must determine what is best for them, not just individually but as a whole." He wanted to be sure she understood. "I cannot allow one man to divert a stream to run a mill if it means that three others will not have the water they need for their stock. I am responsible for all of them, and I must live up to that responsibility."

"But sometimes people see you as autocratic?" There was laughter but also sympathy in her eyes. He could see it.

"Sometimes I must be. I cannot simply do as I please."

She nodded. "I understand that. But one can become so accustomed to being the one who must make the decisions that one does not realize that it is not always necessary."

She was looking up at him and he could see the smile tugging at her lips. She was laughing at him. To his surprise, he did not mind. He found he rather liked it. "You have been talking to my sister, I see." He shook his head ruefully as her smile broadened. "You would not believe that when we were children, she bullied me mercilessly. Perhaps I am simply getting my own back." She did laugh then, and he smiled in return. "No, I had simply failed to see that she has recovered from her years with Talmadge. When she returns from her trip, I will endeavor to consult her, not decide for her. Now, are we friends?"

"Of course." She turned to look off to the side and noticed a building almost hidden by the trees.

He hesitated, uncomfortable, when he saw what she was looking at. "That's only an old summer house." He had almost managed to forget it was here, to forget it existed. But she looked at him with curiosity—something in his tone must have betrayed him—so he gestured her toward it. It was only a summer house, after all.

A short path led to the building, a simple hexagonal structure of wood, painted green as if to help it blend into the surrounding woodland. The door was locked, but he bent down and removed a key hidden under a rock. He stared at it for a moment, then said with what he hoped was a careless laugh, "Not, perhaps, the most secure of hiding places, but it is only locked to keep children from getting in and injuring themselves."

They stepped into the single room. Within was a bed, a chest to hold blankets, and a wooden table and two chairs. A simple stone fireplace covered one wall of the hexagon, with fire tools standing at its side and a candlestick and tinderbox on the mantel. There was no glass for the windows but there were shutters that could cover them.

Kate stood in the center of the room and turned around slowly. "How unusual. I have never seen a summer house that was not situated to take in the view. This one is hidden in the woods, as if it is a refuge. And with a bed. Does someone stay here?"

"I have been known to. When I was a child, I would stay here whenever my parents had one of their parties." She looked at him oddly and he realized he had to offer more explanation. "I would hide here. My parents were somewhat extravagant personalities, and their parties involved extravagances of behavior as well as expenditure. The behavior of their guests—well, it would give one some understanding of the French Jacobins. They made the house unsafe for children."

"You stayed here alone?" She sounded shocked. He had not been able to keep the bitterness from his tone.

Trying for lightness, he continued. "Not always. Before her marriage, Alice joined me. With, I might add, the connivance of her governess and my tutor. Should our parents by any chance have asked for us, they were told we were ill. And the cook always made sure we had plenty to eat." She looked stricken. He did not want her pity, so he forced a smile. "Don't look so horrified. I always thought of it as an adventure. What boy does not want to run away at times, and I also had the honor of protecting my sister."

She looked at him steadily. "One does not think of a duke, or a duke's heir, as being in need of protection. It is difficult to think well of your parents."

He shrugged. "I always had your aunt and uncle. On occasion, when the weather turned nasty, we stayed with them. And after Alice's marriage, Merton's grandfather, the old earl, made sure to have me to visit when my parents were coming down with a party."

"Good friends can make all the difference in one's life."

He wondered at the distant look in her eyes and made a guess. "Your vicar?"

"Indeed. Without him, I would be ignorant, indeed."

"You had no governess?"

She laughed at that. "Hardly. My mother taught me my manners and my letters, but Dr. Finley opened the world of books for me. And others taught me that goodness and kindness do exist—a lesson I sometimes forget."

She had to learn that goodness and kindness existed? She should have been surrounded by nothing else from the moment of her birth. She should have been loved and sheltered. He cleared his throat. "Your aunt said that you are an orphan?"

"Yes." She had turned to stare out the window and spoke without looking at him. "My mother died last autumn, but she had been ill for a long time. Years. A wasting disease."

"I am sorry. And your father?"

That produced a shrug. "He died shortly before my mother fell ill."

"And you were left to care for her alone? That must have been difficult."

A short laugh. "It is not as if he had ever been part of our lives. I do not think I saw him above half a dozen times in my life."

He found himself just behind her—he had moved close to her without even realizing it. His hands reached out to rest on her shoulders. "We were not well served by our parents, either of us, were we?"

She turned, and his hands slipped down and around her. Her face was turned up, only inches from his. "Kate," he murmured, cradling her face in his hands before he brought his mouth down to just barely brush her lips.

It was such a gentle kiss at first. His lips brushed hers softly once again. Then they moved across her cheek. Her skin was so soft. She gave a little gasp and shivered when he kissed her neck and he smiled, pleased by her response. When his arms slid around her to pull her close to him, her arms reached up around his neck.

He returned to her mouth and ran his tongue across her lips until they parted and he entered, tasting her, deepening the kiss hungrily. He felt her soften against him and groaned. It was as if he had been starving all his life and had finally come upon a banquet.

✦⟫⟫✦⟪⟪✦

YES, OH, YES. She sighed with pleasure at the feel of his arms around her, his mouth on hers, and her arms went around his neck to cling to him. Held against him, she breathed in the scent of him—no perfumes or pomades, just him, just Ashleigh. Peter. She could feel him, all along her body. She could feel the solid strength of him. And it did strange things to her own body. Pressing up against him, her breasts seemed to swell and grow sensitive in a way she had never known before.

When his tongue teased at her lips, she parted them in surprise, and when his tongue entered, she gasped in more surprise. It was all so intimate, so pleasurable. She felt herself melting against him, as if her bones had dissolved. Her knees were buckling under her. If he were not holding her, she would fall, she would be naught but a puddle on the floor. She wanted nothing more than to be here, to be part of him, to lose herself in this moment. All thought had vanished. She was nothing but a mass of yearning sensations. She knew only one thing.

She wanted Peter.

✦⟫⟫✦⟪⟪✦

WITHOUT CONSCIOUS THOUGHT—HE would swear it was unconscious—he turned with her and began to move toward the bed. Had he been conscious, he would have realized that the chair was in the way. As it was, the chair went over with a crash that brought them both to their senses.

She jumped away from him, her eyes slowly coming back into focus, her mouth swollen, looking so delightfully confused, so deliciously mussed with her bonnet knocked off, her spencer undone and her bodice loosened.

Her bodice loosened? Good God, had he done that?

She had noticed her disarray, and gasped. She turned away and tried to put herself to right. He should apologize, he knew, but all he wanted to do was pull her back into his arms and keep her there forever. A groan of longing escaped him, and he forced himself to step back.

"Kate, I, I don't know what to say."

She gave him a quick glance and then looked away again.

"I know I should apologize. I know I should not have kissed you, but I cannot honestly say I regret it." He smiled at the memory of the kiss. He could not help it.

That brought a small smile from her as well. "No more can I. I do not recall offering any protest. Nothing was done that I did not desire." She looked down and shook her head. "But it was not wise, Your Grace."

"Peter. Can you not call me Peter?"

The smile faded, and she shook her head, still without looking at him. "No, Your Grace. That would not be wise either."

She was right. He knew she was right. But watching her face disappear inside the bonnet hurt. She belonged in his arms, and the absence of her hurt. When she moved to the door he burst out, "May I at least walk you home?"

Halting in the doorway, she turned partly toward him, but still not looking at him, and shook her head. "No, Your Grace, I do not think…"

"… that would be wise." He completed the phrase with a sigh, and stood at the door to watch her disappear into the woods. He was behaving like an idiot, and he knew it. A reckless idiot who was endangering the reputation of an innocent young woman. When he had encountered her in the bookstore, it had been an accident. He should have simply greeted her and let her go on her way. He should not have walked home with her. He knew that perfectly well. Yet he had.

Then he had seen her walking by the river. There had been no need for him to wait for her. And even if he did wait for her, he could have invited her to walk at Kelswick and then left. No need to walk her home. No need to watch for her, watch for another chance to walk with her. He was being a fool.

He stood at the door, gripping the lintel, and watched her leave. His fingers turned numb as he clenched the rough wood. Off to the side, he caught sight of Hector still standing patiently by the path.

He should not have left his horse saddled for so long. One more thing that he should not have done. That he had not expected to be gone so long did not matter. His behavior was irresponsible.

Not as irresponsible as that of Kate's father, of course. What kind of man leaves his wife and child alone and unprotected. Had he no sense of honor, of duty?

Then he remembered the question about Kate's name. Perhaps her mother had not been a wife. Perhaps it had not been a wife and child but a mistress and child. Many men would feel no responsibility to them at all. Such an attitude might be deplorable, even contemptible, but it was all too common.

That did not excuse his own behavior to Kate. Whatever her mother may have been, may have done, Kate was innocent.

He turned back into the room, picked up the chair and heaved it against the wall.

He didn't want to be wise.

He wanted to be happy.

He didn't want to be responsible.

He wanted Kate.

# CHAPTER ELEVEN

*Somerset*

DRESSED SOBERLY IN a sturdy but respectable coat of black worsted, breeches and with a simple stock at his neck, Howard Hall looked like a moderately successful attorney. He looked so much the part that Sir Richard Langley assumed that was what he was when he was ushered into Sir Richard's study.

Hall looked hesitant. "I do apologize for intruding on you this way, Sir Richard. I had asked for Sir Bertrand Langley, and was told that he was deceased?"

Sir Richard, a paunchy but pleasant fellow no more fashionably dressed than his visitor, nodded cheerfully. "Three years ago. Out hunting. The horse balked at a fence, but my father went over it anyway."

"My sympathy. It must have been a shock for you."

Sir Richard shrugged. "More of a shock for my father, but at least it was quick and clean. He wouldn't have cared to linger." When Hall seemed unable to think of an appropriate response, Sir Richard continued. "Why would you be looking for him? Can't believe he would have gotten himself mixed up in any lawsuits. He always said only fools go to law, and I won't say he was wrong."

Hall smiled slightly to show the proper appreciation of the jest.

"Actually, it was not Sir Bertrand I was seeking but his daughter, Miss Frances Langley."

"Franny? Good God, haven't thought about her in years."

"Dear me, is she also deceased?"

"Not so far as I know. Though I might not know, come to think of it. Haven't heard a word from her since the old man disowned her."

"Dear me."

Sir Richard threw a sharp glace at the visitor. "Why might you be looking for my sister?"

"I am afraid I cannot tell you precisely." Hall gave an apologetic smile. "I can, however, assure you that my finding her will be in no way to her detriment. Quite the contrary."

"Money, eh?"

Hall lowered his eyes. His expression was that of a man maintaining a discreet silence.

"Franny." Sir Richard sat back, eyes unfocused as if looking into the past, until he began to smile. "She always was a stubborn one, you know, and the bravest of us. The only one who would really stand up to our father. Hope she ended up better than poor Mary did, for all she married a viscount. Never heard from either of them after they married, but every now and then someone would bring us word of Newell and another would know something of Mary. Well, they're both dead now."

"Both? Both sisters?" Hall asked sharply.

"Hmm? Oh, no, no. I meant Newell and Mary."

"I see. Did they, by any chance, did they have children?"

Sir Richard shrugged. "Someone once mentioned a son who was living with Newell, but that is all I know. Poor Mary. She wasn't even allowed to keep her child."

Hall coughed diffidently. "Of course, it was your other sister, Frances Langley, I was seeking."

"Ah, yes, of course. Well, we never heard from her either after she married Andrew Darling."

"Andrew Darling?"

Sir Richard grinned. "Good-looking fellow, he was. And crazy about Franny. It was right comical to see him dangling after her. But he was only a clerk at Williams & Co., the big shipping company up in Bristol. My father wouldn't hear of it. So they ran off together. And not Gretna Green either. It was a special license. Andrew wouldn't hear of anything less for Franny." He flushed slightly at Hall's look of surprise and then grinned. "I was a witness at their wedding, though I never told my father. He was in a real fury. He'd intended her for Newell, you see. The only thing that calmed him down was Newell saying he'd take Mary instead."

Hall blinked. "Then that marriage was not a love match, I presume."

Sir Richard snorted. "The only thing Newell loved was the dowry. Poor Mary." With a sigh, he pushed back from his desk. "I'm afraid I can't give you any more help than that. But if you do find Franny, you might tell her I wouldn't mind hearing from her, now that Father's gone. Wouldn't mind a bit."

⫸⫷

A TRIP TO Bristol came next. There, Hall, still in his sober attorney guise, found several people at Williams & Co., now Williams & Sons, who remembered Andrew Darling. The manager of the branch, Harold Quist, had been merely an errand boy at the time of Darling's elopement, but remembered it vividly.

"Oh, my, yes, I doubt any of us who were here at the time will ever forget Andrew Darling's elopement. It was the most exciting thing that ever happened in this office." His eyes twinkled in his cherubic face. "You must realize that though we are a shipping company, all we do in this office is move papers about. It is those on the ships who have the adventures."

"I was wondering if anyone might know of Mr. Darling's current whereabouts," Hall put in diffidently. "Or Mrs. Darling's."

Lost in remembrance, Quist smiled. "We all knew about the romance—the young ones of us, that is. Every time she came to visit her friends here in Bristol, he would be out the door the minute we were finished and on her doorstep two minutes later. Comic, it was. And then after they ran off, Sir Bertrand came charging in. Ranting and raving he was. He wanted Andrew thrashed, hanged from the nearest lamppost, thrown into the sea, anything you could think of."

"Yes, I understand he was quite upset. But Mr. Darling?"

"Well, the reason Sir Bertrand came here, of course, was that he wanted Mr. Williams to dismiss Andrew at once. Old Mr. Williams, that is. These days Mr. Williams is the old man's grandson. He heads the firm now and keeps his office in London."

Hall made an effort to keep his impatience from showing. Obviously, he was going to have to let this fellow spin out his tale.

"Yes, Sir Bertrand was shouting and screaming, smashing his cane on Mr. Williams' desk, accusing him of encouraging the scoundrel—I am softening his language, you understand?"

Hall managed a tight smile and nod.

"Mr. Williams, of course, took umbrage at that. Took umbrage." Quist savored the word. "And, of course, Andrew was a valued employee. He'd been something of a pet of Mr. Williams', and everyone could see he was destined for important things. So he wasn't dismissed, not a bit of it."

"Then he is still here in Bristol?"

"No!" Quist chortled and slapped his thigh. "He was promoted! Mr. Williams put him in charge of the London office. That was only a branch office in those days, though it's our main office now. That was Andrew's doing."

"He is in London, then?" That was a bit of a surprise. Here Farnsworth had sent him chasing all around the country, and she might be sitting there right under his nose.

Quist shook his head regretfully. "I wouldn't know. I remember he retired some years back, not long after old Mr. Williams passed on. I seem to recall that he moved to the country, but I couldn't tell you where. Could be I never knew. But they could probably tell you in London."

❄❄❄❄❄❄

In London, Hall decided it might be wise to be less direct in his inquiries. He did not want word getting back to Darling that someone was searching for him and his wife. As it turned out, the search was almost ludicrously simple.

A few days drinking in the taverns where shipping clerks stopped before they headed home, and he soon discovered that Andrew Darling had been a respected and successful figure in the shipping world. Although his office was in London, his home had been in Lewes even before he retired. He had died a few years ago, but his widow was still living there in comfortable circumstances—very comfortable circumstances.

The next step was equally simple. A day in Lewes was all it took to discover that Mrs. Darling had a niece residing with her, a pretty young woman who went by the name of Kate Darling.

Hall had once more the appearance of a gentleman when he went to report to Farnsworth, and the butler had no difficulty in admitting him and ushering him into the library. The earl greeted him expansively and listened to his report with growing enthusiasm.

"I have her!" His hand slapped down on the desk and his eyes glittered. "I will go down there at once and fetch her myself. You will assist me."

The earl's exuberance surprised Hall, who had always considered

Farnsworth a cold, controlled man. "Do you not think, my lord, that task might best be left to her brother?"

"That fool? Do not be absurd."

Hall persisted. "Nonetheless, as her guardian, he has some legal standing. You do not. Were you to carry her off, it might be considered kidnapping."

Farnsworth waved the protest away. He stood up and began marching about the room. "No one would dare to challenge me. We are talking about an old woman and a girl. You need not fear."

"They might have friends," Hall continued doggedly. "The situation should at least be investigated more thoroughly. You cannot even be certain that this is the girl. I never saw her."

The earl swung about with a snarl and almost stumbled. Righting himself with a hand on a chair, he glared at Hall, who stood his ground, impervious.

"Very well," Farnsworth snapped. "Go down there and investigate. Discover whatever it is that you think needs to be discovered. But do it quickly. Remember, you will not be paid until Katherine Russell is under my roof."

Hall's look of calculation might have given another man pause. Farnsworth never noticed it.

# CHAPTER TWELVE

*Sussex*

FRANNY WATCHED WITH some concern as her niece took off her bonnet and laid it on the cabinet by the door. It was not that Kate looked upset or unhappy. It was more that for the past few days she had somehow removed herself. A week or two earlier, Franny had thought that she was beginning to look forward to the future with eagerness, as if she had finally begun to trust that she had a future. She had been behaving like a young woman looking forward to life.

She had been turning into the girl Franny had hoped she would be.

But recently, she seemed—not frightened, but detached, as if she were observing her life rather than living it. Franny did not like it.

"Have you been for a walk, dear? To Kelswick?" Franny tried to sound cheerful, rather than inquisitive, as she walked with the girl into the parlor. Judging from Kate's slightly twisted smile, she had not succeeded.

"A walk, yes. To Kelswick, no." Kate wrinkled her nose. "I decided it might be... unwise to impose too much on the duke's kindness."

Franny bit her lip. She thought—she feared she understood what Kate was not saying. It was a pity. In so many ways, she and the duke were well matched. Still, there were difficulties as Kate had pointed out before. Peter—Ashleigh—was proud, determined to bring no dishonor to his name. He had overcome his parents' reputation and now the dukedom of Ashleigh was viewed with respect. He would not want to do anything to endanger that respect, to provide food for the gossips.

Kate had her pride as well. She would not accept help that she saw as charity and she was determined that no one would pity her for the behavior, the misbehavior of her father and brother. But that meant that she could not present herself as what she truly was, a well-bred gentlewoman. Why did she think she had to discard the advantages her past gave her in order to escape the wrongs?

Before Franny could comment, Kate smiled brightly—too brightly—and changed the subject. "I have been to see Mr. Prufrock, and I think we have come to an agreement." Franny's face must have fallen because Kate took her aunt's hands and squeezed them. "Really, Aunt Franny, it is for the best. I will enjoy learning how to run the shop, and it means I will be able to support myself for the rest of my life if need be."

Franny wanted to shake the girl. "You do not seem to realize what that will mean for you. You will not be able to go back."

"Go back? Have you gone mad?" Kate looked horrified.

"No, no, I do not mean back to your brother or even back to Yorkshire." Franny shook her head impatiently. "But once you work in a shop, you will no longer be a gentlewoman. You will be looked down on, sneered at, by creatures like Lady Wilton. It is not..." She sucked in a breath and held it before going on. "It is not pleasant."

Kate began to laugh, shaking her head. "Pleasant? Pleasant? Here in this house, these last months—did you not realize? This has been the first time my life could ever be described as pleasant." She looked at her aunt and held out a hand. "Please, Aunt Franny, do not look so stricken. I do not mean to say I was always unhappy. Mama and I managed well enough before she fell ill, and we had friends and neighbors—there was often cheer and laughter. It is only that everything was always shadowed by worry and uncertainty."

"But you need no longer feel uncertain. Surely you know how happy I am to have you here. And I have been thinking. Now that my father is dead, we could go to my brother. He could protect you, and you would not have to hide under an assumed name."

Kate looked at her aunt with real amusement. "Your brother? Oh, really. In all the past thirty-odd years, he never once even wrote to my mother, no less came to see her or invite her to stay with him. Nor have you heard anything from him, have you?"

Franny shook her head ruefully.

"Then do not be foolish. If he never had the courage to stand up to your father, or the energy to find you after your father was dead, where do you think he would find the strength to defy my brother or Farnsworth?"

"You may be right," Franny conceded, "but then we could simply wait. It is only a matter of months before you are twenty-one. And once you are of age, once your brother can no longer touch you, I am sure Alice or Miranda would be pleased to take you to London, introduce you to the society you belong in."

"The society I belong in?" Kate shook her head again, still laughing. "And what society is that, pray tell? My father was a viscount and my mother the daughter of a baronet, but I have never lived the life of the aristocracy, the life of the *ton*. I have not even lived the life of a gentlewoman. By a twist of fate, I can translate Greek and Latin, but I cannot speak French or play an instrument. I have mended many a sheet and darned stockings by the dozen, but I cannot embroider or do any sort of fancywork." She held out her hands. "Look. Are these the hands of a lady?" They were not as rough and red as they had been when she arrived, but neither were they soft and lily white.

Franny held her niece's hands and looked at her sadly. "But my dear, once you begin working in a shop, you will never be able to marry the sort of man you should wed, the sort of man you could love. Do you not want that?"

"I would not mind marrying if I could find someone like your Andrew, someone who loves me and whom I love. But I do not wish to be in a position where I must marry to have someone to support me, to protect me, to keep me safe. I want to be able to do that myself. Since I have inherited no fortune, I will be safe only if can support myself. Otherwise, I must always be at some man's mercy. Now, Mr. Prufrock has said he will take me on as an assistant and teach me the business. Next January, when I am of age, he will sell me the shop, the stock and goodwill, for £500. Do you think we can sell the pearls for that much?"

"The pearls?"

"The necklace my mother gave me, the one your father sent her."

"Ah." Franny nodded, but she was not happy. "Kate, are you certain this is what you want to do?"

They both knew what she was asking. Did Kate really want to put an end to any possibility of a marriage with Ashleigh? Franny thought her heart would break at the look of pain that crossed Kate's face.

"It is for the best. I am sure of it." She sounded quite calm, but when Franny put a hand on her shoulder, she collapsed with her head on Franny's shoulder, heaving heartbroken sobs. "Why does it have to be so hard?"

Franny led the girl to the settee and held her while she cried herself out. Eventually, Kate sat up, wiped her eyes with the handkerchief Franny handed her, and blew her nose.

"I must say, it would have been easier if I had never met him. Or if he had a wart on his nose." Kate managed a wobbly smile.

"That's my girl," said Franny.

THAT EVENING, THE two women sat across from each other at a small table in the parlor, the pearls spread out on a cloth between them. One might have expected them to view the necklace with delight, to try it on or to hold it up to see the way the pearls glowed in the candlelight. Instead, they seemed to view it with gloom.

Kate poked a finger at the loops of the necklace with as much trepidation as if she had been prodding a snake. Franny spread the double strand out into a circle. It was a large circle.

"Have you any idea how much they are worth?" asked Kate.

Franny shook her head. "No idea at all. Do you?"

Kate shook her head in turn. Then she laughed. "A fine lady I would make. I can put a price on a milk cow, or a fine fat pig, but I could not tell you if these things are worth £10 or £10,000. What are we to do?"

Franny frowned. "If we try to sell them ourselves, we will almost certainly be cheated. A jeweler will suspect right away that we do not know the true value, and he will be perfectly correct. Under ordinary circumstances, I would ask the duke for assistance." She looked up and smiled wryly. "That would not, I collect, be a good idea in this instance."

"No, it would not." Kate gave a crooked grin.

"But I think a London jeweler is almost certain to give us a better price than a jeweler here in Lewes. Besides, I would not want the neighbors to be speculating on why we are suddenly selling jewelry." She chewed on her lip as she considered options. "I really would not care to ask anyone in town for help. They are gossips, one and all." Then she smiled. "But Mr. Bancroft has returned. I saw him in town yesterday. I'm sure he would be willing to help, and he frequently goes in to London."

"He will not mind?" Kate looked uncertain.

"I am certain he will not. But…" She hesitated. "I think it would be best if we do not go to Kelswick. I will send a note and ask him to call on us here."

>>><<<

STEPHEN BANCROFT SAT in his office next to the library at Kelswick staring out the window. It was raining, but he did not notice the drops blowing against the panes. It had been raining when he came in, but he had not noticed that his coat was damp. Sooner or later, he would notice that his feet were wet, but that had not happened yet. He was simply staring at nothing in particular.

He did not know what to do.

A year ago, this would have been an unusual state of affairs.

Now, it seemed almost chronic.

The trip to Longwood had left him in turmoil. It had been wonderful. It had been agony. He had seen Alice every day, been with her almost constantly. They had not simply done well together. There had been ease and comfort between them. She had no notion of his feelings, of course. He was certain he had given no hint. But traveling with her and Clara, dining with them—it was as if they were a family.

He had not thought he missed being part of a family. It was, after all, some twenty years since his parents had died and he had been deposited at Kelswick. No one had quite known what to do with him, so he had been handed over to the old steward to be his assistant. Yet he was still a cousin, and so had been on easy terms with Peter and Alice. They had all been friends.

They still viewed him as a friend, he thought. Or an older brother. The problem was that he found it impossible to think of Alice as a friend. Even more impossible to think of her as a sister.

He had brought them back to Kelswick, and he had helped her place advertisements for a new steward. She had asked him to help her with the interviews. She was planning to live there, and she needed a steward she could both talk to and trust. They needed to find someone quickly because the estate couldn't be left with no one in charge for too long.

Then Alice and Clara would be moving to Longwood, leaving him behind.

Alone.

It was all impossible, of course. She was the daughter of a duke, the widow of an earl. He was, at most, the distant connection of a duke. Alice's fourth cousin. He had worked it out one day. They shared a great-great-grandfather.

It was not that he was poor. He could easily afford to buy an estate of his own, though he had never felt it necessary to do so. Nothing like Kelswick—that was quite out of the question. But he could buy something like Longwood, and Alice had seemed as if she would be perfectly content on an estate like that.

Still, she had spent the years of her marriage moving in the highest circles of society, among people he did not know, people who would not be at all desirous of making his acquaintance. He could not ask her to turn her back on that world, or worse, to have that world turn its back on her. To have people pity her.

And now, there was this blasted necklace snaking along on his desk.

What was he supposed to do with it?

He knew what he had been asked to do, and he could accomplish that easily enough. However, he was not at all certain that was the right thing to do.

Why had they asked him to do this and not Peter? He would have thought Peter the logical one to ask—surely a jeweler would offer a far better price to a duke than to a steward, especially a wealthy duke who might be a future customer. Was there some reason? Yet they had not mentioned any need for secrecy. Should he discuss it with Peter?

He glared at the necklace as if it were the source of all his confusion.

Ashleigh came in just then, holding a sheaf of papers. Bancroft stood up and transferred his glare to the duke. He knew things had piled up a bit while he was away, but he had no wish to deal with his elegant cousin at the moment. His glare faded as he realized that Peter did not look his usual immaculate, assured self. In fact, he looked remarkably, unducally uncertain.

Before Bancroft could say anything about the duke's mood, Ashleigh noticed the necklace and frowned. "You are buying pearls, Stephen? Who is the lady?"

Bancroft flushed and produced a slightly twisted smile. He did not care to think about Ashleigh's reaction if he knew that the only lady he would wish to purchase jewels for was Ashleigh's sister, who doubtless already owned far more jewels than he could ever offer. "No," he said. "I have been asked to arrange for the sale of this necklace."

Ashleigh's frown deepened. "Alice is not selling her jewels, is she?"

"No, no," Bancroft assured him. "Franny Darling and her niece asked me for assistance. This necklace belongs to Miss Darling, and she wishes to turn it into cash."

"It belongs to Kate—Miss Darling?" Ashleigh picked it up and ran the pearls through his fingers. "It is very fine."

Bancroft shrugged. "I am afraid I would not know. I thought I would take it to Rundell, Bridge & Rundell. It would have made more sense for them to ask you to take care of this. After all, you know the jewelers. I know you have made some purchases there, and they reset some of Alice's jewels for her. Bridge will give me an honest price, will he not?"

"Hmm? Oh, yes, yes. Honest enough, I am sure." Ashleigh was still fingering the necklace. "Was she distressed at selling it? Miss Darling, I mean. Is it an heirloom perhaps?"

Bancroft looked at him curiously. "Distressed? Rather the opposite I would say. She said something about it representing so many mistakes. Then Franny said all that was in the past and best forgotten—that they needed to concentrate on the future."

"She didn't say why she wanted to sell?"

"No, and I did not care to ask. I wondered, of course. I was afraid perhaps Franny was in some sort of financial difficulties that she did not want anyone to know about. But Miss Darling would doubtless be willing to help her. Have you heard anything that might suggest Franny is in need of money?"

"No, not at all."

"Or perhaps it is Miss Darling who needs the money. She may have inherited debts that she feels obliged to pay."

Ashleigh was standing there, lost in thought, still holding the necklace.

Bancroft frowned at him. "Peter?"

"Hmm? Oh, yes. I will come with you, I think. Yes. We can go into London tomorrow."

"If you like. But Peter, why didn't she just ask you to sell it for her? I don't understand."

The duke shook his head and walked away, still holding the necklace. Bancroft sat down again, with one more puzzle to fret over.

ASHLEIGH SHUT HIMSELF into the library and sat down behind the vast mahogany desk. He did not like the thoughts that were running through his head. The pearls continued to slither through his fingers. They represented mistakes to her, but whose mistakes? Hers? Her mother's? Had this been the price of her mother's honor? Or had it been the price of hers? She would never have sold herself, not knowingly, not Kate. But she was young, her mother had been ill for years, she was without a father to protect her. It would have been too easy for some villain to seduce her with lying words.

His hands tightened, strangling the pearls. Had the villain given her these to salve his conscience? Someday, he would discover his name, the blackguard who had stolen her future. He was a dead man.

She had not sold the pearls for luxuries, she had not even sold them when she was in need, yet she had no sentimental attachment to them. If anything, Stephen said, she seemed to have an aversion to them.

Because they were, for her, a reminder of shame?

Why was she selling them now?

The bookshop. Of course. That was it.

She wanted to buy Prufrock's bookshop. She was selling them to provide her with a way to support herself in the future.

That was impossible, of course. It could not be permitted. Even if she simply owned the shop and did not work in it herself.

He realized that he was holding the pearls so tightly that he was in danger of breaking the thread. He slowly loosened his grip and laid the necklace carefully on the desktop. After all, it was not the necklace he wanted to strangle. It was the man who fathered her and then deserted her. It was the man who had stolen her innocence.

He had to find some way to make life easier for her, to give her the future she deserved.

The best way would be to find her a husband. He knew this was the best solution for her. There was no way to deny that. She needed a husband who would protect her, who could provide her with a secure position in the world. Her poverty did not matter. He could see to it that she had a dowry.

Alice would help him. If Kate appeared in London sponsored by the Duke of Ashleigh and the Countess of Talmadge—no, that would not work. He could not sponsor her. It would be far too awkward for both of them. She would never accept that. But Miranda...she liked Miranda and might accept her help.

If Kate were sponsored by the Countess of Talmadge and the Countess of Merton, suitors would be falling all over themselves in an effort to win her. She could not marry a title, of course, not with her questionable birth, but the world was full of younger sons, gentlemen, any of whom would be honored to have her for a wife. Honored? They would be delighted, eager. He could picture them slavering over her.

He was strangling the pearls again.

# CHAPTER THIRTEEN

T HEY LEFT KELSWICK early in the morning for the ride into London and made a brief stop at Ashleigh House to clean up and refresh themselves. In most establishments, an unexpected arrival of this sort would have sent the servants into paroxysms of accommodation, but not at Ashleigh House. True, the stable grooms were not entirely prepared for visitors, and there were some slight adjustments to be made. The straw in Hector's stall was several days old and had to be replaced; a stall for Pippin, Bancroft's gray, had to be prepared; and John Coachman was not perfectly satisfied with the gloss on the town carriage. Nonetheless, its team of four matched blacks had been exercised regularly and soon stood patiently in the square, awaiting the duke and his cousin.

Within, of course, under the watchful eye of Gregson, who had been butler at Ashleigh House for decades, everything was always prepared for all eventualities. Hot water was whisked to the duke's room within minutes of his arrival, and a light collation soon followed. Since the duke's own valet was still in Kelswick, Tompkins, a footman with aspirations who often valeted for visitors, was on hand to make sure the duke's appearance was immaculate before he left the house. He gave Bancroft a good brushing as well.

As they walked down the stairs, Bancroft watched his cousin almost glide along, quickly yet without any hint of hurry, not hesitating as he approached the carriage, knowing that the steps would be lowered in time for him to ascend. He smiled slightly and wondered if Ashleigh had any idea how unusual his life was.

Probably not.

A SHORT TIME later, they were ushered into a private room at Rundell, Bridge & Rundell by Mr. Bridge, a thin, self-effacing but sharp-eyed man, and offered a glass of Madeira. The heavy velvet drapes over the windows muffled any noises from the street and the solid door shut out the front of the shop most effectively.

When the wine had been poured and biscuits offered and refused, Mr. Bridge felt it permissible to inquire, "How may I help you, Your Grace?" Although he usually knew what was in the offing when one of his customers requested a private interview, in this case, he was uncertain. The usual reason was a sudden need for money—gambling debts as often as not. But he had never heard any whispers about the Duke of Ashleigh's gambling, nor any other hint that the duke might be having financial difficulties, and this was the sort of thing Mr. Bridge made it his business to know.

A request for privacy might also mean that the duke wished to purchase something for a lady and did not want anyone to know the identity of her benefactor. However, the duke was unmarried and buying gifts for a mistress would hardly qualify as scandalous. In addition, he had Mr. Bancroft with him. In Mr. Bridge's experience, people who sought secrecy for embarrassing reasons did not bring along a witness.

Mr. Bridge was curious but managed to display no surprise when the duke drew a velvet bag from his pocket and poured a necklace of pearls onto the desk. He nodded and reached out with a finger to touch the pearls. He nodded again and looked up. "You wish to sell these, Your Grace?"

A slight smile lifted the corners of Ashleigh's mouth. "No, at the moment, I merely wished to have the necklace valued."

Mr. Bridge looked sharply at the duke, then nodded again. He picked up the two strands and let them slither through his fingers. They were large pearls, beautifully matched. The luster seemed excellent, but he needed a glass to examine them for flaws. "May I take this into my workshop, Your Grace?"

The duke waved a smiling permission.

It did not take long. Neither Ashleigh nor Bancroft had taken more than a sip or two of the wine before the jeweler returned and placed the necklace before the duke. "It is, as I am sure you know, of excellent quality. The pearls are remarkably large, well-matched and almost flawless. You inherited them?"

"No." Ashleigh sounded a trifle bored. "They belong to a friend."

Mr. Bridge permitted himself a slight smile. "The reason I ask is that the clasp is somewhat old-fashioned, and if your friend intends to wear them it would be wise to have them restrung. The thread is quite worn in places."

Ashleigh waited.

Mr. Bridge sighed. "As to the value, that naturally depends on a variety of circumstances. If the necklace were brought to me, I would offer perhaps £800."

Ashleigh raised his brows. "And if you were offering it for sale?"

The jeweler smiled. "I would ask for £1200. I might not get it, of course." That won him a smile in return from the duke, so he asked, "Is there anything else I might do for Your Grace?"

The duke had stood and was returning the pearls to their velvet bag. He paused and tilted his head. "Yes, I believe there is something. You might keep an eye out for emeralds. I might be in the market for emeralds. They need not be terribly large, but they must be perfect."

⟫⟫⟫⟪⟪⟪

ONCE THEY WERE seated in the carriage for their return to Ashleigh House, Bancroft turned to Ashleigh with a scowl. "Would you care to explain what that was all about? Miss Darling most definitely asked me to sell it for her, not have it valued."

Ashleigh had been lost in thought. He stared at Bancroft for a moment before he realized what his cousin was saying. "Oh, that. Just withdraw £1200 from the estate account and give it to her."

"But why not simply sell the pearls for her?"

"I do not know how she feels about them, if she really wants to sell or simply thinks she needs the money for her idiotic bookshop scheme. I will keep them for her in case she decides she would like them back."

"Idiotic? Why idiotic? Twelve hundred pounds is more than enough to buy the bookshop and still have enough over to keep her until she is established."

"It is not just idiotic. It is insane." He ground the words out.

"Peter, what are you about? And what was that about emeralds? What is going on?"

Bancroft looked concerned, but Ashleigh just gave a sharp shake of his head and turned to look out the window.

Whoever gave her those pearls chose badly in more ways than one. They did not suit her. Pearls were wrong for her, especially those pearls. They were valuable, but they were too large for her. She was too delicate, too fragile. They would hang on her like a chain. If she were his, he would drape her in emeralds. He could envision her with emeralds winking in her hair, emeralds hanging from her delicate neck, emeralds, and nothing else.

What was he thinking? He must be out of his mind. She was not his. She could not be his. He should never have mentioned emeralds to Bridge.

STEPHEN HAD GIVEN her the money. He reported that she and Franny had been amazed. It was far more than they could have expected—enough to keep her for years. There was no need for her to become a shopkeeper, yet according to Stephen, that is all they were talking about. Why? Ashleigh could not understand it. She had no need to rush into it as if she had no choice. Did she not realize that there were other possibilities for her? Why was she still so determined on a ruinous course?

He found his sister in her sitting room. She was sitting at her writing table with swatches of fabric spread before her, but she was gazing out the window.

"Alice, I need to talk to you," he said peremptorily. "I need your help."

She turned slowly from the window and gazed at him unseeing, until his words seemed to reach her. Then she gave her head a shake and smiled at him. "Of course. What is the problem?"

He flung himself down into a chair and promptly bounced up again to begin pacing about the room. It was not an easy room in which to pace, given the number of small tables bearing delicate china figurines. He caught a shepherdess just before she smashed following an encounter with his leg. He glared at the statuette before replacing it carefully and striding away to stand by the window. "What on earth do you want with all these silly folderols?"

His sister gave an amused shrug. "I don't really know. They are the expected decoration in a lady's boudoir and give the maids something pretty to dust. Now, suppose you tell me what the problem is."

Ashleigh transferred his glare to the carpet, as if its green swirls had given unpardonable offense. "It's Miss Darling. She has this bee in her bonnet about becoming a shopkeeper, of all things. Can you imagine anything more ridiculous?"

Alice continued to look amused. "I do not know that I would call it ridiculous. It strikes me as quite admirable. She has no fortune of her own and does not wish to be dependent on her aunt's charity."

"What nonsense." Ashleigh had begun pacing again. "She is a lady, not some shopkeeper. She needs a husband to take care of her. The only sensible solution is for her to marry." If she were married, no longer nearby where he might encounter her at any moment should he wander in that direction, perhaps then she would no longer fill his thoughts, haunt his dreams.

Alice was looking at him consideringly. "Did you have a groom in mind?"

He waved the question away. "No one in Lewes would be suitable. I thought we might take her to London. If you present her, take her about, she will have offers aplenty."

"She has no dowry. She will have offers from widowers looking for a mother for their children or old men looking for a nurse for themselves. I doubt she would consider either preferable to supporting herself in a shop."

He waved that away, too. "I can provide her with a dowry."

Her eyes widened at that. "I think it most unlikely that she would agree to such an arrangement."

"I would not tell her, of course."

Alice sat very still, looking at her brother. "I am not at all certain that you know what you are about. However, I will tell you that Miranda and I have talked of this very thing. It could not be now, of course. It is nearing the end of the Season. We thought we might invite her to come to London next spring."

Ashleigh frowned. "Why wait so long? There are always people in London—balls, routs, what have you."

"But with a smaller selection of possible bridegrooms when one attends out of Season. What is the great hurry?"

"I just do not want her to do anything irrevocable." He ran his hand through his hair. "If she ever sets herself up as a bookseller, she will never be able to marry a gentleman, to have the kind of life she deserves."

His sister smiled faintly. "Do you truly believe that my marriage was more desirable than the Darlings'? Happier? Preferable in any way?"

He took a deep breath and exhaled slowly. "No, and I will always regret that I was too young to do anything about it. But this is different. I am not my father, to pass my daughter along to one of my cronies because he took a fancy to her. We need to find her a husband who will take good care of her. You probably know more people in the *ton* than I. Can you think of any likely candidates?" Alice was looking too amused. He snapped, "This is not a joke."

"Very well, let me think." She still looked amused but she had tilted her head consideringly and tapped a finger on her cheek. "There is Carraby's son. He has always struck me as a pleasant young man."

"Young George? Don't be ridiculous. The fellow's a fool."

"No fools then. Josiah Western? He is making quite a name for himself with his botanical studies."

Ashleigh snorted. "Botanical studies. The man's a dried up old twig himself."

"What of Charles Conigsby? He's certainly not dried up. Quite handsome in fact."

"Are you mad?" Ashleigh looked at her in shock. "He knows every brothel in London and they all know him."

Alice began to laugh. "Oh Peter, if you could only see yourself."

"Very well," he said stiffly, "if you do not wish to assist me…"

"Do stop being silly." She sighed. "I will talk to Miss Darling and her aunt and suggest a Season or two in London. Perhaps Miranda will wish to talk to her as well. They have become good friends, you know."

"Thank you." He relaxed slightly.

But the next day, Lady Talmadge returned from a visit to Hawthorne Cottage with a puzzled look on her face. She had just handed her bonnet to a footman and was removing her gloves when her brother came into the hall. "Well?" he demanded.

She shook her head slightly, handed her gloves to the footman, and directed him to take her things to her room. Then she took her brother's arm and led him back into the library.

The moment the door was closed, he asked, "What did she say?"

"She said no. Oh, she thanked me very politely and expressed her appreciation conscientiously, but the answer was most definitely and most firmly no."

He frowned in disbelief and began pacing once more. "That is ridiculous. You can't have put it to her properly." Lady Talmadge gave an exasperated sigh, but her brother waved it away. "She must have thought you were offering charity." He stopped and looked at his sister. "Do you think she was simply nervous about appearing in society? Could that be it?"

"Peter, we are talking about Kate Darling. Was she intimidated by the Wiltons? By Selina Webster? This is a young woman who knows her own value."

"Then what is it?" He was pacing again, and running his hand through his hair. "She must be convinced. You will have to speak to her again."

"I am not at all certain that would be wise." Lady Talmadge spoke slowly. "I think the problem has something to do with London itself. When I suggested going there, her first reaction seemed to be panic. She looked truly terrified. And Franny Darling looked frightened, too. They both pulled themselves together almost at once, but even when they were both smiling and thanking me, there was real fear lurking in their eyes."

"Did you not ask her what the problem is?"

"If she does not wish to tell me, I have no right to pry. And neither do you." She held up a hand when he was about to speak. "No, Peter, you cannot decide that you know what is best for her and simply order her to obey."

He gave a short, angry laugh. "Are you planning to reproach me for arrogance?"

She looked at him sharply. "I was going to suggest that you stop to consider why it is that you are so determined to see her wed."

*London*

HALL WAS ONCE more ushered into Farnsworth's library. This time, the earl was already on his feet, almost bouncing with eagerness, barking out "Well?" before Hall was even fully in the room.

Once the door was closed, Hall, who had a marked distrust of eavesdropping servants, moved into the center of the room before he spoke. "There is, I think, no doubt that the young lady is Miss Russell. The description fits, and the timing does as well. She arrived in Sussex only a few days after she disappeared."

"Of course she is Katherine. You have identified the house? Noted her customary comings and goings?" The earl was having difficulty restraining his impatience.

Hall sighed. "There may be some difficulties. She has acquired some powerful friends."

"In Lewes?" The earl gave a contemptuous laugh.

"In, or rather near, Lewes. Her aunt is a friend of the Duke of Ashleigh. He and his sister, Lady Talmadge, have befriended the girl. As have the Earl and Countess of Merton."

Farnsworth frowned briefly, but promptly regained his certainty. "They will be no problem. I have never met them, but I have heard them spoken of. Ashleigh is a sanctimonious prig, fanatically averse to scandal, and I understand Merton is besotted with his wife. They will not disturb themselves over the disappearance of a nobody like Katherine Russell."

"Do not underestimate them. The Duke of Ashleigh is well-respected, and the regent himself attended Merton's wedding."

The earl sneered derisively. "What will they do, call out the watch?"

"Anything they do could prove disastrous. Anything." Hall spoke emphatically. "If you intend to go through with this, you will need to devise a plan to take the girl without arousing suspicion, especially suspicion directed at you."

Farnsworth slammed his hand down on the desk. "Enough! The room that is being prepared for her is almost ready. As soon as all is ready, you will drive me to Lewes and we will take her. She will regret having defied me. Yes, she will regret it."

The earl was smiling again as he waved Hall from the room. It was a smile that did more than merely worry Hall. He had spent months tracking down this girl and had received little of the promised payment. Now, he found himself wondering if he dared continue with this assignment at all.

There had been commissions from Farnsworth in the past, but the earl had always approached each situation with cold calculation. Hall's own tasks had been to investigate people's pasts, locate people who thought a change of address made them invisible, point out the danger of failing to pay one's gambling debts—things of that sort. If he sometimes skirted the law, he did not smash it.

This arrogant dismissal of danger was a change, and not a change for the better.

Hall had not survived this long by ignoring danger.

He did not like this. No, he did not like it at all.

# CHAPTER FOURTEEN

I T HAD BEEN cloudy all day and now dark clouds were rolling in. The rain would begin soon. He really should turn and head for home. There was no point in going to the top of the hill. He knew that. She would not be coming. She had made her choice, and she would not be walking at Kelswick any longer. But still, he had to look.

Hector knew where to stop when they reached the crest. They had been stopping there for days now. He looked down at the path that led from Hawthorne Cottage, the empty path leading to the woods. The woods were empty too—no.

Not empty.

He caught a glimpse of, of something. Movement. It was doubtless just some creature seeking shelter before the rain, a rabbit perhaps.

But it was near the summer house.

He turned Hector down the hill and headed for the path.

It was probably nothing but a rabbit or a badger, but it might not be.

It might be... he refused to even think her name. But it might be.

At his urging, Hector quickened his pace.

The door of the summer house was open, and he could hear—no, not hear, *feel*—someone inside. He looped Hector's reins around a branch and went in.

She was standing by one of the windows, her hand on the shutter, looking out, utterly still. Her dress looked familiar. He must have seen it before. It had yellow stripes, perhaps an effort to bring some sunshine into a gloomy day. Her bonnet hid her face though, and a shawl hung from her arms. His heart was hammering in his chest— could she hear it?

THE CHANGE IN the light when he stepped into the doorway startled her. She spun about and when she saw who it was, she knew she should not have come. Especially since her heart gave a little leap of joy. No, she should not have come.

"You came," he said. He was not quite smiling, but there was a lightness in his expression that had not been there when they last parted.

She looked away, fearing that her face would betray the happiness she felt at the sight of him. It had been foolish to come here, trying to relive that kiss they had shared. Madness. The kiss had been madness. He had to know that as well as she did. Her worst madness, though, was this longing to preserve the memory.

She took a deep breath to bring her emotions under control. "Pardon me, Your Grace. I should not have intruded here."

"Don't be foolish. There is no intrusion. You know that you are more than welcome here, at any time." He reached out toward her.

Avoiding his hand, she shook her head. "No, Your Grace. I should not be here. It was foolish of me to come. We both know that." Ducking her head, hiding behind her bonnet, she tried to slip past him.

"Kate!" He caught her arm.

She stopped but did not turn to him. "Please, Your Grace."

He pulled her closer, and reached out to turn her face to him. He cupped her cheek gently and brushed his thumb lightly over her mouth. "Don't leave, Kate. Don't leave me," he whispered. "I can't bear to lose you."

"Please, don't make it more difficult." She tried to turn away.

"Stay with me."

Why was he making this so difficult? It was so painful, but she had to speak. "That is impossible. You know that."

"Do I?"

His stupidity made her want to weep. "If you don't know it, you should. You don't understand. You don't know about my family."

"It doesn't matter, Kate. None of that matters."

"Of course, it matters!" The words burst out of her. "It will always matter. You don't know what happened."

"Yes I do." He pulled her into his arms, knocking her bonnet aside, and pressed kisses into her hair. "I do know. I know," he murmured softly.

"You know?" She tried to pull away, panicked. "How could you know?"

"There's no need for you to worry about that." He held her tighter. "I know all that I need to know. I know I love you. I want you with me always. You and I, we are all that matters. You and I, Kate. I will take care of you. We will be together always."

She looked at him fully then, but she was still shaking her head. "You can't mean that. The past..."

He covered her mouth with his, and all her protests melted in the sweetness of that kiss. When he finally lifted his head, she was clinging to him. Her longing for him had turned her limbs to jelly. "What's past is past," he said. "Only the future matters, and the future is ours. I love you, Kate."

For so long, she had dreamed of hearing those words. Was this only another dream? Did she dare to believe this was real? She reached up to run her fingers lightly along his cheek. "Are you certain? Truly certain?"

He smiled down at her. Those smiles of his were so rare, so precious. "Truly. And you?"

"Oh, Your Grace, Peter, I love you so." How she had longed to say

166

those words to him. Now, once the words had been spoken, it was as if all the passion and hunger chained up inside her had broken loose. She pulled his head down and kissed him with a fervor she had never known before. The fire of desire deep inside her was threatening to consume her. She was so shaken that she could barely stand.

"Kate, my Kate," he murmured as he dropped kisses on her face, on her neck. "You are mine now, only mine."

"Yes. Yes. You cannot know how I have longed for this." Her voice was the barest whisper.

He moved her toward the bed, undoing her dress, unhooking her stays on the way. His hands were trembling.

"Peter, what...?" She was all confusion again.

He silenced her with another kiss and whispered, "You are mine, Kate, tell me you are mine."

She was trembling as well, her hands fluttering against him. "I am yours," she whispered in reply, and he kissed her possessively.

Soon, her hair, that glorious flaxen mass, was tumbling down over her shoulders and he was twisting his fingers in it, breathing in its fragrance. Her clothing had fallen away and his followed, half-torn off in his eagerness. At least his boots were unfashionably roomy so he could kick them off without entirely letting go of her.

He could not let her go. "It will be all right, my love. My dearest love. I will always take care of you. I will never hurt you." She fluttered in his arms like a tiny bird, and he soothed her with kisses and caresses until she was lying beneath him on the bed. He could not think. All he felt was need, hunger.

She was still trembling, and he could hear her little cries—a moan of pleasure when he kissed the soft skin on her neck, a gasp of surprise when he rubbed his palm across her nipple and it hardened, a sharp gasp when his hand slipped between her thighs.

Her hands fluttered over him in small tentative caresses. In between kisses, tiny half-questions escaped her—"What...? Should we...?"—but he was too hungry to possess her, too eager to go slowly and calm her nervousness. He could not wait. He had to have her now.

"Next time, I will go slowly," he promised as a moan escaped her, "next time," as he drove into her. She shrieked, and dug her fingers into his shoulders.

*Mine,* he thought. *Mine.*

〉〉〉❈〈〈〈

KATE'S TURMOIL SUBSIDED slowly. She had no way of knowing how to deal with the enormity of what had happened. She did not even know the words with which to think about it. Peter was lying with an arm and a leg weighing down on her. She wriggled and turned enough to see him.

He was asleep.

That shook her further, though she could not think why it should. Still, that he should be able to sleep after the extraordinary, the truly overwhelming thing that had happened, seemed impossible. Her world had been overturned, and he fell asleep? She wriggled enough to get herself out from under him and stood up. The rain had begun in earnest, and she could hear it pounding on the roof of the summer house.

She winced. She was sore and extremely sticky. She would need a bath as soon as she reached home. She looked down at him. He was still sleeping, but he was also smiling. She had heard that men enjoyed this far more than women. Apparently, it had not been painful for him. Strange to think that this was what she had been longing for. Or rather, this was what she had *thought* she was longing for.

Still, she was determined not to cry. This was a normal part of married life and she would need to get used to it.

With a sigh, she gathered her scattered garments and dressed herself. Her hairpins were strewn about, but she thought she had located enough to make some order of her hair.

She was just putting in the last pin, still trying not to cry, when he woke up. He grinned at her with an appallingly smug look on his face. Men clearly enjoyed this far more than women did.

"Why are you getting dressed?" he said lazily.

"I must get home, Your Grace. My aunt will be wondering what has happened—" She broke off abruptly and began again. "My aunt will be wondering where I am." She wanted her voice to sound even, but she was afraid it did not. She turned away and reached for her cloak.

"Your Grace?" He sounded amused. "What happened to Peter? What is the matter, Kate?" He came up behind her and wrapped his arms about her.

She leaned back against him, unable to help herself, relishing the comfort, the safety of being sheltered in his embrace. There was something wonderful about simply being held by him, no matter what else had happened. She could manage the other so long as she could feel this closeness.

"There is no need to run off. No need to be upset. Don't worry, my love. I will take care of you. I will always take care of you. You will never need to worry again." He nuzzled her neck. "I'll make a settlement on you, buy you a house, a carriage if you like, and..."

She stiffened. In her mind his words seemed to echo over a great distance.

Could he have just said what she thought he said? She did not want to believe what she had just heard. He could not have said what she thought he said. He could not have meant that.

It was impossible.

He must have felt the change in her, because his voice trailed off.

She pulled away and turned to face him. The horror must have shown in her face.

"Kate, what is it? What's the matter?" He looked distressed.

"You will buy me a house? Is that what you said?" she whispered as she backed away, watching the confusion spread across his face. "You will buy me a house? Great God in heaven, what have I done?" She snatched up her shawl and clutched it in front of her. "You said you loved me. How could you love me and... all those fine words about honor... how could I be such a fool? I thought you were different. I believed you. I trusted you. I fell in love with you. But you are no different from my brother and Farnsworth. You said you loved me, but all you wanted was to make me a *whore!*" Her voice had been growing louder until it ended in a cry of pain.

"No, Kate, no! Never that." He reached toward her.

"Don't touch me! Do not touch me!" She stumbled backward until she reached the wall, then turned and ran out the door.

"Kate! For God's sake, Kate, come back here! It's raining." He stepped back to the bed, snatched up his trousers and began to pull them on.

That was when he saw the blood.

There was quite a bit of blood.

He reached out hesitantly and put a finger on the smear. It was still damp. He sat down abruptly and stared at it. What had he done?

He closed his eyes.

She had been nervous, frightened, not because a previous lover had been rough or brutal, but because there had been no previous lover. She had been so tight. That cry, when she dug her nails into him—it had been pain, not passion as he thought. As he had wanted to think.

How could he not have noticed, how could he not have realized that she was an innocent?

What had he done?

Why hadn't she stopped him?

Damnation.

His gut twisted.

He had convinced himself that she was experienced because that was what he wanted to believe. That would make everything easy for him. Waves of shame washed over him until he thought he would drown. He wished he could drown.

He did not know how long he sat there before he pulled himself together and dragged his clothes on. He had to talk to her, though he did not know what he was going to say. What could he say? To explain—how could he explain? But he had to talk to her.

It was still raining when he rode up to Hawthorne Cottage and tied Hector to the gate. Kate must be soaked, but he had not passed her so she must have reached home. He banged on the door and Molly opened it halfway.

"Is Miss Darling here?"

Molly nodded, but opened the door no further.

"Let me in. I must speak to her."

The maid just looked at him, wide-eyed, and held the door half-shut.

"All right, Molly. I will see to our visitor." Mrs. Darling stepped into the doorway and looked at him coldly. That look, where there had always been warm welcome, brought home the enormity of what he had done.

"Kate," he said, "I must speak with Kate."

"But Kate does not wish to speak with you. Please leave."

"Franny, you do not understand. I must speak with her." His voice was thick with despair.

She shook her head. "I understand only too well, Your Grace. I blame myself in part. God forgive me, I told her she could trust you, that you were an honorable man. I never dreamed you could be so arrogant, so cruel. After everything that she has been through…"

He shook his head wildly and tried to speak. Then she began to close the door. He put out a hand to hold it open and roared, "Kate!"

"Do not make things more difficult." Franny Darling's face was an implacable mask of cold contempt, the face that had always smiled at him before. "Now, I could call Jem in from the garden and ask him to remove you from my home, but I fear he would find it uncomfortable to lay hands upon a duke. I ask that you spare us all further distress and simply leave." She stepped back and closed the door in his face.

He leaned against the door as the rain blew against him. He did not move until his horse whinnied a complaint, recalling him to the present.

He mounted, turned the horse into the lane without thought, and then galloped all the way home.

# CHAPTER FIFTEEN

ASHLEIGH STORMED INTO the library where his sister was sitting, going over the accounts from Longwood. He stood in the middle of the room, looking about him wildly, then picked up a china ornament and threw it violently against the wall. It made an explosive crash as it shattered into a thousand shards.

Lady Talmadge looked at him. Never had she seen her controlled brother smash anything. Certainly not deliberately. Very carefully, she put down her quill, covered the ink bottle, and leaned back in her chair.

He spun around to face her. "She cannot have expected me to marry her!"

"She? Would you by any chance be speaking of Miss Darling? My friend, Kate, who has been a guest in our house? Who has befriended my daughter?"

"Of course," he snapped, pacing back and forth. He came to the wall and slammed his hand against it. "For God's sake, I'm a duke. I can't marry just anyone. She must know that."

"Must she? Curious. I don't know that. Most people think they know that a duke can do anything he pleases. But then I confess, I have begun to question a great many things I am expected to know."

He just shook his head and turned away.

"Perhaps you would be good enough to tell me just precisely what has happened."

He flushed darkly. "I assured her I would take care of her. I told her I would buy her a house."

She noted the flush but decided not to comment on it. "Ah. You would buy her a house. That was the sort of offer you made to a woman who is a friend of mine." She made a slight sound of disgust and looked away. Minutes passed before she looked at him again. He was still leaning against the wall, still not facing her. Afraid to face her, she thought. As well he should be. "Had you given any thought as to where this house would be?"

"Where?" He looked confused by the question, and then shrugged dismissively. "I am sure there are any number of suitable houses hereabouts."

"Really, Peter, think. You are not usually so stupid. You can hardly set up your mistress in a house in Lewes. The neighborhood would be quite scandalized. And consider how poor Kate would feel. She has made friends here, and they would all turn away from her. Being cut by friends is far more painful, I am sure, than being cut by strangers. Then there is the dreadful predicament you would create for Mrs. Darling. She is quite fond of her niece, I believe, and she would be forced to either cut herself off from her niece or be cut herself by all her old friends. No, really, it would not do at all."

He did look at her now and frowned. "That is nonsense."

She looked at him with narrowed eyes. He was not such a fool that he would not see the truth of what she said.

He sighed and looked away. "Very well. It would not have to be right here."

"It is really a pity. I have enjoyed her company and so has Clara. And then Kate and Miranda have also become good friends. We will all be sorry to lose her acquaintance."

He started to speak and then stopped.

She saw him come to the realization that if he made Kate his mistress, he could never again bring her into his home, allow her to meet his family and friends. Was he really such a fool that he had never considered all of this?

She continued, "No country town would do in any case. All it would take would be one visit from you. People would see at once that she is being kept and then no one would even speak to her. She would be so completely isolated that she would be fortunate if the butcher would sell her meat. No, it will have to be London, one of those streets where gentlemen set up their mistresses. You will know them. At least there, she will have the other whores for company."

"Do not use that word! That is what she said when she... but I don't mean that at all."

She stood up and leaned forward and slapped her hands on the desk. "Then she at least faces reality. You object to the *word*? How dare you! You are the one who proposed the reality, no matter how many pretty words you choose to wrap it up in. But you had not actually thought about the reality, had you? Such little details as the fact that any children she bore you would be bastards, that should you marry or tire of her and dismiss her she would have no hope of a decent future. She would have no choice but to be *that word* you do not wish me to use."

"I would not let that happen."

"But it would happen. You could not prevent it. It would not harm you, of course, but it would destroy her. Did you think that you could somehow keep her separate from the rest of the world, on a little island with only you two?"

He stood there with his head bowed. "Yes," he whispered at last. He was staring at his fists, clenched around nothing. "Yes, I suppose I did."

"Oh, Peter, you poor fool." Her expression had softened from anger to sadness. "I never thought to be ashamed of you, but I am. And to think that I was worried that you would take it badly when I told you my plans. I am moving to Longwood, and if he will have me, I am going to marry Stephen. At least now I no longer need to give a fig for your opinion."

With that, she swept out of the room. Ashleigh stood there looking most unducally uncertain. What she had said was slowly sinking in, but it was her final statement that first penetrated. "Bancroft? She is going to marry Bancroft?" He stumbled for a moment, then hurried after her.

The steward had just arrived in the hall, apparently on the way to his office, and Lady Talmadge was standing beside him, a hand on his arm to halt him. He looked, as always, solid and reliable, respectable rather than stylish. Next to him, Alice looked polished and elegant, even with ink stains on her fingers. Bancroft was looking down at her hand, as if wondering what it was doing there.

"Bancroft? Bancroft has presumed to propose to you?" Ashleigh looked outraged.

Bancroft spun about to look at Ashleigh, then turned back to Lady Talmadge in confusion.

"Don't be ridiculous," said Lady Talmadge, facing her brother calmly. "It has become clear to me that he would never so presume. I have concluded that I shall be obliged to propose to him." She turned to the steward, who was now looking stupefied. "Mr. Bancroft, you cannot have failed to notice that I hold you in the highest esteem, and I trust I am not mistaken in my belief that you return my regard. Dare I hope that you will do me the great honor of consenting to be my husband?"

Bancroft opened his mouth, but no words came out. He began to smile and tried again. "My dear Lady Talmadge, this is so sudden." The words seemed to choke him and he pulled her into a fierce embrace. "Oh, God, Alice, I love you so." She laughed exultantly and their kiss ended the need for conversation.

Ashleigh stared at them, unnoticed and ignored. Then he turned and flung out of the house. A few minutes later, he was mounted and galloping down the drive.

>>><<<

SEVERAL HOURS LATER, well past the dinner hour, Ashleigh arrived on foot at Schotten Hall, leading a limping horse through the gloomy drizzle. The horse was escorted to the stables, where it would receive the attentions of the head groom, a man Ashleigh trusted to give the steed the best of care. The groom who led the horse away looked at Ashleigh nervously, as did the footman who let him into the house, where Ashleigh himself was escorted into the library, a room he had always liked. It was not overly crowded with books, since the Earl of Merton, like his grandfather before him, was not much of a reader. What the room did have was a good fire, comfortable chairs, and a full decanter of brandy. It was to this last that Ashleigh directed his steps while he awaited Merton's arrival. The first glass was tossed back in an instant, the second more slowly, and he had just poured his third—or perhaps it was his fourth—glass when Merton arrived.

"You need to have the brandy decanter refilled."

Merton raised his brows. "So I see," he said slowly, taking in the duke's appearance. Ashleigh was disheveled, his cravat was hanging askew, and his boots were covered with mud. "What the devil is going on?"

Ashleigh shrugged. "I went for a gallop and my horse came up lame. I was closer to here than to home, so…" He shrugged again and swallowed half the glass of brandy.

"Of course. That explains perfectly why you are busily getting foxed. You never get foxed. I refuse to believe a lame horse is the cause of this."

Ashleigh scowled at him, topped up his glass and carried it carefully over to a chair by the fireside. He sat there, legs stretched out in front of him, cradling the glass and staring morosely at the fire. "I've made a bloody muck of things," he said finally.

Merton sat down opposite him and waited. The silence stretched out.

Finally, Ashleigh spoke again. "Alice is going to marry Bancroft."

"Is that what has you in a stew?" Merton asked in surprise. "Surely you saw that coming."

Ashleigh frowned at him. "You knew about this?"

Merton laughed. "I would wager everyone who knows them saw it coming. She blushes like a school girl every time he comes into the room, and he stammers and trips over his feet like a school boy. Then he stares at her with a look of utter adoration and she tries to pretend she doesn't see it. Don't tell me you had not noticed."

"But he's a steward, for God's sake, even if he is some distant family connection. How can my sister marry a steward? Could she not choose someone suitable?"

Merton glared at his friend. "I cannot believe you are saying this. Your father arranged an eminently suitable marriage for her when she was fifteen, and she spent the next, what, fifteen years? sixteen? being miserable and beaten down. Now she has recovered herself—and remember that you wanted her to recover herself—and found a man she loves, a man who loves her, and all you can do is complain because it touches your pride? Are you truly so high in the instep that you would deny her some happiness?"

Ashleigh had returned his gaze to the fire. "No, of course not. I want her to be happy, truly I do. It is only... it is only the surprise, I suppose. I did not see it coming. It appears I fail to see a great many things."

Merton did not consider himself the most observant of men, but he had no difficulty seeing that whatever was troubling Ashleigh, it was not his sister's proposed marriage. It had to be something more serious. He settled back down and waited.

The brandy vanished from Ashleigh's glass.

Finally, Ashleigh spoke. "Kate—Miss Darling—hates me."

Merton could not suppress a chuckle. "Surely not. I would wager a good deal that she loves you."

"She did. She said so. But not anymore. Now she hates me." When Merton tried to make protesting noises, Ashleigh simply shook his head. "No, it is true. I have made a mess of it, a terrible mess."

"What could you possibly have done to make her hate you?" Merton asked with a smile.

"I asked her to be my mistress."

"*What!*" Merton stopped smiling.

In response, Ashleigh smiled bitterly. "You see? After that, what could she do but hate me?"

Merton went over to the decanter, poured himself a brandy, and took a deep swallow. "You do know that she is my wife's friend, do you not? In fact, since she appears to have no family other than Franny, Miranda asked me to stand as a brother to her. Do I need to challenge you?"

Ashleigh said nothing but directed a look of misery at his friend.

Merton began pacing. "Whatever possessed you to do such a thing? She may be poor, but she is a lady. Surely even you could see that. What were you thinking?"

Ashleigh lapsed into moroseness. "I wasn't thinking, I was only wanting. I'm obsessed with her, Tom. I can't think about anything but her. I ride around my fields and I wish she was with me. I try to read, and I see her face instead of the page. And at night—oh, God, Tom, at night! You have no idea."

"I do have some idea," replied Merton dryly. "But why in heaven's name did you not ask her to marry you?"

"Because I am a duke. I am a bloody duke. And now she has a horror of me." He leaned back and shut his eyes.

Merton looked at him carefully. "You asked her to be your mistress. Is that all you did?"

Ashleigh flinched.

"By God, Peter, I should call you out. She has no father or brother to do it, and she is my wife's friend."

The duke drew himself up. "I seem to recall that you and Miranda..."

"I always intended marriage and Miranda and I both knew it."

It probably was not possible for Ashleigh to look any more miserable, but he seemed to. He leaned back and covered his eyes with his arm.

"That is what Kate thought? That you intended marriage?"

Ashleigh nodded.

They both sat there in silence, Ashleigh with his head bowed. Finally, Merton spoke. "Ah, Peter, you damned fool. You will have to make it right. You will have to grovel, and I do not think you will enjoy it." Merton paused when he heard a snore and realized Ashleigh had fallen asleep. He considered ringing for a footman to help him move Ashleigh to the couch but decided to leave him where he was. He deserved a stiff neck to go with the aching head he would have in the morning.

# CHAPTER SIXTEEN

ASHLEIGH STIRRED AND winced. His neck was stiff. He awakened sufficiently to realize he was not in his bed, and pried his eyes open. He was not in his room, either. He was... he was in Merton's library. Memory came rushing in. He closed his eyes again, and swallowed to keep down the bile of self-disgust. How could he have been so dishonorable? How could he have used Kate so miserably?

Could she ever forgive him?

He could not bear to lose her. He would beg her to marry him, but would she accept him? After his arrogant, selfish, idiotic behavior yesterday, would her pride make her throw his proposal back in his face? Because God knew, she had pride aplenty.

He heaved himself out of the chair and held on to it, swaying slightly, as he waited for his head to stop spinning. He rubbed a hand along his unshaven cheek and looked down at his stained and wrinkled clothing. With a laugh of self-contempt he thought of the times he had chastised Merton for his disheveled appearance. No matter what the state of Merton's clothes, his soul had always been clean and honorable. He wished he could believe the same of himself.

The door opened and Merton came in, along with the bright light from the hall. "Ah, you are awake. I came in to warn you. Miranda will be down soon and is looking for a dull knife with which to flay you."

"I suppose you had to tell her."

"Yes, as a matter of fact, I did. She is my wife, you see, and that is one of the things we do. We tell each other things."

Ashleigh flushed, and Merton watched him.

After what seemed like hours, Merton spoke softly. "What are you going to do?"

"Find Kate. Make her listen to me. Beg her to marry me." Ashleigh closed his eyes and took a deep breath. "I can't lose her, Tom. I can't."

Merton nodded. "Do you want to clean up? Have something to eat?"

Ashleigh shook his head. "Can I borrow a horse, though? Hector came up lame on the way here yesterday."

"Of course. Take Belial." He grinned at Ashleigh's look. "No, that's not a comment on your behavior, nor on the horse's. Belial's good in the mud, and the roads are a mess after all this rain. He'll get you to Lewes safely."

⟫⟪

KATE WALKED QUICKLY along the riverbank, keeping pace with the tumbling waters, swollen by all the recent rain. She had cried herself out last night, and now anger was beginning to replace the sorrow. The anger was mainly at herself for being such a fool. There had never been any real possibility of marriage—deep down, she had always known that, even when she was deceiving herself into thinking that his words meant marriage. Dukes marry the daughters of important families, wealthy families, not the penniless daughters of families with contemptible reputations.

Now, her stupidity had ruined everything. Not only her chances of keeping him as a friend but also any possibility of taking over Mr. Prufrock's bookshop. She must remember to tell him that he needed to find another buyer. There was no way she could stay in Lewes, not where she might see Peter—Ashleigh—the duke—she did not even know what to call him now. It would be intolerable for her, and perhaps for him as well. At least once she moved away, she could think of him as Peter and remember that he had once said he loved her.

Had he meant it? Perhaps. But that obviously wasn't enough. Not for him. When she thought about it, he had not lied to her. He had never mentioned marriage. No doubt, it never crossed his mind that there was anything dishonorable in what he had proposed, nothing dishonorable for a duke, that is. No one would ever suggest that he should not take a mistress, and the woman's loss of honor meant nothing.

How could he have thought that? How could he claim to love her and then seek to condemn her to a life of shame and humiliation?

There was no point in thinking about him. It hurt too much. Instead, she needed to decide what to do now, where to go.

Not back to Yorkshire. They had probably already looked for her there, but they might go back, and she could not be certain that no one would let her brother know if she returned. Many people would assume that she belonged in his care. Nor could she go to her mother's family in Shropshire. They would also look there. No place like Bath or Brighton, where gossip about newcomers might reach London.

Her mouth twisted angrily. She was so ignorant. She knew nothing of the world, nothing even of the country in which she lived. Aunt Franny had said she would go with her, but that was another source of guilt. He had been Aunt Franny's friend, and she had ruined that as well. It was not that he would become her aunt's enemy—she would never believe that of him. But her actions, her fall, had destroyed the ease and comfort between her aunt and the duke's family. Lord and Lady Merton, as well, she was certain. They would all stand by the duke, not with someone whose very existence would now be an embarrassment for him.

Like a fool, she had convinced herself that what she wanted was possible, and her idiocy, her stupidity had ruined things for her aunt as well as herself.

Very well. She had been a fool, but she would survive. She had survived her brother. She had survived Farnsworth. She would survive this. There were other places, other towns, other shops. She would make a life for herself. She would.

She strode along, oblivious to her surroundings. With her head down, she saw nothing but the path at her feet. The river, tumbling over rocks and catching on fallen branches, was loud enough to drown out any noises from the road. So it was that she never noticed the scarlet carriage passing by on the road from London. The passenger in the carriage never glanced out, so intent was he on his own thoughts.

It was nearly an hour later when she finally trudged back up the road to Hawthorne Cottage, footsore and exhausted, but no closer to a decision about her future than she had been when she set out. Still preoccupied with her own thoughts, still staring down at the road as she walked, she was almost upon the scarlet carriage before she noticed it and recognized the crest. Not just the crest but the man standing beside it, leaning on a walking stick. He had obviously been watching for her, and when her eyes met his, he smiled.

It was a terrifying smile.

She froze momentarily, like a frightened rabbit, before she spun around and began to run, but it was too late. She ran right into a man who appeared in the road behind her. He grabbed hold of her and began to drag her back. She tried to pull away, to wriggle out of his grasp, and did manage to drive an elbow into his gut.

He let out a grunt, but didn't loosen his hold. "Please, Miss, I don't want to hurt you. Just come along."

She threw her head back and connected with his jaw, but that probably hurt her more than it hurt him because all he did was say, "Please, Miss, this doesn't help." When she tried to drag her feet, he lifted her enough so she could do nothing but kick futilely at the air.

He carried her toward the carriage where Farnsworth was waiting.

He stood negligently, resting one hand on that damned cane of his. He was, as always, dressed elegantly, even formally, in breeches and white stockings, with a silken waistcoat. When she had been dragged in front of him, still twisting and flailing, he bowed with mocking courtesy. "Miss Russell. You missed our earlier appointment. That was most ill-advised of you."

"You can't do this." She would have screamed, but the struggle was leaving her winded. "You have no right."

"I am the Earl of Farnsworth. That is all the right I need."

"You are a filthy, disgusting pig."

His smile turned to a sneer. "I will make certain that you pay for that discourtesy. You will soon regret having defied me."

She lifted her head and spat in his face.

None of them moved as the spittle trailed down Farnsworth's cheek. There was a sudden intake of breath from the man holding her, but no other sound. Even the breeze had stilled, and the birds were silent, as if nature, too, were waiting.

Then Farnsworth's face turned purple with rage and his backhand blow knocked her back against her captor, hard enough to make him stagger. Dazed though she was, she could feel his grip loosen and began to struggle again.

ASHLEIGH SLOWED BELIAL to stare, puzzled, at the unfamiliar carriage in front of Hawthorne Cottage. Two strangers stood near it, one dressed as a workman of some sort, the other as a gentleman in an almost arrogant display of wealth. When the workman turned slightly, he realized that the man was holding Kate captive and kicked the horse into motion.

Then he saw the blow.

His roar of rage could doubtless have been heard across the Channel as Belial thundered toward the group. The two men turned at the noise and stepped apart, sudden fear showing in their eyes. He threw himself off the horse, which continued to gallop at the man brandishing a cane, who slipped as he tried to run for the coach. Ashleigh charged at the man holding Kate. He flung her at Ashleigh and ran. She crashed into him hard enough to knock him off balance, landing them both in the ditch beside the road.

From the corner of his eye, he saw the workman grab the other man, throw him into the carriage, and jump in himself. The carriage was already driving away and he could do nothing to pursue it. Kate was still striking out blindly, kicking and clawing, crying out in protest without any words. Ignoring the blows, he pulled her into his arms, murmuring over and over, "It's all right, it's Peter, I have you, my darling, you're safe now."

She calmed down enough to raise her head and look at him. "Peter?" she asked in confusion.

The trembling began then, and he held her close while she quivered in his arms, sobbing and gasping for breath. When the shaking finally slowed, he picked her up and carried her to the house, whispering soothing murmurs and endearments.

The door was standing ajar, but he did not notice the oddity of this. He carried her into the parlor, and laid her on the settee so he could kneel beside her. The mark on her cheek was vivid against the pallor of her face, and his hand curved around it, not quite touching her. "He hurt you," he said flatly. "He will pay, I promise you."

Still shivering, she looked around fearfully. "Where is he?" she asked in a whisper.

"He's gone—fled. You're safe now."

Her eyes were still darting around the room and she twisted around for a better look. It was only when she bumped into his arm that she seemed to realize he was there. "Peter?" She blinked in confusion, a confusion that seemed tinged with fear. "How did you come to be here? Why are you here?"

"Please don't be afraid. I have to talk to you. I have to beg your forgiveness." He lifted her hands to his mouth to press kisses on them. "Forgive me, Kate. Please, forgive me. I know I behaved like the worst sort of arrogant fool, but you have to forgive me, you have to marry me. Please say you forgive me, I beg you. Say you will marry me."

Kate shook her head impatiently. "You don't understand, you don't know…" She broke off abruptly. "Aunt Franny. Molly. Where is everyone? What did he do to them?" She leaped to her feet and swayed slightly. He reached out to steady her, but she pushed away and ran from the room. "Aunt Franny! Where are you? Aunt Franny!"

Franny? He had completely forgotten about her aunt.

Her fear was turning into panic. This was obviously not the time to try to talk to her. First this crisis, whatever it was, had to be dealt with. He hurried after her and took hold of her arm to pull her to a halt. "Calm down. Stop and listen. Do you hear anything?"

Like a trapped creature, she swung wildly from side to side then stilled when she caught the faint tapping sound. "Where?"

"Back there." He led her through to the back of the house and down to the kitchen.

Her cries of "Aunt Franny?" brought a banging from the pantry door. She tried to lift the bar from the door, but her fingers kept slipping until Ashleigh took it from her. The moment he lifted it, the door swung open. Franny Darling came tumbling out to grasp her niece in her arms. Right behind her were Cook and Jem, Molly and the other two maids. The women seemed unharmed, though they were sobbing and shrieking. The elderly gardener, who had a gash across his cheek and was limping badly, was muttering curses.

Kate and Franny were alternately clutching each other and frantically checking for injuries, all the while gasping "Are you all right? Did he hurt you?"

Ashleigh took charge and began to snap out orders.

He told Jem to sit down on a chair, checked to make certain that the limp was caused by a bruise, not a break, and sent Molly for water and bandages. Cook was told to start making tea for everyone. He herded Kate and Franny back into the sitting room without their even realizing that they were moving and settled them on the settee, still talking over each other. He stood apart from them, leaning on the back of a chair and waiting for them to wind down.

Eventually, they did so, and could manage to speak to each other, though they were still clutching hands.

"Was that the man, Kate?"

Kate nodded.

"You poor child. I had no idea—is he quite mad?"

"Oh, Aunt Franny, I am so sorry. Did he hurt you?"

"No, though he knocked poor Jem down with that nasty cane. Then that fellow with him waved a pistol around and locked us in the pantry. Disgusting fellow."

"This is all my fault. I should never have come here. I swear, I would never have come if I had thought he might harm you."

"Nonsense. Where else would you go? Next time, we will be prepared." Franny was recovering her spirit. She reached up to touch Kate's cheek. "But your poor face. Did he do that?"

Kate nodded. "I must leave right away. He will be back, I am sure of it."

Franny opened her mouth to protest, but then stopped and nodded slowly. "How did you manage to get away from him this time?"

"Peter—the duke rescued me."

They both turned to look at him, as if just then realizing his presence. He bowed slightly into the silence.

"I suppose I must thank you, Your Grace." Franny did not smile at him, and her tone remained formal. "But I must also ask what brings you here?"

"I came to beg. To beg pardon of Kate, and also of you, but above all to beg Kate to marry me." He was watching Kate carefully and she had been looking at him. But at his words, she dropped her eyes and shook her head. His heart sank. "Kate, please…"

"You do not have to do this, Your Grace. You are feeling guilty, but there is no need. It was my own foolishness that made me think you meant marriage, and I was mad to think it possible."

"No, Kate, I was the fool yesterday." He was beside her on his knee again, holding her hands. "I love you, Kate. I cannot lose you. Marry me, please, marry me."

"Stop this nonsense," she snapped, pulling her hands loose and stepping away from him. "This is preposterous. You know nothing of me, of my situation. You don't even know who I am. You must listen to me." She held up her hands to hold him off. "Please," she added, as if in an afterthought. He rose slowly and returned to stand in his earlier position.

After a deep breath, she began. "My name is Katherine Russell. My father was Viscount Newell." She looked at Ashleigh and gave a short laugh. "You are unlikely to have met him in the Lords, or in any of the gentlemen's clubs. From all I know of him, he spent his time in the hells and stews, and my brother shared those… interests. My mother and I lived on his estate in Yorkshire, where we tried to wring enough income from it to pay his debts." Ashleigh frowned angrily and opened his mouth to speak, but she ignored him. He gripped the back of the chair before him.

"My father's death a few years ago changed nothing—it simply meant that it was now my brother's debts that needed to be paid. But things became more difficult with my mother's illness. By the time she died, there was little left. My brother appeared for her funeral, but then departed again when he realized there was nothing else to sell. I remained, managing with the help of friends and neighbors. Early this year, my brother returned. He announced that he had decided to take me to London to live with him."

She looked at Ashleigh then. "Yesterday was not the first time I have given in to foolishness, convincing myself that things were as I wished, and not as they are. I was pleased by his decision. I looked forward to seeing more of the world, perhaps finding a husband, having a home of my own, some safety and security." Her mouth twisted in a grimace, and she looked away again.

"My mistake was not realizing that there was something he could sell—me. He owed many thousands of pounds to the Earl of Farnsworth, and he offered me in payment of the debt. So I ran away and came here."

Ashleigh felt the blood leave his face. "My God, Kate!" She was heaping coals of fire on his head. She had escaped from *that* and he had offered...

Could a sound be more bitter than the laugh she uttered? "Believe it, Your Grace. And since I am not yet of age, I remain legally in my brother's power. Now, I must leave here before he comes or Farnsworth returns."

He turned away, slammed his hand against the wall and leaned there until the raw anger and shame that were choking him subsided enough for him to be able to think. What he had done—after what she had gone through, his behavior—there was no excuse for him. And he had thought an apology would be enough to win her?

What he wanted no longer mattered, but her safety did. He straightened and turned around, taking charge once more. "You are right. You cannot stay here. You will come to Kelswick. You, too, Franny, and the servants as well." Franny began to protest, but he overruled her. "If he is mad enough to try to kidnap Kate this way, in broad daylight, there is no way to know what else he might do. No one is safe in this house, but not even your earl will be mad enough to come near Kelswick."

Kate shook her head firmly. "I'm sure that is very kind of you,

Your Grace, but this is my problem, and I will take care of it. I am very grateful for the assistance you gave me today, but there is no need for you to involve yourself any further. Aunt Franny should be safe enough once I am gone from here."

"Nonsense." He spoke quite as firmly. "You will both be safe at Kelswick for the present, and once we are married, no one will dare to touch you." He had not expected to say that, but no sooner had he spoken the words than he realized that marriage—marriage to him— was the ideal way to protect her.

"Married?" Now she looked at him as if he were a madman. "Have you heard nothing I said?"

"It is the perfect solution. Once we are wed, your brother can do nothing." Surely she could see that this would be the best thing for her.

"Perfect? Oh, yes, that is the perfect solution. Well, I am sorry, but I will not be married because you feel guilty for something that was as much my fault as yours."

He flushed. "That is not why I want to marry you."

"Of course not!" She curled her lip at him. "You want to marry me so that you can destroy everything you have spent years trying to accomplish. I heard what you told me of your parents. Think of all you have felt obliged to do to make up for their behavior. Yet compared to my brother, they were saints."

Her anger was a relief. At least she no longer trembled with fear. "No," he said judiciously, "definitely not saints."

Ignoring his interruption, she continued, "And you certainly have never wished to associate yourself with a family as... as contemptible as mine."

"You know, I find I do not care a fig about your family." He found he was actually feeling quite cheerful, something he would not have believed possible last night or earlier this morning. Perhaps Fate was giving him a chance to make up for his behavior. If it came to a struggle between his pride and Kate's, he had at least a chance to win. "I do, however, very much want you for my wife."

She threw up her hands in exasperation. "You have taken leave of your senses."

He smiled. "And you haven't said the only thing that might give me pause. You have not said you don't love me. Even though after my contemptible stupidity yesterday, I was afraid you would hate me."

"Your Grace..."

He touched a finger to her lips. "Peter. Call me Peter, Kate."

"Peter." It came out with an exasperated sigh. "You are not listening to me."

"I assure you, I have heard every word."

Franny coughed loudly, and he turned to meet her eye. Though the friendly welcome of the past had not yet returned, at least she was not looking at him with the contempt she had shown last night.

"He makes a certain amount of sense, Kate," Franny said. "We have no way of knowing what that creature will do, and we need time to make plans. You don't have to marry him if you don't want to, but we will be safer at Kelswick until we decide what to do next."

Kate started to speak, but then could not miss seeing the look of fear that shadowed the older woman's eyes.

"I will take Kate with me now," Ashleigh said. "Lock the door—all the doors—and do not open them to anyone until I return, or Bancroft comes. I will send people to help you pack."

Franny simply nodded.

"Aunt Franny!" Kate could not keep the protest in.

"This is the most sensible thing to do at the moment," Franny told her niece. "We must be practical. What can you or I do against armed men? And how could we protect the servants? At least at Kelswick, we will all be safe."

Ashleigh looked suddenly serious. "And Franny, pack everything that is important to you. If this earl is mad enough to attempt a kidnapping in the middle of the day, who knows what else he is mad enough to do."

"GET US OUT of here as fast as you can!" Hall shouted to the coachman as he shoved Farnsworth into the carriage and clambered in behind him.

Farnsworth was still empurpled, spittle flying as he sputtered in fury. "How dare you lay hands on me! What? Would you have me run from some idiotic yokel? You clown!" He brushed himself off as if Hall's touch had soiled him, then called to the coachman, "Turn this carriage around."

Hall overrode the order, calling up, "Keep going if you want to avoid the hangman." After peering through the window to make sure there was no pursuit, he said, "That was no yokel. That was the Duke of Ashleigh."

"That clod? That unshaven, slovenly oaf?" Farnsworth barked a laugh. "Your fears have blinded you. He could have been driven off by a word."

"Believe me, that was Ashleigh. I've seen him often enough. And it appears his feelings for the young lady go beyond a polite acquaintance."

"Presumptuous boy." Farnsworth straightened his coat and adjusted his cuffs. "He cannot have her. She is mine."

Hall did not bother replying, but kept a careful watch out the rear window until they reached London.

# CHAPTER SEVENTEEN

LADY TALMADGE WAS at the escritoire in her sitting room, once more making lists, this time of things that needed to be packed.

Her brother burst in after a perfunctory knock, carrying a fuming Kate Darling over his shoulder. He plopped her down in a chair and turned to his sister. "Explain to her that she must marry me. It is the only sensible thing to do." Then he left, slamming the door behind him.

Lady Talmadge stared at the door in astonishment. Her brother did not slam doors. It was one of the things—one of the many things—he did not do. She turned to look at Kate, who had leaped up as soon as he set her down, and was now standing there simmering with a mix of emotions. Lady Talmadge was not entirely certain what was in the mix, but she was fairly certain that anger and exasperation took up a goodly proportion of the brew. She was not greatly surprised. Provoking exasperation was one of the things her brother did well. He did it to her often enough.

Kate, who had been glaring at the door, turned to Lady Talmadge. "I must apologize for this intrusion, my lady."

"My lady? I thought we had agreed that I was to be Alice." Then she noticed the red mark on Kate's cheek and her eyes widened. "Never tell me my brother did that!"

It took Kate a moment to realize what Lady Talmadge was talking about. She lifted her hand to her cheek. "No, no. On the contrary. He came to my rescue and has been more than gallant."

"Then you must tell me what this is all about." She went over to Kate and led her to a settee where she could sit beside the girl.

Kate allowed herself to be led but persisted in shaking her head. "I have to get away from here as quickly as possible."

"Away from here—from Kelswick?"

"Not just Kelswick." Kate waved a dismissive hand. "From Aunt Franny, from Lewes, from anyone around here. It's no longer safe here. I have to go someplace where they can't find me."

Alice was now thoroughly confused. "I understood from what Peter said that he had proposed marriage...?"

"He is being ridiculous." Kate shook her head angrily. "Your brother cannot possibly marry me. It is quite impossible."

"Are you already married?"

"Of course not," Kate said impatiently.

"Well, I am reasonably certain that Peter doesn't have a wife hidden away in the attic, so I do not see that it is impossible. And—forgive me if this distresses you—I thought from what my brother said that yesterday you did think it possible."

Kate flushed. Not the delicate pink of diffidence but the harsh red of humiliation. "That was because I did not realize... I had forgotten... I thought..." She took a deep breath before she spoke again. "I will not be married because your brother is feeling guilty. Nor will I be married because he pities me."

Lady Talmadge frowned. "I don't think I understand."

Kate stared at her hands. "I had managed to convince myself that it was all over. That what was past was past and could no longer touch me." Suddenly she began to shake, though whether this was with fear or with anger, the older woman did not know.

Alarmed, Lady Talmadge reached over to grip Kate's hands tightly. "It's all right, Kate. Everything is going to be all right." The older woman watched carefully until the tremors subsided.

"Ridiculous, isn't it?" Kate managed a tremulous laugh. "I wasn't nearly so frightened when I ran away from London. But now I feel as if he can reach out and snatch me up no matter where I go. And I will endanger anyone who tries to help me." She saw Lady Talmadge's confusion. "You must think me mad. I must tell you the whole ugly story."

Which she did, staring at her hands the whole time. It was not until she finished that she raised her head to look at Lady Talmadge. "So you see, I cannot marry your brother. I would bring nothing but shame and disgrace to his name."

Lady Talmadge, who had reacted to the story with the same horror, fury and admiration that had animated her brother, pulled the girl into her arms for a hug. "My poor Kate, why did you not tell us? We could have protected you."

"You forget that my brother is my legal guardian."

"Legal nonsense. A guardian is supposed to guard. Now, you must let Peter take care of this. He loves to take care of problems and he is really very good at it. I think one of the things that has been driving him wild is that you seemed to be handling your problems yourself without any assistance from him. He is not accustomed to that."

"Even a duke cannot change reality. Anything he attempts to do will simply involve him—all of you—in a sordid scandal at best. No. This is my problem and I will find a way to handle it. I will not let those creatures defeat me. I will not!"

"I admire that spirit." Lady Talmadge smiled. "I am very glad that Peter brought you here, so you will be safe while we determine our best course of action."

Kate continued to shake her head. "I cannot stay here. That will only bring trouble down on you all. I promise you that I will leave as soon as I can determine where to go."

"That would be truly foolish. This is no time to be turning yourself into a martyr." Lady Talmadge was pleased to see that Kate flushed uncomfortably at that. "You will do much better to continue being furious with your brother and that dreadful earl. I will be able to forgive you if you refuse my brother because you decide you cannot put up with his managing ways, but not if you decide to make him miserable in a misguided effort to protect him."

Kate's head snapped back and she opened her mouth to defend herself, but could not seem to find the words with which to do so.

"Listen to me." Lady Talmadge gripped Kate's hands. "Do not underestimate the power of a duke. You do not want to cower behind him? You want to fight your own battle? Fine. But think of this. No knight ever went into battle without a shield, and Peter makes a very good shield. He also serves as a very good weapon, a weapon you can wield in this battle."

It was easy to see this thought taking root in Kate's mind, and the anger and resentment in her expression eased into a cautious hope.

Lady Talmadge rang the bell and told the maid who responded, "Tell Mrs. Quilby that Mrs. Darling and Miss Russell will be staying with us for a while." She turned to Kate to say, "You might as well use your own name again," before returning to the maid. "Ask her to see that rooms are prepared for them. I think... I think perhaps the Columbine suite would do. And if you would, bring hot water for washing, and a pot of tea." Turning to Kate, she said, "You will feel better once you have had a chance to clean up a bit, and then we will talk some more."

SEATED ONCE MORE in Lady Talmadge's sitting room, Kate had to admit that Alice had been right. She did feel better now that she'd had a chance to wash herself, brush off her dress and neaten her hair. She felt even better after having drunk a cup of tea and eaten half a dozen of the tiny strawberry tarts.

Better, but not entirely at ease.

The sitting room was, like everything at Kelswick, immaculate and perfect in every detail. The ceiling was festooned with flowers and flourishes of baroque plasterwork that trailed down onto the walls, every inch of it in perfect repair. The pale blue silk hangings on the walls were pristine, apparently impervious to any smuts or soot produced by the coal fire that must have been needed to keep the room warm during the winter. Withal, the overall impression of the room was of comfort.

With delicate care, Kate put her cup and saucer down on the marquetry table beside her chair. Gesturing about her, she said, "I am not accustomed to a life like this, you know."

"Few people are," Lady Talmadge observed dryly.

"Yes, but I do not wish you to suffer under a misapprehension. I know I told you that my father was a viscount, but I never lived in anything resembling noble splendor. I grew up with my mother in a manor house that was crumbling around us, three-quarters of it completely uninhabitable."

"I hope you do not mean to convince me that you are a poor little urchin dragged in from the gutter. I saw you slap down that toad Wilton without turning a hair, and your look at his mother would have frozen the blood in her veins if she had any."

"I did, didn't I?" She was surprised to find that she wanted to smile at the memory. It was probably not well done of her to take pleasure in such things but she could not regret her show of pride. "How dreadfully rude of me."

"No need to worry. I am certain she never noticed. I have never seen any signs of perception in her. Nonetheless, I have difficulty believing you will find yourself uncomfortable in society."

"Not uncomfortable. My mother made certain I grew up with all the necessary social graces." This memory also brought pleasure, but it was bittersweet. "We would pretend to be 'at home'. I would be the lady of the house and she would be assorted visitors, some pleasant, some foolish. And, of course, we had many friends in the neighborhood. I did not grow up in isolation. Indeed, I had a very happy childhood. It was only when my mother grew ill…" Her voice trailed off.

Lady Talmadge prodded. "This was after your father's death?"

Those last years had been difficult, but Kate dismissed the temptation to self-pity with a shrug. "Yes, but his death was unimportant. You can have no idea how little he and my brother impinged on our lives. Shameful though it may sound, it had been so many years since I had last seen Humphrey that I did not recognize him when he arrived for my mother's funeral." A bitter laugh could not be restrained. "So you can see why I sometimes forget how much power he has over my life. It was barely a month that I spent with him in London, and he used it to destroy me."

"What utter nonsense." Ashleigh strode into the room. "Destroy you. Really. You must get over this tendency to melodrama. I fear it will be quite exhausting over the breakfast table." He bent over to drop a light kiss on her cheek before moving on to the tea table. "Ah, good. I was told that Cook had made strawberry tarts and I am glad to see you have left me some. You will not mind if I finish them off."

"Much good it would do me to object." Lady Talmadge watched with amusement as the last of the tarts vanished into her brother.

With a contented sigh, he dusted off the crumbs of pastry and turned back to Kate. "That is something you will have to remember. I am exceedingly fond of strawberry tarts and I hope you will have Cook make them frequently when strawberries are in season." He smiled at her look of confusion. "Little attentions like that are important in a marriage."

The exasperation returned. How could he simply ignore everything she had told him? "Your Grace, you persist…"

"Indeed I do, Miss Russell, indeed I do."

"You seem to have forgotten my situation…"

"No, my love, you seem to have forgotten that I am a duke. Or perhaps you do not entirely realize what that means. If I stand in the middle of London and say that this morning I saw the sun rise in the west, I will be surrounded by people who swear they saw the same thing. I assure you that once you are my duchess, the entire world will have forgotten your family."

He had called her "my love". Those two words were all she heard, at first. But eventually, the rest of his words penetrated. Kate was torn between hope and despair, but anger trumped them both. "What arrogance. You are a duke, and rivers will part for you, tides will turn for you, and all the world will leap to do your bidding."

He blinked in surprise. "Well, hardly that," he began.

"Precisely that," she interrupted. "Do you realize that is exactly Farnsworth's attitude? He is only an earl, of course, but I warrant you his assurance is almost equal to yours."

"You cannot possibly compare me to that, that vile creature." He flushed with anger. "You know I would never hurt you." He stopped abruptly, realizing that he had hurt her.

Her anger subsided as quickly as it had flared up. "No, I know you have never meant to harm me, or anyone else. You try to protect us all. But you don't seem to realize that you are vulnerable, too."

"Vulnerable? Me?"

"Yes, you. If nothing else, Farnsworth will create a scandal," she warned, "and that will harm you if you are in any way connected with me."

"Farnsworth may try, but he will not succeed. I can protect myself and I can protect you." He put his hand to her cheek and turned her to look at him. "You are safe now. Safe from your brother, safe from Farnsworth, safe from everything. I swear it."

She wanted to believe it, she truly did, but she could not and tried to turn her face away.

He stopped her. "If you do not believe it yet, you will. Stephen is with your aunt, helping her to oversee the packing, and he will escort her here. I will send the announcement of our betrothal to the London papers this afternoon..." He broke off and, ignoring Kate's protest, turned to his sister. "Shall I send the announcement for you and Stephen at the same time?"

Lady Talmadge started slightly at the question, but then smiled. "You have decided to stop being an ass then?"

He smiled back, shamefaced. "I was twenty-seven different kinds of an ass yesterday..."

"At least."

"... but I do wish you and Stephen all happiness. He is one of the finest men I have ever known."

"Thank you." She kissed her brother on the cheek.

"And you will be married from here? It would give me great pleasure."

"If you do not think it will distract from your own celebrations. Kate, would you mind?"

Kate felt as if she had fallen into a whirlpool. She had completely lost control of her life. This was not right. "No," she said. "This will not do." Then she saw the look of hurt on Lady Talmadge's face, and jumped to her feet to grasp the older woman's hands. "No, no, I do not mean that... I am making a muddle of everything." She turned to the duke. "I mean that I cannot marry you, Your Grace." There, that was said as firmly as she could manage.

Ashleigh stood there looking at Kate, an uncertain smile on his face. "Alice, could you excuse us for a few minutes?"

"Peter, you are not to bully."

"Sister mine, you may choose to make your proposals in front of an audience, but some people prefer privacy." His eyes remained fixed on Kate.

Lady Talmadge raised a hand in mock surrender. "Very well. Just remember, Kate, you can leave whenever you choose." Then she leaned over to whisper in Kate's ear. "A weapon. Think of him as a weapon."

Think? When he was looking at her that way? She could not even turn her eyes away from him.

"Kate?" His voice, so strong and cheerful a few minutes ago, now sounded strained. "Kate, yesterday you said you loved me. Did I destroy that? I know I was a fool. I behaved like a brute, a swine, the worst sort of blackguard." He had seized her hands and was holding them over his heart. "Can you forgive me? Can you let me try to redeem myself? I swear I will do everything within my power to make you happy. Let me try." He raised her hands to his lips and pressed kisses on them.

Tears were welling up in her eyes—she could feel them, and willed them not to fall. She was falling apart but she needed to be strong. All she wanted was to lean against him, to have him wrap his arms about her, holding her safe. But she could not. If he was going to be her shield and her weapon, she could not let him misunderstand. "Your Grace"—she felt him stiffen—"Peter"—his eyes lifted to look into hers—"you know I love you. That's why…"

She was unable to say anything more. He was pressing kisses on her eyes, her temples, her mouth, nibbling on her ear, then moving along her jaw and returning to her mouth. His hands were caressing her, holding her close. The knowledge that she should pull away was of no use. She was lost in the joy of being held in his arms. She melted against him and returned kiss for kiss, caress for caress.

How long their embrace lasted neither could have said. Ashleigh was the one who finally pulled back, though his hands were still on her shoulders. "No, I will show you that I am not without honor. I will show you that I am capable of restraint—though very little of it, where you are concerned."

Shaking her head seemed to have no effect on his smile. She had to speak. "I cannot marry you, Peter."

The smile did not diminish as he heaved a sigh. "And what is the problem now, my sweet? You did say you love me, did you not?"

"That is precisely why I cannot marry you. I know you think that Farnsworth cannot touch you, and perhaps you are right. But he can create a scandal that will touch me." Peter chuckled, so she struck him on the chest. "Why will you not listen? You must pay attention to me."

"Where did you acquire this yearning for martyrdom, my sweet? You are making a remarkable mountain out of a very small molehill."

"You keep laughing at me, but it is no laughing matter. You yourself told me how you hated the scandals your parents created."

"And what scandals have you created?"

She pushed away and stalked across the room before turning to face him, arms akimbo. "Have you already forgotten? My brother tried to *sell* me, to use me to pay his gambling debts."

"Deplorable, dastardly, utterly beneath contempt, but hardly a scandal of your creation. Indeed, not scandalous at all until it becomes generally known. And that, I think, is unlikely to happen."

"I ran away and made my way here from London alone."

"Dangerous, though necessary, but brave and honorable rather than scandalous."

"My father..."

"There is not a family in the *ton* that does not number a witless gambler in its ranks." He had been coming closer and closer and now enfolded her in his arms once more. "Trust me. We will see you safely free of your brother and his friend. Then, if you truly do not wish to marry me, I will not hold you to it."

She was in his arms, the place she wanted to be, the place she always wanted to be. She leaned against him—she could not help it—feeling the strength of him, breathing the clean scent of him. This was where she felt safe, the place where she felt more complete than ever before. He thought she might not *want* to marry him? She did not know whether to laugh or weep. "The problem is not my wishes, as well you know. I must be certain that I will not bring you harm. You must promise me that you will not try to force a marriage between us if I will bring scandal and dishonor in my train."

"You will not..."

"You cannot know what will happen. My brother is a fool and Farnsworth is dangerous. There is no way to know what they may do between them. I must have your promise."

His jaw was tense as he looked away, and he could not answer at first. Finally, he said, "I do not think I can make that promise."

"You must," she said insistently. "I will not be responsible for your ruin."

He gave a stiff nod. "Very well, I promise that I will not hold you against your will. If, when this is finished, you wish to leave, I will not stop you. Will that do?"

She nodded in return. It would have to do. The problem was that she was not at all certain that she would be able to find the strength to leave if she needed to.

⟫⟫⟩⟨⟨⟨

AFTER DINNER, THEY all gathered in the library. Although she had been in this room a number of times, Kate found herself once more awed by its grandeur, to say nothing of the hundreds—no, thousands—of books that lined the shelves.

"You'll grow accustomed to it." Peter grinned at her. His good humor or his arrogance—she was not sure which—had returned.

She settled herself primly in the small armchair he led her to. "I am not sure I like it that you can so easily read my thoughts."

Leaning over her, he whispered, "Can you read mine?" Her blush brought a smug look to his face and he sat down beside her, his chair close enough to hers that his leg brushed her skirt and his fingers on the arm of his chair were not an inch from hers.

His proximity did not put her at her ease. Instead, her body was far too aware of his nearness, and his every glace raised the temperature of her blood. It was as if she had left her common sense behind when she left Hawthorne Cottage.

Seated nearby, Franny remained tense, as if she had not entirely recovered from the shock of the morning. Stephen, however, seemed somehow larger than he had been before. One could never have called him timid or diffident, but he had always somehow held himself in reserve. Today, when he was sitting beside Alice, they both seemed alive with happiness.

It was Stephen who began by asking if there was any plan for dealing with Farnsworth and Newell.

"Not a plan, precisely," Peter said. "I thought the first step should be to have the announcement of our betrothal in the paper."

"Without seeking her brother's permission? I hardly recognize my punctilious brother." Alice looked at him with fond amusement.

"I assure you, I asked Franny's permission with all due ceremony."

Franny was busily shaking her head and clenching her hands. Now that Kate had calmed down a bit, she seemed to be the one most affected by the morning's events. "I really do not understand what you think this will accomplish, Peter."

"Several things." He grinned happily. "First, it will announce our betrothal to society without any mention of Kate's brother, and I think he is not well known to society, is he, Alice?"

His sister shook her head. "I had never heard of him. Farnsworth, however…" She made a moue of distaste. "I never met him, but his name was occasionally mentioned, not with admiration. Even Talmadge considered him too disreputable to know, so he would never have been introduced to me."

"Well then, people's first notice of Kate will be as a young lady of good family from Yorkshire. They may have heard of her father as a gamester, but there is nothing unusual in that. Her brother, we will simply ignore."

Kate could not stand it any longer. He seemed to be actually enjoying this. "That is all very well and good, Your Grace, but there is no guarantee that my brother will ignore *me*."

"Now, now, Kate, I thought we had done with that 'Your Grace' nonsense." He was definitely enjoying himself. "There are two possibilities. The most likely is that your brother and Farnsworth will acknowledge themselves defeated and creep back into their holes like the curs they are. The other—and this is a possibility only if one or both of them are somewhat deranged—is that they will make another attempt to kidnap you. That, we can foil easily enough, and simply making the attempt would be enough to land them on a ship for Van Diemen's Land."

She glared at him. "You want it to be the second."

He returned grin for glare. "I confess, it would give me great pleasure to thrash both of them. But I fear they will not be so foolish as to give me the opportunity."

"Yet you insisted that Aunt Franny and I stay here for safety's sake."

"And I still do." He held up a hand to halt any protest from Franny. "They do not yet know that you are under my protection, nor do they know of our betrothal. I will sleep easier knowing you are safely under my roof, even though I think any danger from them is unlikely."

# CHAPTER EIGHTEEN

T HE DUCAL HOUSEHOLD was awakened in the early hours of the morning by a hammering on the door. By the time Ragwell, the butler, had made himself sufficiently presentable to appear in the front hall, a large disreputable creature was standing there grinning. Ragwell blinked. The disreputable creature, who seemed to be streaked with soot and smoke, and whose clothes were torn and filthy, bore a remarkable resemblance to James, one of the footmen. But James normally stood at attention in the hall in pristine glory.

Ragwell did not have a chance to demand an explanation. The duke, wrapped in a banyan of scarlet silk embroidered with dragons, came hurrying down the stairs, calling out, "James, what has happened?"

"They came back, Your Grace, just like you said they might. Tried to burn the house down. We put it out easy enough, and we caught one of them." He was grinning proudly. "The other got away, though, and we could hear a carriage driving off."

"Good lad." The duke clasped the footman's filthy shoulder, much to Ragwell's horror. "Where have you put him?"

"We tied 'im up, and Will's keeping watch over 'im in Mrs. Darling's garden shed," said James, losing his aitches in his excitement.

By now, most of the household had arrived, and James was basking in the attention. He winked at one of the parlor maids and turned to Franny, whose eyes had widened at the mention of her garden shed. "No need to worry, Mrs. Darling. They tossed lamp oil on the back door and set it afire, but we beat it out before it could catch 'old. No damage, or nothing that a fresh coat of paint won't put right."

"They set my house on fire?" Franny sat down abruptly on the stairs. Kate and Alice hurried to join her. Alice wrapped her shawl around the older woman before turning to her brother to demand an explanation.

Ashleigh was grinning again. "Just as a precaution, I set some men to keep an eye on Hawthorne Cottage."

"You knew this would happen?" Kate sounded aghast.

"Knew? Certainly not. I thought nothing would happen, but it seemed only sensible to be forehanded."

Franny was pale and shivering despite the shawl and Kate's arm about her. "If you had not insisted we come here, we could have been burned alive. And if you had not left men there to guard it, my home would be ashes. We are greatly indebted to you."

"Nonsense, Franny. Let there be no talk of debts between us. I have ever thought of you and Andrew as more parents to me than my own ever were, and we will soon be related by marriage as well." With a hand on each one, he drew Kate and Franny to their feet. "Now, may I suggest that you ladies all retire to your rooms and sleep peacefully for the remainder of the night while Stephen and I have a talk with our intruder?" Kate opened her mouth, but before any sound could come out, he said, "And no, you may not come with us. You would be a hindrance, not a help."

Kate looked rebellious but Alice came over and spoke softly. "He's right, you know. If you are present, they will be obliged to behave like gentlemen and that will likely get them nowhere." As she ushered Kate and Franny up the stairs, she spoke over her shoulder. "You will, of course, tell us all in the morning."

"But of course." Ashleigh swept a courtly bow.

Everyone disappeared, leaving James with Ashleigh and Stephen, who looked at the duke with no small degree of surprise. "You are enjoying this, aren't you?"

Ashleigh cocked his head and considered. "You know, I do believe I am."

IN THE MORNING, the ladies of the household were up with housemaids, much to the consternation of the housemaid who had just opened the curtains in the breakfast room and had no idea how she was supposed to dust and sweep with the room occupied. At least it was too warm to need a fire. She snatched up her brush and dust pan and tried to blend into the woodwork, hoping they were just passing through.

"That's all right, Jenny, is it?" Lady Talmadge smiled at her. The maid nodded. Lady Talmadge smiled again. "Continue with your tasks elsewhere and don't worry about this room."

The maid fled. She had never seen ladies up so early in the morning and didn't know what to make of it. It just wasn't natural. And when she ran down to the kitchen to warn Cook that the ladies had already appeared for breakfast, she thought Cook would faint dead away.

By the time Ashleigh and Bancroft arrived, not too much later, both tea and coffee had appeared, along with toast and butter and jam. It was as well for Jenny's nerves that she did not see those gentlemen. After all, housemaids have nerves just as ladies do, though they are not generally permitted to indulge in them.

Ragwell did see them arrive, and came close to indulging in a fit of nerves himself. He had never seen his duke so... so.... he could not even put it into words. The duke was unshaven, he wore neither coat nor cravat, his shirtsleeves were rolled up and Ragwell could have sworn that the duke's knuckles were bloody. Mr. Bancroft looked slightly better in that he retained his coat, but that was not enough to console Ragwell. The duke, *his* duke, who had never appeared other than perfectly turned out since the age of twelve, not only looked like a ruffian but seemed not in the least distressed by his appearance and had not the slightest hesitation about presenting himself to the ladies in this condition. Had the sun risen in the west, Ragwell could not have been more disconcerted. Nonetheless, he stood by, his face as impassive as he could make it, as Ashleigh entered the breakfast room.

"Ah, coffee. Excellent," said the duke. "Ragwell, ask Cook if she could manage a couple of beefsteaks for us. I find myself quite ravenous this morning."

The butler departed silently.

"You have shocked poor Ragwell beyond description," said Alice with a laugh. "He will never be able to view you with proper awe again."

Kate, however, had spotted the bloody knuckles, and seized Ashleigh's hand to examine them.

"Now, now, there's nothing to worry about, my sweet." He gave her hands a squeeze. "And Franny, you will be pleased to know that James was quite correct. There was no damage to your house except for a bit of scorching on the back door, and that is being put right as we speak."

"I do not think any of us were worrying about my door, Peter," she said dryly. "We are a trifle more concerned about the people who were endeavoring to set the fire."

Settling himself into his chair at the head of the table, Ashleigh drained a cup of coffee and signaled for another before he spoke. "You will also be pleased to know that no one was trying to kill you."

"Immensely consoling," snapped Franny. "So if anyone had been killed or injured, it would have been purely accidental?"

"Precisely." Ashleigh grinned. "The idea was that a fire started at the back of the house would have sent everyone out the front. There were two more men in hiding there, and their task was to scoop you up, Kate, and carry you off in the confusion before anyone could realize what was happening."

"Oh." She thought for a moment. "That might actually have worked. But who sent them? I cannot imagine my brother having the intelligence to work out such a plan, and it seems insufficiently brutal for Farnsworth."

That last comment gave Ashleigh a moment's pause. She had spoken quite calmly. He felt an icy tightening in his chest at the realization that his Kate had been so exposed to brutality that she could speak of it in such a matter-of-fact way, but he managed a smile. "It appears that the plan belonged to a gentleman named Hall. Do you know him?" Receiving only a blank look and a shake of the head from her, he continued, "He is the sort of gentleman one employs when one does not wish anyone else to be aware of the tasks for which he is being employed. In this case, it appears he was employed first to find you, Kate, and now to retrieve you."

She pursed her lips. "Rather as if I were a misplaced parcel. I really do not care for being treated like a, like a piece of merchandise." She took a deep breath and glanced again at Ashleigh's knuckles. "Did he just volunteer this information or did he require persuasion?"

A deep chuckle came from Bancroft, who was seated next to Lady Talmadge and appeared to be holding her hand under the table. "There was no difficulty. I simply pointed out to him that arson is a hanging offense, and if he did not give us the information we wanted, we would have no choice but to hand him over to the magistrate."

"And that was all?" Kate sounded skeptical.

Bancroft shrugged. "And then Ashleigh pointed out that the hangman wouldn't care if bits of him had been broken off, bits like fingers. He took one look at Ashleigh and began to chatter away."

HALL NURSED A pint of ale in a corner of the Mitre Inn. The public room was crowded with people wanting to talk about the events at Hawthorne Cottage the night before. Some of the tales were quite wild. One had a crowd of Luddites attacking the cottage with axes and the duke himself driving them off. Another had a madman planning to put the entire town of Lewes to the torch.

Well, thought Hall, perhaps that last one wasn't entirely wild. He had a strong feeling that Farnsworth might, indeed, be mad.

One thing was clear from the talk, however. Mrs. Darling and her niece were staying with the duke. He had spread the cloak of his protection over them. No one seemed in the least surprised at this.

He took a sip of ale and considered his options. He could go to the duke and tell him what Farnsworth had been attempting, but he doubted anything he had to say would be news to the duke. One of his men had been captured, and the fellow had no reason to keep silent if speaking might get him out of punishment. Hall could not blame him. He would do the same himself. Unfortunately, that meant he himself had nothing to sell to the duke.

Unless he went back to Farnsworth to find out what he planned to do next. That might be worth something.

He took another sip and considered. One problem was that Farnsworth was unlikely to actually have a plan beyond marching in and seizing the girl. If Hall was around, Farnsworth might insist on his cooperation. That could be nothing but disastrous. Farnsworth seemed to consider that his title made him immune to danger. Even if that were true, it would offer no protection to Hall.

No.

His only safety lay in keeping as much distance as possible between himself and Farnsworth.

He stood up, tossed a coin on the table to pay his reckoning, and left the tavern. No one noticed his departure.

It was a pity about the money Farnsworth owed him, but it would do him no good if he was swinging from a noose.

He collected his horse and set out for London. There were plenty of places where he could go to cover. He would not be found unless he wished to be found.

# CHAPTER NINETEEN

*London*

CRACK! FARNSWORTH'S STICK smashed down on the table uncomfortably close to Newell's hand. He would have removed his hand, but he was not certain he would remain vertical without the table to lean on.

It didn't seem right. Perhaps falling asleep in the library was not quite the thing to do, but it was his library, and if he chose to sleep it off there, he didn't see why Farnsworth was making a fuss.

Come to think of it, he didn't see why Farnsworth was there at all. Something about the paper. It was on the desk, and that was what Farnsworth had been smacking with his stick. Newell tried to focus on it.

"You traitorous scum!" Farnsworth was shouting. "How dare you try to do this to me?"

Newell tried shaking his head to clear it. A bad idea. He gave up trying to keep vertical and slid down to sit on the floor.

Apparently, that was a bad idea, too. Farnsworth grabbed his shirt and hauled him back up.

He winced. "Do about what?" he managed to croak out.

Farnsworth was shaking the paper in his face now. "Do you expect me to believe you did not know about this? Did you think I would allow you to get away with it?"

The shaking paper was making Newell dizzy. The whole world was making him dizzy. He could feel himself sinking lower as his knees slowly gave way.

He came to with a gasp. He was lying on the floor, awash in cold water. Farnsworth was still there, standing next to the footman, who was holding a bucket, now empty. A newspaper was clutched in the earl's fist, and he was leaning on his stick. Red blotches were spattered across his face, and he spoke through clenched teeth. "If you think betrothing your sister to a duke will solve your problems, you are sadly mistaken. She is my property, and you will retrieve her for me." He flung the paper down. "You have until Thursday."

Newell blinked his eyes, but the earl was gone. He could hear that blasted walking stick tapping down the hall. Pulling himself up to a sitting position, he picked up the paper and peered at it. It was folded to the announcements, and he tried to make sense of the births, deaths and marriages until he came to the betrothals.

The Duke of Ashleigh and his sister? That was impossible. But it said Miss Katherine Russell, of Grassington, daughter of the late Viscount Newell. How could that be? Where could she have ever met a duke, no less one as top-lofty as Ashleigh was reputed to be?

He kept staring at the paper long after he had absorbed the words, long after the footman had crept silently away. If his sister was going to marry the Duke of Ashleigh, if this was really true, all sorts of things were possible. A duke, *this* duke, at least, was rich. He could pay off his debts, get out of the hands of the moneylenders, get free of Farnsworth.

No. He felt a chill as he realized Farnsworth would not let that happen. Of that, he was certain. If he did not get hold of Katherine, if he did not turn her over to the earl, he did not know what Farnsworth would do.

He did know that whatever Farnsworth did, it would be unpleasant. Very unpleasant.

Newell hauled himself to his feet and wiped his sleeve across his face. His hands were shaking, and he knew it was not simply the effects of last night's debauch.

He had to get cleaned up. With that announcement in hand, the moneylenders would almost certainly advance him some more, enough to be able to do something. Maybe after a drink, he would be able to think what that something might be. He had until Thursday, after all.

"Watkins!" he shouted. "Watkins! What the hell day is it today?"

*Sussex*

ASHLEIGH AND BANCROFT spent the morning at Schotten Hall, bringing Lord and Lady Merton up to date on Kate's situation. They were suitably horrified, and Merton uttered the appropriate imprecations on the heads of Newell and Farnsworth. Lady Merton seemed not at all shocked at her husband's language. In fact, she nodded approvingly, and offered a number of suggestions as to what might be done with the villains.

Ashleigh looked at her with a new sense of admiration. "You have an estimable view of what should be done with your enemies, Miranda."

She gave him a level look. "I do not take kindly to threats against those I love."

"No more do I. We are allies in this, then?"

"Indeed."

He put out a hand. She took it, and they smiled approvingly at each other.

Paying no attention to them, Merton demanded, "When do we get to thrash them?"

Bancroft snorted.

Ashleigh grinned most unducally. "I have baited the hook with the announcement of our betrothal. I do not anticipate a prolonged wait."

The wait was even shorter than Ashleigh had expected. By the time he and Bancroft returned to Kelswick, a letter had arrived for Kate, a letter that had been delivered by hand. She was waiting for them, and thrust it into Ashleigh's hands as soon as he crossed the threshold.

"Can you believe it? My brother obviously thinks me a complete fool. He tells me to meet him in the garden tonight at midnight. Midnight! I ask you, can he display no originality of thought?"

Ashleigh had to laugh. It seemed that she was even more outraged by the insult to her intelligence than she had been by the threat to her person. Still smiling, he took the letter into the library, where Franny, Alice and Bancroft crowded around him to see what it said.

"Heavens!" exclaimed Franny. "He dares to accuse Kate of flouting his authority? The presumption of the scoundrel!"

Ashleigh laughed. "I am amazed. I never thought he would be so cooperative." He handed the letter back to Kate. "If you will excuse me, I must send a message to Merton. He will never forgive me if I leave him out of this, though he may find it difficult to persuade Miranda to remain at home. Come along, Stephen. We must make our preparations for this evening."

The ladies watched them stride off to the library. Small explosions of outrage continued to burst forth from Franny, but Alice took Kate's arm and moved toward the stairs. "Do you know," she said, "I do not think I have ever seen my brother this way. He is actually enjoying himself. I cannot remember him ever being so, so *buoyant*. I understand that this is all difficult for you, but I cannot help but be pleased to see my brother thus."

"Difficult?" Head tilted to the side, Kate considered that. "No, this is not difficult. Not any longer. It was difficult when I kept thinking that Humphrey would suddenly appear to drag me back, and I would be unable to stop him. I feared that no one would help me, that no one *could* help me. But now? With all of you beside me, I find I am looking forward to confronting him, to telling him just what I think of him."

"Ah, you must marry Peter. I do so want to have you for a sister, and then I will be able to claim Franny for an aunt as well." She took the older woman's arm with her free hand so they ascended the stairs three abreast. "You two will be such excellent examples for Clara."

AT THE APPOINTED hour, she stepped slowly along the garden path. The path of pale pebbles was wide, and the moon was bright enough to light the way, but tall shrubs loomed on either side, so she walked cautiously. The chill of the night made her grateful for her cloak. She wanted to think it was only the temperature that made her shiver.

The gate leading to the road was already in sight when she heard footsteps just behind her. She had been expecting it, waiting for it. That did not prevent the shock of fear or the sick feeling as she admitted to herself that, yes, a brother could be guilty of such a betrayal.

Before she could turn, or even decide in which direction to turn, rough hands grabbed her arms, and as she started to scream, someone stuffed a rag into her mouth. She tried instinctively to break free, but before she could manage more than an ineffectual kick, a sack had been dropped over her head and she was knocked to the ground while a rope was wrapped around her.

Struggling did no good as she found herself tossed over a shoulder and, shortly thereafter, tossed across a horse. That it was a horse was quite clear from the smell, though she was inclined to think that even through the sack, the horse smelled better than the man had. A rider joined her, and a hand kept her from falling off as the horse broke into a jarring trot.

It wasn't a long trip, for which she was most grateful, though it was easily the most uncomfortable of her life. When she was hauled off the horse and tossed over a shoulder once more, she had a moment of panic. Had she been able to push the rag out of her mouth, she could have let out a scream that would be heard in Timbuctoo. As it was, the best she could produce was a muffled grunt accompanied by a frantic wriggle. Even that only won her a smack on the head, cushioned by the sack but hard enough to make her feel momentarily dizzy.

"Stupid bitch."

She heard the mutter. It was the first time either of her captors—she was fairly certain there were two of them—had spoken. Neither the roughness of the voice nor the coarseness of the epithet offered reassurance.

She was not carried far before she heard a door open and she was unceremoniously dumped on the ground. Landing on her hip, she made a muffled sound of pain.

"'Ere she is. We'll 'ave our pay now." The same voice, followed by the clink of coins.

"There. At least you could have put her in the coach for me." An educated, though petulant, voice, this one. The accent of a gentleman, though she would not care to call the speaker such.

The door slammed open, and she could hear footsteps, voices, as a number of people came in.

"I am afraid this little transaction is at an end."

Peter's voice, and it was high time he arrived! She wriggled uncomfortably.

There was a confusion of sounds—bumps, thuds, grunts. The sound of fist against flesh. A crack that might have been bone breaking. She was picked up again, but not roughly this time. Instead, she felt cradled in an embrace, and then she was gently laid down.

She could hear muttered curses and the sound of a knife sawing through the rope until it loosened. The sack was pulled quickly off her, and she snatched the rag from her mouth herself. There was Stephen, bending over her, his eyes so worried, checking her all over, carefully. "Are you hurt? You must be bruised at least. They were treating you so roughly... oh, Alice!" His arms wrapped around her and he was holding her tightly and murmuring endearments.

She managed a strained laugh. "It was my idea, remember. Would you have denied me my adventure? Did you doubt I could do it?"

He leaned his forehead against hers. "Never that. What I had not fully realized was how difficult it would be to watch you tossed about when I could not step in to protect you. Never again. To preserve my sanity, you must never put yourself in danger again."

Her laugh came a bit more easily this time. "It is a bit lowering to be treated like a parcel, picked up here, delivered there."

He lifted his head and looked at her carefully. Then he smiled a bit. "Would you like to kick them? The ones who carried you off are over there." He indicated two ruffians who were piled in a corner, tied up and watched over by three of Ashleigh's larger footmen.

She looked around and realized they were in a barn, the abandoned one not far from Kelswick on the London road. "I would rather kick the creature who arranged this."

Bancroft gestured to the middle of the room. "You may have to wait your turn."

Ashleigh was driving his fist into the gut of a man with a bloody nose who was flapping his arms in what might be a gesture of surrender. He crumpled into a heap and lay there shivering. Ashleigh was about to haul him up to be hit again when Merton put a restraining hand on his arm. "Now, now, Peter, a bit of forbearance if you please." Ashleigh glared at his laughing friend.

Lady Talmadge watched with interest. "Is that Lord Newell?" When Bancroft nodded, she said, "I believe it is my turn now." She walked over in no apparent hurry and kicked the fallen creature in the ribs. She smiled, satisfied, at his grunt.

Merton grinned at her, then he and Bancroft hauled the man to his feet.

"Lord Newell, I believe," said Ashleigh.

The fellow nodded, breathing roughly, looking resentful. "Did Farnsworth send you? I told him I'd bring her to him. You didn't have to do this." Then he saw Lady Talmadge and frowned, confused. "A woman? What's a woman doing here? Who are you?"

She smiled. "Your doom, I believe."

"Indeed," said Ashleigh. "This lady, whom you paid these, ah, creatures, to kidnap, is Lady Talmadge, widow of the late Earl of Talmadge and sister of the Duke of Ashleigh. I am Ashleigh." He inclined his head slightly.

Now Newell was looking frightened, shaking his head, wide-eyed. "No, no, must be some mistake, all a mistake. Never kidnapped anyone."

"Definitely a mistake," said Ashleigh. "Kidnapping is, after all, a hanging offense, even for a peer."

"No, never kidnapped anyone. Word of honor." What color there had been in Newell's face was fading rapidly. "Just meant to get my sister. That's all. Not kidnapping. Farnsworth said it wasn't kidnapping. Couldn't be kidnapping. Not when she's my sister."

"Unfortunately for you, it is most definitely kidnapping when the lady abducted is *my* sister." Ashleigh looked at him with contempt, then turned to the grooms. "Tie this one up as well. We will send a cart to transport them back to the house. Lock them in one of the cellars for the night."

"No," protested Newell loudly as the grooms tightened the ropes. "You can't do that. Just wanted my sister. Wouldn't kidnap anyone. Word of honor as a gentleman."

But no one was listening.

>>>><<<<

JEREMIAH JORREY, ATTORNEY at law, had, of course, made all speed to
travel to Kelswick the moment the duke requested his presence. One
does not delay when a duke calls, especially when that duke is
wealthy, powerful, and one's most important client.

Although the duke had been most gracious, addressing him cour-
teously and ordering his comfort seen to, Jorrey could not feel at ease.
He had been apprised of the situation, which was indeed shocking.
Quite shocking. Then there were the documents the duke had
requested him to draw up. To say they were unusual was the least of
it.

And he had always thought the duke such a pattern of propriety. A
bit high in the instep, but he was a duke.

Perhaps that was the explanation. The Duke of Ashleigh would not
be the first duke to consider himself above other mortals and so not
bound by the rules that restricted others. After all, what the duke
appeared to be planning was not dishonorable. No, no. One might
even call it generous. Still, it was, well, unusual. Jorrey did not like the
unusual.

He sighed and returned to the document he was drafting. It was
not particularly complicated, which was just as well. There were a few
law books here in His Grace's office—more probably this was His
Grace's steward's office—but Jorrey had not needed to consult them.
The matter may have been odd but it was really quite straight-
forward. All three matters were. Jorrey did not see why there had been
any urgency about it, but when a duke wanted something done
immediately, it was done immediately.

At the smaller desk in the office, Jorrey's clerk was industriously
making two fair copies of each document. Jorrey looked at him with
approval. The lad had been recommended by Lord Merton and he was
working out quite well. They should be finished with the documents

quite quickly.

>>>><<<<

IT WAS EARLY afternoon by the time a footman brought the message that Jorrey had completed his tasks. The entire party had been gathered on the terrace, trying to pretend they were actually interested in their books, needlework, or sketch pads, and they heaved a collective sigh of relief that the waiting was over.

They made an impressive parade as they walked to the library. Ashleigh and Bancroft looked perfectly polished, their coats and breeches fitting with nary a wrinkle, their boots sporting a mirror finish, and their linen so fine and bright it could have been taken for silk. Even Merton had managed to get through this much of the day without destroying his cravat or tossing aside his coat.

Kate may have been the smallest of the ladies, but she was not the least elegant. Her dress of peach muslin had a scalloped hem decorated with embroidered scrolls just short enough to allow a glimpse of matching slippers. Her hair had been carefully arranged by Lady Talmadge's maid into an elaborate bun, threaded with ribbons to match her gown, and small ringlets framed her face. As she walked beside Ashleigh, her hand on his arm, she felt like a queen. When he looked down at her and smiled, she felt like an empress.

Lady Talmadge, walking with Bancroft, was almost giddy with pride in her performance the night before. She kept telling herself that she was a sedate matron, a widow with a fifteen-year-old daughter. But when she saw the admiration in Bancroft's eyes, when she felt the warmth of his hand when he pressed it over hers, she knew herself to be the heroine of her own romantic adventure. And he was her hero.

Lord and Lady Merton, being less affected by the situation, were nonetheless eager spectators, looking forward to the next act in this drama. As expected, Miranda had refused to be left behind. The baby was not due for another five months, she pointed out, and frustration would do her no good at all. Anyone who expected her to miss out on the next act in this drama clearly did not know her very well. Few people knew her as well as her husband did, and Tom had asked only that she remain in the house with Kate while they rounded up the kidnappers.

Bringing up the rear was Franny Darling, perhaps the most subdued member of the party. As polished in appearance as the others, in a deep purple gown and matching turban, she was less certain of ultimate success in this matter. Then also, she was about to have her first glimpse of her nephew. She could remember Mary's sorrow when her son was removed from her care, the long letters she had written, the misery of them only relieved after Kate's birth gave her a new reason for existence. Could anything make up for the misery that had been inflicted on her sister, first by their father and then by Mary's husband? Perhaps it was well that Mary had not lived to see the perfidy of that son whose departure she had once mourned.

They arranged themselves in the library. Ashleigh was seated behind the broad mahogany desk, on which the only items were an inkwell, quill, and blotter. The others were seated in a row on either side of him, creating the effect of a judgment tribunal. Ashleigh nodded to a footman who left the room and, moments later, Newell was brought in.

He was no longer bound, but the footman at his side had more to do holding him up than trying to prevent his escape. Filthy and disheveled, Newell stumbled along until he finally stood before the duke. He looked from side to side, as if unable to comprehend what was happening. He could find no sympathy in any of the faces.

Franny's eyes widened in shock and she grasped Kate's hand. "This, this *creature* is your brother?" At her niece's short nod she opened her mouth but closed it, unable to think of anything to say.

Newell had finally recognized his sister. "Katherine? Katherine, you have to come with me. You must."

Kate looked at him coldly and said nothing.

"Katherine, you don't understand. You don't know what Farnsworth will do to me." He tried to step closer but the footman prevented him.

"I believe you are the one who does not understand, Newell," said Ashleigh. "Miss Russell is betrothed to me. Judging from the letter you sent her, I believe you saw the announcement."

"But she can't marry you." Sweat was making muddy tracks on his face. "Farnsworth... she is promised to Farnsworth." His voice squeaked with desperation.

"Really?" Ashleigh regarded him impassively. "There was talk of marriage, was there? Did Miss Russell receive a proposal? Did she accept one?"

Newell turned an unbecoming red, licked his lips and darted his eyes around the room. "My permission. She needs my permission to marry."

"I have the approval of her aunt," Ashleigh said as he gestured to Mrs. Darling, "a far more respectable guardian than you, you must allow."

Torn between horror and disgust, Franny burst out, "You appalling reprobate! I cannot believe my dear sister gave birth to such a one as you."

This time, Kate grasped her aunt's hand to offer comfort.

Ashleigh ignored the interruption and continued. "However, to make certain there are no unnecessary complications, my attorney has prepared a document, giving your permission for our marriage. You need only sign it." He nodded a signal to one of the footmen, who promptly withdrew.

Newell blanched and shook his head violently. "No, no I can't. You don't know Farnsworth. You don't know what he is capable of. You have no idea what he'll do to me if I don't give him my sister."

The duke smiled coldly. "Your worries about Farnsworth are misplaced. You seem to forget that you attempted to kidnap Lady Talmadge. My only reason for allowing you to escape the hangman's noose is the wish to spare my future wife the embarrassment of a scandal."

Newell's knees gave out and he collapsed on the floor, a quivering, moaning wreck.

Merton could not stand it any longer. With a look of revulsion on his face, he said, "For God's sake, Newell, pull yourself together. At least make an effort to pretend you are a man and stop sniveling."

"The fool doesn't even seem to realize that he is being offered a lifeline," said Bancroft.

"Enough!" said Ashleigh. "Now listen to me while I tell you what will happen." The footman had just ushered Jorrey and his clerk into the room, and the duke waved them to the desk. "You have the documents prepared?"

"Yes, Your Grace." The lawyer had taken one horrified look at the creature on the floor, stepped cautiously around him, and now kept his eyes carefully on the desk. He laid the papers, separated into three piles, before the duke.

Ashleigh nodded his approval. "Your clerk and Merton will witness the signatures." He turned back to Newell. "Now, this is what is going to happen. You are going to sign the document giving your agreement to your sister's marriage to me and this other one, turning guardianship of your sister over to your aunt, Mrs. Darling. After that, since we are going to be related by marriage, I will undertake to pay off your mortgages and any other nongambling debts."

Newell had looked up hopefully at that, but when the word "nongambling" reached his mind, his look of panic returned. "But Farnsworth..." The duke silenced him with a glare.

"It would be simpler and cheaper to let the creature hang," Bancroft broke in. He looked coldly implacable, with no hint of his usual kindness.

Ashleigh permitted himself a slight smile. "You must understand," he told Newell, "that Lady Talmadge is betrothed to Mr. Bancroft here, and he is not inclined to pardon your treatment of her last night."

Newell simply stared helplessly.

"As I was saying, I will pay your nongambling debts. You will not need to worry about Farnsworth because you and your colleagues from last night will be on your way to the West Indies. I have arranged passage for you on one of my friend Merton's ships." Merton smiled.

Newell seemed about to speak, but Ashleigh ignored him. "I believe you are something of a gambler. Well, when you arrive in Kingston, you will present a letter I have prepared to my agent there. He will give you one hundred pounds, which should enable you to live for a year. I will wager that you don't survive that year. If you do, on the anniversary of your arrival, you will apply to my agent for another hundred pounds. We will repeat this arrangement every year, and you will, under no circumstances, attempt to return to England."

At this, Newell simply looked horrified. "But, but you can't do that to me."

"I assure you that I can. And to make certain that you do not attempt to return, you will sign a confession of your attempt to kidnap Lady Talmadge."

"But I didn't. I never tried to kidnap her. I only wanted my sister."

"Do you seriously think I would permit you to humiliate your sister by having you publicly confess what you intended to do to her?"

"But I'm a viscount," Newell blustered. "I have property, an estate. What will become of that?"

"Ah, yes, I was coming to that. You will turn the management of your estate over to your aunt and your sister. After all, you have never actually managed it yourself so that will mean little change. Any income from it shall be theirs to do with as they please." Ashleigh smiled briefly at the lawyer, who was pursing his lips in disapproval.

"Jorrey here shares your disquiet at leaving the management of an estate to two women, but I have assured him that I will be glad to give them my best advice should they need it."

The smile faded as Ashleigh turned back to Newell. A black cap on his head might have been appropriate. "Well, what will it be? The West Indies or the hangman?"

Newell gnawed at his lower lip. "What about Farnsworth? When he finds out…"

"You will be well out to sea before Farnsworth knows anything."

Newell's resigned nod was enough. Jorrey held out a quill, and the defeated viscount stepped up to sign.

⫸⫷

KATE WATCHED THE others leave the library, chatting triumphantly, until the door closed and she was left alone with Ashleigh. "I can't quite take it in." She shook her head slowly. "My brother, Farnsworth… you made it all just disappear. You actually did." She sketched a wave with her hand and looked at him with something like awe.

"I told you I could." His smile was slightly smug, and she had to think the smugness had some justification. But then the smile faded and he came to stand before her, not quite touching. His voice was low, thick with emotion. "You are safe now, you know. You can choose freely, without fear. What will it be, Kate? Will you marry me?" All the ducal arrogance had dropped away.

She wanted to smile, but could not. She lifted her eyes to his and wanted to believe what she saw there. When she lifted her hand to caress his cheek, he grasped it, and turned to press a kiss in her palm.

"Is it really true? I will not bring you any harm?"

"Only if you refuse me. Only then." He held her hand tightly.

"Oh, Peter, I want so much to be your wife. I can't believe it's really possible." She was smiling now, and laughter began to bubble up. "I love you so."

"Kate!" He pulled her against him and held her so tightly she thought she would have the weave of his coat imprinted on her cheek. "Kate." He loosened his grip slowly. "Come for a walk with me, Kate."

She went along with him and they walked for a long while in silence, a happy, companionable silence, she thought. Then she realized that they were nearing the summer house, and her steps slowed. There was no rain this time, but the surrounding trees kept it in deep shadow.

"I know," he said, his mouth twisting, "this place does not hold the happiest of memories for you. But I have something I must tell you, and I think that this is the place for it."

She let him lead her in, but her steps were not eager. Nor were his.

"Merton said to me one day that he and his wife tell each other things. That is one of the things being married means to them." He looked at her. "That is the kind of marriage I want. No secrets, no hiding. I want truth and honesty between us."

"Do you think I am hiding something? I assure you, Your Grace, you have all my secrets now."

He smiled briefly. "Well, I will never have any difficulty in knowing when you are angry with me. You will call me 'Your Grace'. But that is not what I meant. I have to tell you something, something of which I am bitterly ashamed."

"Peter, if you are talking about that day here, we both misunderstood. I am also at fault for thinking things were true because I wanted them to be true. I lied to myself. You did not lie to me."

"At least your lies to yourself painted me as a nobler character than I was. My lies to myself were more selfish."

She laughed at that. "You, selfish? My brother is selfish. And I think I may be selfish in wanting to marry you. But you?"

"Yes, me. You don't know the tales I spun to convince myself that making you my mistress would not be dishonorable, that it would be to your benefit." He reached out and ran his fingers along her cheek. "I wanted you. I wanted you from the moment I first saw you in your aunt's house, when you were so annoyed that I mistook you for a servant. And every time I saw you, I wanted you more. Everything about you fascinated me. It didn't help that I told myself that I couldn't have you, that you were the Darlings' niece. I wanted you in a hundred different ways."

She smiled at him. "Is that a confession? I felt the same way, longing for you, and knowing that I could not have you. Why is that so dreadful?"

"It isn't. Your mistake was thinking me a better man than I am. The problem is the lies I told myself to justify having you, to let me try to make you my mistress." He watched her face, but could see nothing more than curiosity in it. "Clara let slip that you were Franny's niece, not Andrew's, so your name was not really Darling. That, with the things you had said about your father's lack of care made me think you were illegitimate."

"Ah." She smiled slightly. "Well, I can see where that would be an explanation."

He had to continue. "And when I saw the necklace—it was so valuable, and went so ill with your poverty when you arrived— Stephen said it represented mistakes to you, and Franny said the past should be forgotten. I thought some scoundrel had seduced you and given you the necklace as payment."

There was no smile on her face now. "I assure you, if any man had offered me payment for my favors, I would have thrown it in his face. Her father sent those pearls to my mother after my father died. They were her mother's jewels. It was the first time he had ever done anything to help her, to help us, and it was too late. She was already ill, already dying. I did not feel kindly toward him." She looked at him. "That was all it took to make you think so ill of me? You could have asked me, you know."

He nodded. "So you see, I am sadly lacking in honor."

The silence stretched out, until she smiled. "But then, if none of this had happened, this encounter here, you would not have come riding up the road and rescued me when Farnsworth tried to carry me off." He turned away with a dismissive gesture. "No," she insisted, "you did rescue me. I don't want to think what would have happened had you not arrived just then. And since then, everything you have done since then—you have been my knight in shining armor."

He shook his head helplessly at her, and could not keep a smile from appearing as he spread his arms open. "Kate, my dearest Kate, you unman me. You turn my failings into virtues. How will I ever manage to live up to your picture of me?"

"No need to worry about that. I will find ways to puncture your self-esteem whenever I see you growing too arrogant." She came into his arms and pulled his head down for a kiss.

Sometime later, he lifted his head and rested his cheek on her head. "There is one more apology I must make. That day, the way I took you—I hurt you. I should never have been so rough. I gave you no pleasure, nothing but pain."

The silence stretched out as she remained in his arms, leaning against him. At length, she said, "Do you mean it isn't always like that? It doesn't always hurt?"

"God, no!" She was going to give him a chance? There was hope? He was pressing kisses on her hair, on her face. "Let me show you. Let me show you what it should have been like. What it can be like."

First came fear, but then she felt the longing rise in her, that strange longing she could not name, the longing that had kept her awake so many nights. While he waited patiently for her answer, the fear was replaced by trust. She lifted her arms to go around his neck. "Show me," she said, and turned her face to meet his kiss.

He picked her up and carried her into the summer house. It had been transformed. There was a feather mattress on the bed and fine linen sheets. A soft rug covered the floor and curtains at the windows filtered the dim light. On the table was a vase of roses, perfuming the air. He enjoyed her surprise.

"You planned this?" She was not sure if she should feel flattered or offended that he had been so certain of her.

"No, not planned. I dared not do anything but hope."

He went slowly, this time. Each lace he unfastened, each ribbon he untied was accompanied by a kiss. Each inch of skin that he uncovered received a caress. She tingled all over with pleasure and growing anticipation. Unable to wait, she pushed his coat and waistcoat from his shoulders, untied his cravat, pulled up his shirt to enable her to touch his skin. She laughed when his nipples hardened under her caress just as hers did under his and he groaned at her touch.

By the time he laid her on the bed, every part of her seemed to come alive with longing. He touched her in her most private place and she could not breathe. When he slid into her, this time, there was no pain, only a sense of rightness, that this was what she had been waiting for. This time, her gasps were gasps of delight, her cry a cry of pure ecstasy.

Afterwards, when he lay beside her, cradling her in his arms, there was no smugness in his smile, only joy.

# CHAPTER TWENTY

NEWELL HAD BEEN too engrossed in his own woes to mention it, or perhaps it would have slipped his mind under any circumstances, but there had been another man at the barn: the coachman.

Now the coachman was not a particularly brave man, nor was he a particularly foolish one. When he heard the commotion in the barn and saw, through a crack of the door, that his companions were significantly outnumbered, he saw no point in remaining. He might have been able to ride off on one of the horses, but he was a coachman, not a horseman. Besides, he did not choose to risk being heard. He simply disappeared into the woods.

It is a long walk from Lewes to London, the coachman discovered, made even longer by his efforts to keep out of sight. When he finally reached the city some days later, he wanted nothing more than a large quantity of ale, a decent meal, and a bed. These were all to be found in a tavern he knew but, the next morning, as he breakfasted on bread and ale, he considered his next step.

He was not overburdened with funds at the moment, since his preliminary payment in this affair had been only enough to cover the hire of the coach. Although he was not privy to the precise details of the enterprise, he had heard enough to know that the Earl of Farnsworth was involved. He did not, of course, know the earl. Coachmen and earls do not travel in the same circles. However, he had heard of the earl, and the circles in which he had heard the name spoken suggested that the earl was not precisely a model of probity.

The earl would want to know about the debacle that had occurred, and would doubtless be willing to pay for the information. And to pay to keep his involvement secret.

A few discreet questions provided him with the earl's direction and he eventually made his way to the appropriate square. It was, he was pleased to note, a thoroughly respectable-looking residence, in excellent repair, with gleaming paintwork on the front door. Not that he intended to go to the front door. Even if he could win entrance that way, he would not attempt it. He had no wish to advertise his business to anyone who chanced to pass.

No. He went around to the alley in the back, through the gate and then to the kitchen door. The surly fellow who answered the door refused to let him in but, grudgingly, took a message, offering information about recent events concerning a lady in Lewes.

The coachman was not offended. No one of sense allowed strangers into the house. He was willing to wait, thinking it likely that his message would win him admittance once the earl had heard it.

In this, he was quite correct. He was taken to the library, where the earl awaited him with barely restrained eagerness.

"Well? Well?" barked the earl. His eyes glittered, and he was tapping a rapid tattoo on the ground with a walking stick. "Where is she?"

The coachman realized he might have made a mistake. The earl was obviously expecting good news—at least, what would be good news for him. He might not welcome bad news.

The coachman licked his lips. There was no avoiding it, now that he was here. "It was a trap. They were expecting us. I'm the only one that got away."

There was a moment of stillness. The coachman did not dare breathe. Then a red tide of fury rose in the earl's face and a torrent of imprecations spewed from his mouth. He raised the stick and staggered toward the coachman. "Fools! Incompetents!"

Each word was accompanied by a swing of the stick, and the coachman barely managed to dodge enough to stay on his feet and get out the door. He fled back down to the kitchen, where the servants stood like statues, watching the door fearfully. He gave them barely a glance as he raced out.

The upstairs servants also made themselves scarce while the shouts reverberated in the hall and the earl's stick wreaked havoc on assorted ornaments. Eventually, silence returned and so did the footmen usually posted in the hall. When the bell rang, the footman whose turn it was first jumped nervously, then steeled himself and entered the library.

The floor was littered with shards of china and glass but Farnsworth sat at the desk writing a letter as calmly as if nothing had happened. He folded and sealed it, and it was only when he lifted his head that the footman saw the tic twitching in his cheek. "Find Hall and give this to him." The order was barked out and the earl turned away, as if the footman had already vanished on his errand.

There was no direction on the letter, which was hardly surprising, since no one knew where Hall lived. However, the footman knew—all the footmen knew—that one could leave messages in a number of places. When Hall was willing to meet, a message would be returned.

Sometimes, that took a matter of hours. In this case, it took close to a week. At the tavern where the meeting was to take place, the footman thought, at first, that Hall had not yet arrived. He bought a pint at the bar before he spotted his quarry at a table by the wall, his dingy brown clothing making him almost invisible against the dingy brown woodwork.

The letter was handed over without conversation. Hall opened it and read it. He looked startled, the first time the footman had known Hall to show any reaction to anything.

"Do you know what this says?" Hall asked. When the footman

shook his head, Hall gave a tight smile. "Just as well." He tucked the letter in his coat and got up to leave. Before he departed, he stopped and looked back at the footman. "A word of advice. You might want to look for a new position."

*Sussex*

IT HAD BEEN a glorious day. Ashleigh had been out with the builders and the master brewer, examining the site for the new brewery and checking over the plans. If all went well, this year's crop of hops would be used right here at Kelswick, and there would be jobs for all who wanted to stay. When he got home, Kate would be there. She was beginning to feel comfortable at Kelswick, and in twelve days, she would be his wife. If he got back early enough, perhaps they could walk down to the summer house.

A horseman was waiting at the bend of the lane ahead. He was a stranger but looked innocuous enough in his brown, nondescript clothes, neither rich nor poor. He held up a hand, as if asking for a word, so Ashleigh pulled up his horse.

"I wondered if I might have a word, Your Grace." He sounded not quite like a gentleman, but respectable enough.

Ashleigh nodded. "What can I do for you, Mister…?"

He shook his head. "I'm afraid my name would mean nothing to you, but you may call me Brown if you like. I think I may be in a position to do something for you."

Ashleigh said nothing and waited.

Mr. Brown nodded approvingly. "It never does to rush into things, does it? Well, I am what you might call a fixer. People come to me with a problem, and I try to take care of it for them."

"And do you think I have a problem?" Ashleigh sounded vaguely amused.

"No, you misunderstand me. I was not offering you my services, precisely, though we have come into contact before in what you might call a tangential fashion." Mr. Brown spoke softly. "For example, one of my tasks might have been to find a young lady who had run away from home and return her to her family."

Any trace of humor vanished from Ashleigh's face, and he swung around on his horse toward Brown.

Brown held up a hand to ward him off. "Now, finding a young lady that way is a perfectly decent thing to do, one might say, though I won't deny that, on occasion, things turn out to be a bit more complicated than I was told at the beginning. One of the hazards of my profession, you might say. People are not always quite honest." He paused to let Ashleigh pull his horse back a few paces. "But there are things I do not do, not for any amount of money, and I find I consider myself insulted when someone thinks I would do such a thing."

He reached into his coat and pulled out a letter, which he handed to Ashleigh. "You ought, I believe, to read this."

Ashleigh darted a suspicious look at him but took the letter. His eyes widened as he read it. "This is preposterous." He glared at Brown, who shrugged. "This letter is addressed to someone by the name of Hall. Is that you?"

"I have sometimes been called by that name."

Ashleigh continued to glare. "And Farnsworth wants you to kill me?"

Brown shrugged again. "He is a man who is accustomed to his own way."

"But, but this is insane. He must be out of his mind."

Another shrug. "The thought has occurred to me," said Brown.

Ashleigh's outrage slowly faded as he considered that last remark. "Do you mean that seriously?" he said at last.

Brown sighed. "I am not a medical man, of course, but I have wondered. He has the pox, you know, and it affects some that way."

"Good God." Ashleigh's mouth twisted in disgust. "Yet you would have handed Miss Russell over to him."

A shadow of what could have been bitterness passed over Brown's face. "It is not for the likes of me to pass judgment on the behavior of my betters, now, is it?"

"Then why have you brought me this letter? I will reward you, of course. Is that what you want?"

Brown shook his head. "Not precisely. I am thinking of it more as a sort of insurance. This affair could have ramifications, unpleasant ramifications. When that happens, and noblemen are involved, people like me often end up being punished for things that were none of our doing. I would like to think that an honorable gentleman like yourself would prevent such an injustice."

"In other words, if you seem headed for the hangman's noose, you would like me to come to the rescue."

"Something of the sort." Brown nodded diffidently. "Though I hope it will never come to that."

"I do not even know your real name."

Brown smiled. "And I would prefer that neither you nor the authorities ever have any reason to know it."

Ashleigh nodded stiffly. "Very well. I am in your debt. You may call on me should you ever have need of my assistance. You have my word on it."

"Thank you, Your Grace." Brown turned to go, but then turned back. "By the by, you might want to tell Mrs. Darling that her brother would be pleased to hear from her." Ashleigh's look of surprise won another shrug. "Now that their father is dead." With that, he kicked his horse into motion and rode off.

Ashleigh looked after him, thinking that for a Londoner, the fellow looked quite comfortable on a horse. But then, perhaps he wasn't really a Londoner. He was taking the road that led to the West Country.

THAT EVENING, OVER the port after dinner, Ashleigh told Bancroft about his encounter with "Mr. Brown" and showed him the letter. "It's a bit awkward. I'd like to tell Franny about her brother, but then I would have to explain about Brown, and I don't want Kate to be frightened, or Alice either. It will be difficult enough to come up with a reason for going to London at this time." He fiddled with his glass, staring into the wine as if it held answers, but showed no inclination to drink it.

Bancroft looked up from the letter in surprise. "You're planning to keep this from them? Don't be a fool." When Ashleigh looked startled, he went on, "Have you learned nothing? Those ladies do not want to be wrapped up in ignorance. They have more than enough courage and intelligence to deal with this new threat."

"I am not denying their intelligence, but I can protect them. I will deal with the threat."

"Will you? Then think on this. If they do not know there is danger, they will not be on their guard. Were you planning to lock them in their rooms until you deal with Farnsworth?"

Ashleigh raked his fingers through his hair. "I would like to do precisely that. Damnation. Kate is only now beginning to relax, to believe she is safe. And now this. Who would have thought Farnsworth would begin acting like a madman? He says I have been impertinent and must be removed. Insane." He glared at Bancroft. "It is all very well for you. The threat is not against Alice, and you do not have to tell her that your promise was meaningless."

"Is that what troubles you? That you promised more than you can deliver?" Bancroft leaned back in his chair and laughed. "Do you really think Kate will blame you for this?"

"She should. I blame myself." Ashleigh pushed away from the table and began pacing. "I should have taken the threat from Farnsworth more seriously. I should not have expected him to behave rationally. After that attempt to snatch her up in broad daylight, and the fire—I should have seen the danger, the signs of madness. She tried to tell me what he is like. I should have listened to her."

"Peter," Bancroft began gently, but the duke ignored him and continued pacing. Bancroft stood and caught Ashleigh by the arm. "Peter, you did listen to her. That's why you persuaded her and Franny to stay on here instead of going back to Franny's home. Not everything is your fault, and not everything is your sole responsibility. I know you want to protect Kate from Farnsworth and his threats, but that does not mean you must refuse all assistance. I would take it amiss if you were to keep me out of this, and I do not doubt that Merton will feel the same way."

Ashleigh halted and considered. A rueful smile broke through the worry on his face. "To say nothing of Alice. She used to bully me mercilessly when we were children, you know. You must beware. Now that she has recovered from Talmadge, she is returning to her old ways."

Bancroft smiled contentedly. "She only bullied you because you were too stubborn to acknowledge when she was right. And now, I believe, it is time for us to join the ladies."

The room that served as the family sitting room had long windows opening on to the terrace and the garden beyond. These were open, letting in the fresh evening breeze. To the surprise of all, himself included, Ashleigh closed them and drew the curtains before sitting down next to Kate. His sister looked at him, handed him his tea, and suggested to Clara that since she was so tired, she really ought to go to bed.

Clara opened her mouth to protest, but was silenced by a look from her mother. She turned to Bancroft, but there was no help there. So she excused herself with exquisite politeness and went off, radiating resentment as only a fifteen-year-old girl can.

The remaining ladies watched her leave, then turned the weight of their curiosity on Ashleigh, who put down his teacup with a sigh and told his tale.

"I'm sorry, Kate," he concluded. "I truly thought it was over. It never occurred to me that Farnsworth might still be a threat."

She shrugged and answered calmly. "I can't claim to be surprised. No matter how hard I tried, I couldn't make myself believe that he would simply give up. He is a man who cannot believe that anyone would dare oppose him."

"Such wickedness! I can scarce believe it." Franny, the mother hen, looked around furiously. "This cannot be permitted. He must be stopped."

"Indeed, Ma'am," said Bancroft gently. "You may be assured that we will stop him."

"Indeed, we will," said Lady Talmadge. "Have you gentlemen made any plans as yet?"

Ashleigh, who had been watching Kate carefully and seeing more anger than distress, turned to his sister. "I thought to go to London. It will be easier to confront him there. But," he hesitated, "but I would like all of us to go. I do not care to leave you unprotected, where you might be vulnerable to attack."

"You think we would be unsafe if we stayed here at Kelswick?" Kate almost laughed at the thought, but Ashley shook his head.

"You would be safe enough, perhaps, if you never stepped outside the door," he said, "but I fear you might find such restriction irritating."

Bancroft added, "No sensible man would attempt anything here, but he is not sensible. Proposing the murder of a duke? The man is not entirely rational."

Lady Talmadge leaned back and thought. "No, he does not seem quite rational. In fact, he seems quite mad." She looked at her brother. "Do you know any of his family? Who is his heir?"

Ashleigh snorted. "Do you seriously think that he is likely to listen to the remonstrances of his aunts and cousins?"

"No," she snapped. "I think that his family, and particularly his heir, will have an interest in seeing that he does not run amok, bringing shame on their name and, quite possibly, destroying his estate. They might prefer to have him quietly restrained someplace where he can do no harm."

The others looked at her with something approaching awe.

"Bedlam, you mean?" said Kate. Her eyes narrowed in speculation.

Lady Talmadge shrugged. "His family is more likely to find a private asylum for him. But yes, that is essentially what I mean." She smiled at Kate.

"Good God." Ashleigh looked stunned.

His sister turned to him with a frown. "Would that not serve?"

"It would. Indeed, it would. I had just not expected... I had not thought you to be quite so ferocious."

"Be warned, Your Grace," said Franny. "When those we love are threatened, we women are not only ferocious but do not feel ourselves bound by any of your codes of gentlemanly behavior. We will use any weapons that come to hand."

Ashleigh looked to Bancroft for help, but that gentleman was gazing carefully at the Romney portrait of the previous duke and showed no inclination to offer an opinion. Ashleigh cleared his throat. "Yes. Well. Yes." He cleared his throat again. "I will write to Jorrey and tell him to see what he can discover."

# CHAPTER TWENTY-ONE

*London*

A SHLEIGH HOUSE WAS probably what she should have expected after Kelswick, but it was so unlike her brother's house that Kate had all she could do to keep from staring.

It was, of course, perfect in every detail. The sheer size of the building had almost overwhelmed her when the carriage drew up before it—four stories of pale stone taking up an entire side of Portland Square. Then came the hall, with its rose and white marble floor and, high above, a glass cupola. Everything gleamed and glowed with polish. The servants somehow managed to seem invisible, yet they were instantly there to whisk away bonnets and shawls, to open doors, to provide tea.

The housekeeper had escorted her to her rooms—rooms! Not simply a bedchamber, but also a sitting room, a dressing room in which a maid was unpacking her clothes and putting everything away, and even a bathing room with piped water coming from gilded faucets shaped like fish. The rooms looked over the garden, where some late roses were blooming, and a pleasant breeze carried their scent into the room.

She stood in the center of the sitting room and turned around slowly. It was a room that would look like sunshine on the gloomiest days with its pale yellow walls picked out in cream. The windows were draped in a silky fabric of blue and yellow, and the same colors appeared in the coverings of the chairs and settee. A small work table stood between the windows, its top a bouquet of marquetry flowers. It was quite beautiful.

Perhaps if she were taller, she would not feel such a bumpkin amidst all this perfection. Or perhaps, it would make no difference.

She felt him there in the room, behind her, before she heard him. She always knew when he was there. Had this been true from that first day when she opened the door to him or had it developed slowly? That also made no difference. She turned, smiled, and went into his arms.

He held her, nothing more, and she leaned against him, absorbing the strength and safety of him.

Eventually, he spoke. "It will be all right, Kate. All will be well."

ASHLEIGH SAT MOTIONLESS in the carriage. Not a crease marred the perfection of his blue superfine coat, his pale yellow brocaded waistcoat, his biscuit knit trousers. His black Hessians were polished to a mirror gleam. The whiteness of his linen defied the sooty air of London, and the intricate folds of his cravat defied the city's damp atmosphere. A tall beaver sat at precisely the right angle on his head, neither too stolid nor too jaunty. His hands, encased in a second skin of pale yellow kid, rested on the silver handle of his ebony walking stick.

Across from him sat Merton and Bancroft, nearly his equals in sartorial splendor. Bancroft had rejected his usual unobtrusiveness for a waistcoat in swirls of purple and green, and Merton had managed to refrain from destroying the perfection of his cravat or disheveling his hair. He could not, however, match the immobility of Ashleigh's countenance.

"I still say this is a bad idea," he muttered as the ducal equipage pulled up in front of Farnsworth's residence. "What the devil do you expect to accomplish?"

The men had all descended before Ashleigh replied. "If this were a duel, he would be given an opportunity to apologize. As it is, once he realizes that he is known, that he is opposed, he may withdraw." Merton snorted at that, and Ashleigh smiled faintly. "Also, I wish to see him, to judge for myself."

Bancroft shook his head. "We will do it your way. I expect you will have to see for yourself. Just do not be too foolish. A man who hires assassins is not deserving of chivalry."

Ashleigh nodded and led the way up the steps. The door was opened promptly and they entered, placing their cards on the servant's tray. "We would speak with the earl," he said and strolled in, looking casually about the hall.

Minutes later, they were ushered into a library where a man of middle years stood leaning on a cane. His complexion was mottled and his eyes glittered in an unhealthy way.

"You're Ashleigh?" he demanded. At the duke's nod, he barked out, "Well, I see you have come to your senses. Have you brought her? Where is she?"

Taken aback, Ashleigh stared coldly at the man. "You are Farnsworth?"

"Of course I am. What do you think? You are in my home, are you not?"

Ashleigh acknowledged that with a slight nod.

Farnsworth snorted. "Do not play games with me. Katherine is mine. I want the little bitch brought to me immediately." He thumped his cane on the floor.

"You dare to speak of her that way!" Ashleigh sucked in an angry gasp and started for the man, but Bancroft put out a hand. He managed to compose himself before he spoke again. "You do not seem to be aware that Miss Russell and I are betrothed."

He could get no further before Farnsworth broke in, stumbling forward. "No, she is mine! I have her brother's word. I want her. I will have her!" His voice rose furiously.

Ashleigh glanced at his companions. "This is useless." He turned back to the earl. "I have come to give you fair warning. You must put an end to this insane pursuit of Miss Russell. If you do not do so of your own accord, I will be forced to take action of my own. Is that perfectly clear?"

Farnsworth's eyes grew round with anger. "You dare... you dare to threaten me? Do you know who I am? I am Farnsworth!" Spittle frothed at the corners of his mouth. He swung the cane at them though they were well beyond his reach. "No one defies me. I am Farnsworth!"

This time, it was Merton who made to move toward him, and Ashleigh who held him back. They withdrew and left the building, followed by shouts of "I am Farnsworth. No one defies me."

Once back in the carriage, Ashleigh leaned his head back on the squabs and closed his eyes. They were nearly home before he spoke. "My God, that creature could have gotten his hands on Kate. The thought that he might even touch her... and her brother would have let him..."

"Pity Newell's already at sea," said Bancroft. "I wouldn't mind having a further chat with him."

"You would have to wait your turn," said Merton. "But this did clear up one thing. He's definitely got the pox." When his companions looked at him curiously, he gave a sour grin. "Did you see his nose?"

"It looked damaged," said Bancroft, "as if something had struck him."

Merton shook his head. "It's rotting away. He's better dressed than the poxy madmen you see in ports around the Mediterranean or in the

Indies but, other than that, I saw his like too often when I was in the navy."

Ashleigh felt ill.

KATE AND ALICE were waiting nervously at the door when the gentlemen returned. Ashleigh shook his head, but not even that gesture had been needed. The very fact that they wore masks of impassivity was enough to announce that they had no good news to tell.

In the library, Ashleigh picked up some papers and promptly threw then back down. "The man's as mad as a hatter, but according to Jorrey, he has no near relations. Hell, there isn't even an heir as far as anyone knows. And if I challenge him, I will have to kill him in order to stop him. There's nothing else for it. I will have to go to the authorities and have him taken in charge."

"No!" Kate spoke sharply, then repeated more softly, "No. He would fight it, you know he would. The scandal would be enormous. The papers and the caricaturists would have a field day. Your name, your reputation would be destroyed simply because of your connection with me. I cannot allow that."

"Good God, Kate, do you think I can risk leaving that madman at large? He's shown himself willing to use kidnapping, arson and murder to get his hands on you. Do you expect me to stand aside until he succeeds?"

"I will not embroil you in a scandal of this magnitude."

"And I will not allow you to put yourself at risk."

They glared at each other.

"Do stop playing at heroics, you two, and let me think." Lady Talmadge settled herself in a chair and tapped her finger thoughtfully on her cheek. "Not a large party. A small dinner, I think. Yes, a small, select company. That would be best."

"Alice, what on earth are you talking about? We are trying to protect Kate, not launch her into society."

Bancroft put a calming hand on Ashleigh's shoulder. "Let your sister think. She does it quite well."

She shot him a quick glance of appreciation and said, "It would be infinitely better for us to have this handled quietly, but it would also be better for certain others. Consider the case of Earl Ferrars."

Ashleigh frowned. "Ferrars? But that was more than half a century ago."

"Yes," she nodded, "but people still remember it."

"Didn't he murder someone?" asked Kate.

"Yes, his steward, and he was hanged for it," Bancroft said. "A triumph of justice, one might say."

"They may say that in the House of Lords," Merton said. "In taverns, they are more apt to say that a peer has to be found standing over the body with a bloody dagger in his hand before anyone will do anything to stop him."

Lady Talmadge nodded in agreement. "There were complaints that this was far from his first violent crime. They said he would have been brought to justice far sooner had he not been a peer. The case is still brought up from time to time in the radical papers."

"You read the radical papers?" Ashleigh looked at his sister in consternation. "No. Wait." He put up a hand and shook his head to clear it. "What has this to do with dinner parties?"

Lady Talmadge smiled tolerantly at her brother. "With all the recent unrest, the government is worried about riots and rebellion. Sidmouth has been particularly assiduous in uncovering plots and sedition."

"I fail to see what Home Secretary Sidmouth has to do with my affairs." Ashleigh was sounding ducal again.

"He will not be at all pleased to learn that a peer has been running about, committing crimes right and left, considering himself untouchable because of his position. Attempting to kidnap an innocent girl. Torching the home of a respectable widow. Seeking to hire an assassin. Making such behavior—such *unpunished*—behavior public could easily set off a wave of rioting that could have unforeseeable consequences. It could be 1789 all over again."

Her brother looked at her in horror. "You can't be serious."

She sighed regretfully. "No, I'm not. However, I have listened to Sidmouth rant about his conspiracies often enough. It is precisely the sort of scenario he will have no difficulty believing. We will invite him to dinner and fawn over him. Then you will confide in him over port and express your concerns about this madman and the effect on the public when his crimes become known." She paused to think. "We should invite someone else as well. Not the prime minister. Liverpool may rely on Sidmouth, but he prefers to not know about unpleasant details. Eldon, I think. As lord chancellor, he has the power to convene a panel to examine Farnsworth and have him committed without any of it being made public."

The others stared at her in silence until Bancroft shook his head in bemusement. "Did your husband have any notion of what Byzantine plotting was going on in that head of yours?"

"Of course not. I was simply there to arrange the dinners and routs and be attractive and charming to the guests. No one ever desired me to voice an opinion or give advice, so I never did. But I watched. And I listened." She allowed herself a small smile of satisfaction.

Ashleigh was still staring at his sister, but the shock had given way to calculation. "You know, that might work. That might actually work."

Kate remained confused. "I am afraid I do not understand at all. These are powerful men you are talking about. Why would they even be interested, no less willing to help me?"

"They would not be helping you, Kate," said Bancroft. "They

would be furthering their own interests and, in the process, they would be doing a favor for a duke, trusting that he will remember and be grateful enough to cooperate with them in the future."

"A somewhat cynical assessment, but nonetheless accurate," said Ashleigh.

Kate frowned and swung around to look at him. "Does this mean you will be in their debt? Is that wise?"

He shrugged. "Not so deep in their debt that I would ever feel obliged to do anything I would not do otherwise. Remember, Farnsworth is a problem for them as well, though they do not yet realize it. With all the unrest disturbing the country, a mad peer who commits crimes but whose rank makes him immune to punishment could be the spark to set off a conflagration."

Bancroft's laugh rumbled out. "Don't worry, Kate. I have known Peter practically all his life, and I have never yet known him to do something he did not wish to do."

"Three days hence—no, four," said Lady Talmadge thoughtfully. "That will give Cook a bit more time to prepare. Come along, Kate. You are about to receive a lesson in planning a dinner party."

IT WAS A comparatively small dinner, with only ten at table. Nonetheless, Lady Talmadge had seen to it that all the most elaborate silver dishes were on display, including the Cellini salt cellar acquired by the fourth duke when he visited Rome on his Grand Tour. The huge silver gilt tureen on the sideboard had been a gift from King Charles II to an earlier duchess, though this was not, of course, mentioned unless someone happened to inquire.

Twenty bewigged footmen, in the austere Ashleigh livery of black and silver, stood motionless against the walls, stepping forward to serve the ten diners only when given an almost imperceptible signal by the butler.

Ashleigh himself looked far more regal than poor mad George ever had or than the regent could ever hope to. In breeches, as befitted a conservative peer, a black coat, as prescribed earlier by Beau Brummell, and a brocaded waistcoat, his perfect tailoring displayed a masculine figure that needed neither padding nor corseting. Bancroft was similarly attired, though his coat was not quite so snug and his waistcoat showed a pale yellow stripe.

The austerity of the gentlemen's attire served as a foil for the exuberance of the ladies' gowns. Franny was the most sedate in lavender silk trimmed with lace and a matching turban, with a modest set of amethysts around her neck. Lady Talmadge's blue satin was overlaid with a skirt of silver net, and the intricate braids and ringlets of her hair sported a diamond pin holding in place a plume of three blue feathers. Her necklace and bracelet of sapphires and diamonds drew a gasp of admiration from Lady Eldon when she arrived. Kate was a picture of innocence in fine white muslin with intricate white embroidery on the tiny sleeves and bodice and around the hem. The only touch of color was the green sash, just the color of the leaves on the white roses in her hair.

Cook, who had often been frustrated by the duke's indifference to elaborate entertainments, was determined to show what he could do. The meal began with a choice of fresh pea soup with tiny croutons or a clear bouillon garnished with minced herbs, followed by a fish course featuring sea bass in a champagne sauce or turbot in a cream sauce. Then there were vol-au-vents stuffed with lobster or a forcemeat of chicken, braised ducklings, a chaudfroid of game, a roast sirloin of beef with mustard sauce, pies of herbs and greens, oranges stuffed with ices, meringues and syllabubs, all accompanied by fine wines.

The dinner was a triumph. Sidmouth basked in the honor done him by so elaborate a meal for so small a company, and felt pleasantly flattered by the admiration of Mrs. Darling and her niece. An occasional smile lightened his heavy countenance as he responded to their chatter.

Lord Eldon was pleased as well, most especially by the welcome given to his wife, his beloved Bessie. As the daughter of a banker, she had not always been accorded a warm welcome in the *ton*. Here, however, not only had Lady Talmadge greeted her as an old and valued friend but the duke paid her particular attention, and Lord Merton's light teasing had the elderly lady blushing happily.

By the time the ladies withdrew, the guests were in a comfortably mellow mood, and Ashleigh nodded to dismiss the servants.

Sidmouth cast a sardonic glance at his host. Now was doubtless the time when he would discover the reason for all this attention. He lifted his glass and admired the glow of the port in the candlelight before speaking. "Pleasant girl, your betrothed. I don't believe I have seen her in town before." He looked questioningly at Ashleigh.

"No, Miss Russell lived always in Yorkshire and came to stay with her aunt in Lewes only after her mother's death."

"Ah. There's a great attraction in modest country manners." Sidmouth gave a knowing smile. He remembered the former duke and duchess, whose escapades had frequently exploded on the public scene. "And I don't suppose you are in need of a great dowry."

Eldon looked a trifle uncomfortable at such plain speaking, but Ashleigh managed a small smile.

"Right." Sidmouth drained his glass and refilled it. He disliked waiting. "Well then, what is all this in aid of? The dinner has been excellent, and the ladies charming, but I cannot believe you invited us only for the pleasure of our company. What favor is it that you are asking? A place for an indigent relative? A bill of enclosure?"

Ashleigh fingered his glass and spoke slowly. "It is a bit awkward. I do not know quite what should be done, and I am hoping that you gentlemen, positioned as you are, might be able to advise me."

Eldon's white brows came together in a frown. "If this is a legal matter…"

Sidmouth scowled, his mind leaping as always to his major preoccupation. "Treason? Have you uncovered some sort of plot?" He turned his glare on Bancroft and Merton.

"No, nothing of that sort. At least not precisely. My friends here are familiar with the situation, which is why I wished them to be present." Ashleigh looked from Sidmouth to Eldon and back again. "Do you, my lords, by any chance know the Earl of Farnsworth?"

"Know him? I would not say that, precisely." A shadow of distaste crossed Eldon's face. He tended to the puritanical. "I know something of him. However, he has never taken any great interest in affairs of state. I have rarely seen him in the Lords."

Sidmouth snorted. "I would not have thought him the sort of person you would wish to know, Duke."

"I cannot say that I wish to know him. Unfortunately, he has intruded himself into my life rather dangerously. He has developed some sort of obsession regarding Miss Russell and is determined to have her."

"Annoying perhaps, embarrassing even, especially for the young lady, but your betrothal has been announced. Surely that put an end to his persistence," said Eldon.

"All of which is in no way the concern of government ministers," Sidmouth snapped.

"Unfortunately," said Ashleigh, "his actions went well beyond persistence, and have not ceased. He endeavored to abduct Miss Russell, and it was only by chance that I arrived in time to rescue her. Then he sent men to burn down the house in which she had been living with her aunt. Fortunately, I had already removed the ladies and their servants to Kelswick, and the men I left guarding the place were able to capture one of the arsonists and put out the flames."

There was silence while the two members of the government considered this, Eldon shocked and Sidmouth angry.

"These are serious criminal charges, Your Grace." Sidmouth was now sitting stiffly in his chair. "Have you evidence to bring before a magistrate?"

"There are witnesses to both events." Ashleigh removed a paper from the inner pocket of his coat and handed it to Sidmouth. "Then there is this."

Sidmouth started to glance through it quickly, then stopped and read it again slowly before passing it to Eldon. His face was once again impassive when he spoke. "How did you come by this letter, Your Grace?"

"The fellow to whom it was written brought it to me," said Ashleigh. "It seems he does not consider himself a criminal, no less a murderer, and was rather offended that Farnsworth assumed he was available for such a task."

Eldon had finished reading the letter and looked up, aghast. "And Farnsworth signed his name to this? The man must be mad."

Ashleigh gave him a long look. "The thought had crossed my mind."

Eldon started to speak, then stopped. "Mad?" he said slowly. "You are serious?"

Ashleigh shrugged.

At this point Merton broke into the conversation. "Bancroft and I went with the duke to confront Farnsworth and try to bring him to his senses. He was—I do not know quite how to describe it."

"He was raving," said Bancroft bluntly. "Practically foaming at the mouth."

His mouth tight with displeasure, Sidmouth looked around the company. "This is a matter that should be dealt with by Farnsworth's family. I do not see why you are endeavoring to bring us into it."

Ashworth nodded in agreement. "That was my thought. Unfortunately, Farnsworth does not seem to have any family, at least none who are known. I could have charges brought against him, but that would inevitably bring scandal and notoriety down on my betrothed and me. I would prefer to avoid that."

"On the other hand," said Merton, "having a peer going about acting as if he is above the law plays right into the hands of the radicals demanding reform."

"An unpleasant situation," contributed Bancroft.

"In many ways," said Sidmouth tightly.

Ashleigh nodded. "I do not know what the law might be here, but I wondered if you, Lord Eldon, as lord chancellor, might be empowered to institute proceedings? To have Farnsworth examined by a panel of doctors who would, in turn, be able to determine the best course for him?"

Eldon looked no happier than Sidmouth. "I really do not know, Your Grace…"

Ashleigh raised a hand and looked rueful. "I apologize, my lord. I do not mean to put you in an awkward position. It is only that I thought you ought to be apprised of the situation, since there is the possibility that it could erupt into something serious."

Bancroft coughed and examined his glass. "After all, none of us would wish to see another scandal like the trial of Earl Ferrars."

Sidmouth glared at everyone, and was about to speak when a confusion of noise penetrated the room. Ashleigh frowned and stood. The rest followed him as he strode into the hall.

The Earl of Farnsworth stood in the center of the hall, a circle of distressed footmen surrounding him. The earl leaned arrogantly on his cane, a hectic flush on his face. "Ah, there you are, Ashleigh. I have come for Miss Russell. Tell your minions to bring her to me."

"Remove him," Ashleigh said to the footmen in icy tones.

Farnsworth cast a glance over the footmen and his mouth curled in a sneer. "These canaille? They would not dare to so much as touch me." He turned back to Ashleigh and noticed the others behind him. "You have your tame toadies again, I see. And who is this? Ah, more canaille. Sidmouth, the doctor's brat, and Eldon, the jumped-up cit. You keep low company, Duke."

At a gesture from Ashleigh, two of the footmen approached Farnsworth, but he suddenly turned and swung his cane at them, smashing it across the face of one. "You would dare to touch me?"

Merton muttered something and stepped toward Farnsworth, but Ashleigh stopped him. "My play, I believe," he murmured. Two steps brought him to Farnsworth. He snatched the flailing cane with one hand and, with the other, dealt a blow that laid the earl low.

"Neat, very neat," said Merton. "You do these things with a certain flair."

Ashleigh acknowledged the comment with a small bow before turning to the injured footman. The damage was minor, his nose was bloodied but not broken, and Gregson had the man helped below where the housekeeper was prepared for all emergencies. Then, assured that the earl's carriage was at the door, he had the remaining footmen carry the unconscious earl out and ship him home.

Ashleigh turned to his guests with an apologetic shrug. "As I mentioned, he is becoming intrusive."

Eldon looked deeply distressed and was shaking his head.

Sidmouth continued to scowl, and looked searchingly at Ashleigh. "I don't see how you could have planned this demonstration, but it was certainly fortuitous." At the duke's haughty look, he waved a hand dismissively. "No, no, I intend no insult, but you must admit it is a remarkable coincidence."

He harrumphed and stared at the floor, while Eldon made small exclamations of distress. Looking up once more, Sidmouth said, "I will take my leave now, Your Grace, if you will make my excuses to your ladies. I have a number of pressing matters demanding attention."

He looked pointedly at Eldon, who cleared his throat and said, "I, too, if you could let my lady know that we must be leaving."

*Sussex*

IT WAS BANCROFT who first noticed the item. He and Ashleigh had been sitting companionably over a quiet breakfast back at Kelswick, he reading the *Morning Post* and the duke reading *The Times*.

"Good God," he exclaimed. "Did you see this?"

Ashleigh looked up curiously. "Hmm?"

Bancroft handed the paper over, pointing to the headline: "Murder of peer in Mayfair Street, brutal attack on Earl of Farnsworth thought to be the work of footpads."

The duke snatched at the paper and read the brief story through twice. Still staring at it, he said, "Farnsworth was apparently walking home alone in the early morning hours. Does that seem likely to you?"

"Does what seem likely?" Lady Talmadge came in, smiling cheerfully, followed by Clara. Although the question was directed at her brother, the smile went directly to Bancroft, where it was answered by one of his.

Momentarily distracted, Ashleigh marveled once more at the change in his sister, so confident and happy at last. When she repeated her question, he caught himself up and showed her the paper.

She read it and paled. "Farnsworth is dead? How, how extraordinary."

"Who?" asked Clara, her interest caught by the interest of her elders.

"Oh, no one you know, dear. Just someone your uncle once met." Lady Talmadge continued to stare at the paper.

Clara frowned, then her face cleared. "Oh, I know. The Earl of Farnsworth. He's the one who tried to kidnap Kate and burn down Mrs. Darling's house. That will please Kate, won't it?"

Bancroft, who had been in the process of taking a sip of tea, came very close to snorting it all over the table. Her mother sighed. Her uncle demanded, "How the devil did you know that?"

Clara looked affronted. "Everyone knows that," she said dismissively.

"Everyone?" Ashleigh glared at her, and was about to say more, but his sister silenced him with a look. He tightened his lips and stood up. "If you will excuse me, I must go see Mrs. Darling and Miss Russell."

Clara, munching on her toast, watched in surprise as her uncle strode out.

Bancroft was now sitting beside Lady Talmadge and had his arm around her. Without looking up from her, he said, "Clara, I suggest you go for a stroll on the terrace."

His tone was so commanding that she took her toast and left without protest.

"Alice," he said softly. "Look at me."

She was, if possible, even paler than when she had first read the notice. "This was my idea, Stephen. I thought I was being so clever. I never expected…"

"Of course not. None of us did. And for all we know, it may have been footpads. No one's fault, he just chanced to be in the wrong place at the wrong time." She started to speak but he put a finger on her lips. "That is all we will ever know about it."

⟫⟫⟩✻⟨⟨⟪

A FEW MINUTES later, Ashleigh was holding Kate tightly in his arms, his cheek nestled against her hair, hers pillowed on his chest.

"He is truly dead?" she whispered.

"So it would seem."

"It's a shock. I must admit that." She lifted her face to look at him. "Do you believe it was footpads?" His hesitation was enough for her.

"No more do I."

"It is probably a kinder fate than being locked away in a mad-house."

She sighed.

"Do not start to feel guilty, Kate. You are in no way responsible for his madness, and he had to be stopped. Had we shaken him loose from you, he would have fastened on to some other innocent."

"And she would not have had you to protect her, would she?" Kate managed a smile. "But I do not think I would care to have Lord Sidmouth for an enemy."

# CHAPTER TWENTY-TWO

THE GUESTS—THE SPECIAL ones—began arriving several days before the wedding. Dr. Finley, Squire Grant and Mrs. Grant came first to Hawthorne Cottage, which rang with tears and laughter. Mrs. Grant could not believe how much Mrs. Darling resembled her dear friend, Mary. Mrs. Darling was so pleased to see the dear friends her sister had mentioned so often over the years in her letters. And all of them exclaimed over Kate, how well she looked, how happy she looked.

Once that was over, and the new arrivals had been given a chance to freshen themselves, they all gathered in the drawing room for tea and information.

Mrs. Grant began. Putting down her teacup, she turned to Kate. "I am pleased that everything has turned out well for you, but you must realize how terribly worried we have been. And the absence of any information other than your aunt's mysterious assurance that you were safe did not make us rest easy. You must tell us."

So tell them Kate did. But all her efforts to make light of her adventures, to highlight the virtues of her friends and minimize the vices of her brother and Farnsworth, could not make it anything other than a sorry tale.

The squire was outraged. "Should have thrashed that wastrel the first time he came nosing around," he muttered. "West Indies… fever there… good."

Dr. Finley was also muttering, but in Greek, and too softly for Kate to catch what he was saying.

Mrs. Grant had tears in her eyes. "Oh, Kate, my dear, why didn't you come to us? You know we would never have let that creature take you!"

Kate reached over to squeeze the good woman's hand. "They would have looked for me there. They did, didn't they? And I did not want to bring trouble down on you. Farnsworth is—was—powerful."

"But not, in the end, as powerful as he thought," said Dr. Finley. "An amazing example of hubris, was it not?"

The others smiled at him fondly.

Later, when they had a chance to speak privately, Mrs. Grant asked Kate about Ashleigh. "You are not marrying him out of gratitude, are you? Or because he is a duke? Neither one is a good basis for marriage, and I know your mother always hoped you would be able to marry for love."

"Dear Mrs. Grant! I do, indeed, love him. You will, too, as soon as you meet him. There is no need to fear."

That evening, the entire party went to dine at Kelswick, where everyone made much of the guests from Yorkshire. Ashleigh was flattering in his gratitude to them for their friendship to Kate as she was growing up, sought the squire's advice on what needed to be done for the Newell estate, and told Dr. Finley to make free of the Kelswick library while he was here.

Bancroft and Lady Talmadge had been wed the week before but had put off their departure for Longwood until after her brother's wedding. She refused to use her title, however, and insisted on being called Mrs. Bancroft, somewhat to the Grants' confusion.

The next day brought the arrival of Sir Richard Langley. The feelings of the brother and sister, who had not seen each other in more than thirty years, may be imagined. In the face of Franny's happy memories of her husband and her obvious prosperity, to say nothing of his niece's forthcoming marriage to a duke, all he could do was shake his head in bewilderment and say, "Whatever would the old man have said."

On Saturday, Ashleigh and Miss Russell were married in the Church of St. Thomas, across the river from the main part of Lewes. The church was crowded with their friends and well-wishers, and townspeople and tenants lined the road back to Kelswick, where a celebratory feast was laid out under tents on the lawn. The bride and groom smiled and waved and accepted good wishes. But when they withdrew to their room at the end of the day, they could remember very little of it.

They saw only each other.

# EPILOGUE

THE SHEER WHITE curtains were pulled closed, softening the afternoon sun that poured into the nursery. A cheerful fire burned in the grate, with a fire guard securely around it even though young Tom was not even crawling yet. But safety was always important.

Nearby stood the cradle. It was an impressive affair, brought back from Venice by an ancestor several generations back. Painted garlands decorated its sides, and gilding highlighted the edges. Inside was bedding of the finest linen, smooth and silky to caress a baby's tender skin. At least Ashleigh had been assured that was so.

But although the cradle was still swaying slightly, it was empty.

Ashleigh leaned against the door and watched Kate walk back and forth, rocking their son in her arms. She was such a slim creature it was hard to believe that she had given birth to such a strapping baby. Everyone told him it had been an easy birth, and Kate herself swore she would love to have another dozen babes, but he remembered hearing her cry out in pain.

He shook his head. He didn't know about Kate, but he was not sure he could go through that again.

They also told him that young Tom was a remarkably good baby. He was not so sure about that either. Kate had insisted on having the nursery near their room and it had been more than three months before he could count on sleeping through the night undisturbed.

Now it was happening again. Tom had been fussy lately—another tooth coming, Nurse said—but Kate seemed to have found the secret to soothing him. At least he was resting quietly in her arms. She was not quite singing—it was more of a chant. He couldn't quite make out the words, so he came in closer.

*"Arma virumque cano, Troiae qui primus ab oris..."*

He smothered a laugh. He could not believe it. That was Latin verse. *"I sing of arms and the man who first from the shores of Troy..."* She was reciting the *Aeneid* to their son!

"Kate, my love, don't you think Tom is a bit young to be starting his classical education? He's not yet a year old and he doesn't even speak English."

She looked up with a luminous smile. Her smiles had replaced the look of fear that used to shadow her face. He would never get enough of her smiles.

"I don't know any lullabies except 'Rock-a bye Baby' and I've never liked the bit about the cradle falling," she said. "It frightened me when I was small. So I tried this. It makes a nice, rhythmic chant, don't you think?" She turned to let her smile shine on the baby. "Who knows? Maybe when he starts to study Latin, it will somehow seem familiar. But I think I'll skip the battle scenes."

Ashleigh put his arm around her shoulders, embracing them both protectively. "Oh, I don't know," he said. "It seems to me that those were my favorite parts when I was a boy."

KATE LEANED AGAINST her husband, her warrior, who could be relied on to always protect her and their son. It was wonderful to feel safe, she would never deny that. However, she had a suspicion that he really needed a large family to care for and keep him from getting overprotective. Fortunately, that was a real possibility. She was not yet certain, but she had a feeling that there would be another babe for that cradle in about seven months.

# Author's Note

*Madness*

The Earl of Farnsworth suffered from what came to be called general paresis of the insane, the final and fatal stage of untreated syphilis. In addition to the sores generally characteristic of syphilis, general paresis was characterized by loss of control over movement and delusions of grandeur.

There was no cure for him at this point, but neither was there any simple way to control him. Madness, like so much else, was a family responsibility. It was up to the family to take care of the lunatic. (That is not intended to be a slur. Madman, lunatic, imbecile—these were the accepted medical descriptions.)

The most obvious solution was to keep the madman at home. Locking the mad wife in the attic with a keeper, as Rochester did in *Jane Eyre*, was a distinct possibility. Or the "eccentric" uncle could be kept in a separate wing or in a cottage on the estate. Or, if the uncle was not violent, he could live with the family and everyone made the best of it.

The other alternative was a madhouse. Increasingly, people were coming to think of madness as an illness, and many places offered care and treatment. Others simply kept the patients locked up.

If the family could not afford to pay for the patient's care, and could not care for him at home, he might be turned out to fend for himself or end up in Bedlam or some other public asylum.

In all these cases, the decision had to be made by the family, or by the head of the family. However, Farnsworth has no family, and even if he had one, as an earl, he would be the head.

In the absence of family, the Lord Chancellor could convene a Commission of Lunacy to examine Farnsworth and, presumably, commit him to care. It is unlikely this could have been done without publicity, and no one ever wanted that kind of publicity.

### *Kate's necklace*

Before the advent of cultured pearls, pearls were more expensive than diamonds or any other gems. Even given that, figuring out how much Kate's necklace could reasonably be worth proved to be more difficult than I expected. I went to the library and examined books on historical jewelry. There were plenty of gorgeous pictures, but no prices. I asked people at the Victoria and Albert. They said, "That's a good question." The answer was that it's hard to tell. I tried looking at the trials at the Old Bailey. An occasional pearl turned up but with no indication of its size or quality. Then the Library of Congress sent me a pile of photocopies of pages from books and newspapers and the newspapers did have some prices.

An 1830 newspaper had an excerpt from Bourrienne's *Memoirs of Napoleon Bonaparte* that talked about one of Empress Josephine's purchases. She was particularly fond of pearls, and bought a pearl necklace that had belonged to Marie Antoinette for 250,000 francs. That was about £12,000 at the time. However, a queen's necklace, complete with historic associations was surely more expensive than one belonging to a baronet's wife.

In 1882, at a sale of diamonds and pearls, a necklace of 147 pearls in three rows went for £3,400. That's the equivalent of more than £4,000 in 1820. But that was a particularly impressive necklace.

So Mr. Bridge's estimate of £800-£1,200 for a necklace that a country baronet might have given to his wife is my best estimate, too.

# About the Author

When she retired after too many years in journalism, Lillian Marek felt a longing for happy endings and stories where the good guys win and the bad guys get their just desserts. Having exhausted her library's supply of non-gory mystery stories, she started reading romance novels, especially historical romance. This was so much fun that she thought she'd like to try her hand at writing one. So she took her computer keyboard in hand, slipped back into the 19th century, and began.

She was not mistaken—writing romance novels is as much fun as reading them.

Her list of story ideas now numbers more than 80. She may be spinning tales for quite a while.

Made in the USA
Middletown, DE
07 June 2021